THE PROTECTOR

BOOK TWO OF THE NIGHT REALM SERIES

K. R. BOWMAN

THE PROTECTOR

K. R. BOWMAN

ISBN:

Ebook: 978-1-7359097-4-5

Paperback: 978-1-7359097-5-2

Hardback: 978-1-7359097-6-9

PROLOGUE

The Dark

THE CREATURE LURKED IN ITS LAIR HIGH ABOVE THE VALLEY WHERE HIS foes roamed. He watched them carry on their meaningless existence while the cool breeze blew in through the cracks of the shutters, chilling his taut, ink-black skin. The full moon cast a bright light on the forest beneath. And yet, a dark hunger gnawed within him, a hunger for vengeance.

His sightless sockets, devoid of any real vision, pulsed red as rage coursed through his entire body. Evidence of his fury still lay scattered around him as chunks of walls, floors, and ceilings splintered at his feet. Long scars remained on the ceiling where his claws dug deep as he punished the room around him for his failings.

He held her in his grasp. Touched her heart with his claws. A second more, and she would have been dead, the rite completed. The power belonged to him. And yet…

The others scattered after it was over, knowing better than to approach him. Had one been foolish enough to come near he probably would have destroyed them, taking their heart as he should have taken hers. The power coursing through him wanted to rip something apart.

Would he have the chance again? How? He had been there. She had been in his grasp.

He needed to hunt. Get the anger out. Feed on something. Feel their life force leave their body.

He burst through the window, claws piercing the limestone as he launched himself off the ledge. A cool breeze caressed his face, the moon high above beckoned to him. He sprang forward, dropping down the cliff-side. His massive black wings unfurled, catching the air beneath and propelling him upward.

Tonight, he would hunt and feed to take the edge off. But ultimately he knew, he had to find her again and take the power he deserved. The hunger demanded it. He would become the source of the mindless bodies, one way or another.

1

Callum

THAT MONSTER HELD SLOANE SUSPENDED ABOVE ME. HER SCREAMS pierced through the barrage of creatures and Realmers fighting. I fought to get to her, scrambling over fallen rock and debris. The creature held her in its grasp like a lover. Ferocity took over, and I hacked away at anything in my way.

Her screams turned into a high pitch wail, hurting my sensitive ears, but I didn't notice. I had to reach her. I yelled with each onslaught of my sword. Black goo covered my clothes and skin. It looked as if the monster was carving her chest open, but surely not. My eyes could barely make sense of what they saw. Icy air whooshed through the cavern.

A burst of white light erupted the darkness. The creatures screeched and high-tailed it, escaping through the portals. Above me, the creature beat the air with its massive wings, but its claws were empty. Sloane was gone.

What the hell happened?

Fire rushed through my body and tore me in two. I screamed. Pain and loss enveloped me like a dear friend, and I let it. The fire took over. White filled my vision. I sent it after the creature.

It roared and swooped through the cave and out through a portal far above. The portals blinked out as if never there and silence fell like a heavy rock. My fire dissolved the rock around me as it roared. I stood transfixed. Flames crackled and whispered through my mind. *Was this the end?*

———

Irene found me and brought me back to reality, calming my fire. The casualty-ridden battlefield around us had been like one from a movie. Buildings destroyed. Realmers were dead or gone. People missing limbs.

At first, we didn't know what steps to take. Chuck was part of the missing. Several Hunters disappeared. So we floundered for a few hours, trying to find our feet again. I was on a mission to find our friends.

Irene shouted, "Callum! Over here!"

Her bright red hair was like a beacon. It grew fuzzier as the humidity in the mountain increased, so she was easy to spot in the darkness. Sweat and dirt-caked her clothes and streaked her pale skin. Her muscles strained as she lifted a massive rock.

"Hold on, I'll help," I said, as I climbed over fallen walls and posts. "Who is it?"

"Raleigh." She heaved the massive sandstone away, revealing a small hole. Raleigh's big brown eyes blinked rapidly up at us. Dirt and dust covered every inch of her.

"Thought you'd never come," her throat scratched out.

Irene and I leaned down and grabbed hold of Raleigh's arms to lift her out.

"You'll have to grab my forearm. I broke my hand. I think." She held her right elbow toward me, and I pulled. She grimaced as the pain shot through her.

"Sorry."

"It's okay. I'm glad to be out of there." She peered over her shoulder and called down into the hole, "Thanks for the company!"

Irene and I glanced at each other but didn't ask. I didn't want to hear anything about her ghost friends.

Raleigh's bottom lip was split, and her leg was purple and almost black from bruises. She breathed in deep, revelling in the fresh air. Her short-cropped hair stood out at different angles. Deep gashes marred her tattooed arm. The once bright, pretty colors were brown and dark red.

"Come on, let's get you to the medic area. See if they can fix your hand." Irene gently wrapped an arm around Raleigh's middle and helped her to stand.

"Ugh, oh my gods. Hurts like cats on your balls," she said through gritted teeth.

I chuckled and shook my head. Reminded me of Ashlen. Who knew what she would say once we found her.

2

Sloane

FUCKING HELL.

Mud, blood, remnants of some kind of animal, and black slime covered my torn clothes. I ripped the navy sheets off of me and swung my legs around, resting my booted feet on the worn carpet. Artemis still hung around my neck. The needles swung lazily back and forth. My right bicep was slightly numb, along with the majority of my legs down to my toes.

I took a steadying, deep breath. My head swam. *You've got to be kidding me.*

My lungs were on fire as I gasped for breath. Tears sprung to my eyes. I clutched at my chest, rubbing my sternum; except that hurt too. Bright red blood covered my hands. My vision blurred and the room tipped. *How the hell did I get here? Why was I covered in blood and in so much pain? Did I kill someone?*

The blood had smeared across my chest and onto the collar of my black tank top. I frantically wiped and scrubbed it. The picture of the creature's face sprang before my eyes and forever embedded into my memory; his gaping mouth laughed demonically in my face as he tried to separate me from the land of the living. The black holes where his eyes should have been seemed to reach for my soul. *What was that thing?*

Goosebumps rose along my arms, and the hairs on my neck stood to attention. Fear made my nostrils flare, and my heart raced. My only thoughts were to make sure my heart was still in its place, but as I wiped away the caked blood, pale flesh appeared. The skin was smooth, if only slightly pink.

I should have died. How had I gone back home?

I scanned the room. My room. *I was home.* Everything was just as I had left it. My laptop covered in stickers waited for me on my desk. My pictures sat lovingly on the bookshelves and hung adoringly on the golden walls. Even my bookbag still rested by my bed, as if I had dropped it there after walking in from school. The clock on my night-stand read 9:03 a.m. The only thing different about my room was that there were no clothes scattered across the floor. No signs that someone lived there. My room had become a scene of preservation.

How long was I gone? Only a few months? A year?

Time had warped in my mind.

My legs shook as I put weight on them. Something constricted my thigh like a vise-grip. When I looked down, I found a blade in its holster. Holding it in my hand felt right. But in my mind, it should have been glowing. *Masada. The name came to me, but I wasn't sure what it meant.* I slid the knife back where it rested. My fingers dug into the mattress and sheets. I gritted my teeth and slowly leaned forward, tightening my thighs to try and balance. I stood with my arms outstretched. No doubt that I looked like a toddler or acrobat on a tightrope. Standing had never been this hard.

"Okay, this is good. It's progress." I took a deep soothing breath.

Something rumbled. I glared at my stomach, who was the culprit. My door seemed so far away. I carefully took one shaky step at a time. It probably took me ten minutes to travel to the door. I steadied myself against the wall. A bead of sweat ran down my temple. I pathetically pawed at the doorknob. The door cracked open, letting in a little air. I closed my eyes and strained to hear signs of life throughout the house.

"Mom?" I waited. Nothing.

My eyebrows knitted together. I guessed it was a weekday, which meant she'd be at work. I kind of hoped that life had stopped since I wasn't there anymore. But what did I know?

I braced myself against the doorjamb and took a step into the hallway. The house echoed with my footsteps hitting the old wood floors. I wobbled to the next door and pushed it open. My tiny aqua bathroom looked cleaner. The white tiles sparkled. Nothing littered the floor. Even the mirror was streak-free. I shouldn't be too surprised. I was the messy one compared to my mom.

Flipping the light on, I blinked rapidly, and stepped in front of the sink, to survey the damage on my face more clearly.

Who the hell is that person?

I turned my head. The girl in the mirror turned hers as well. I raised my eyebrows, making my forehead crease and hurt. Dark brown mud had dried and caked onto the side of my face. I didn't remember how that got there. *I don't remember much of anything except that my name is Sloane, I've been in the realm training, and something happened that sent me home. Flickers of images kept popping up. Are they images of my life?* More dark, muddy streaks ran along my jaw and neck. My dishwater hair was plastered to my head. The color of my hair was indistinguishable. I traced around my eyes. My fingertips barely brushed the surface of my skin.

I locked eyes with the girl staring back. I truly didn't know her anymore. She looked exhausted. Vast amounts of fear echoed in her blue eyes, so much fear and pain that it was almost unbearable to keep looking into them. It was undeniable this girl had been through some shit. I didn't think that even covered it. She still looked young, but her eyes told her true age. My age. At that moment, I felt eighty-two. I concentrated on the porcelain sink, tapping my finger against the white bowl. I looked to the right to see the shower. It blissfully called to me.

I forgot about everything else and started pulling and tearing my clothes from my body, trying to get away from the dirt and blood. I left the necklace around my neck, keeping her close to me so there wouldn't be a chance I'd forget her. *My necklace I knew for certain was a her, and her name was Artemis. More memories flooded me. Masada was my knife. Gifts from my mother, left behind by my father who was forced to flee, and given to a child he didn't know existed. Something was missing... I knew it would come to me. I would search for it later.*

Artemis had become more of a friend, and Masada a comfort. I tended to personify most inanimate objects or animals so thinking of Artemis as a living breathing extension of me, of my family, wasn't difficult. Because of how I attached myself, it had been so hard for my mom to get rid of my stuffed animals, she knew what they meant to me. I would always be a child at heart.

I stepped into the shower, the cool tile singing to me. When I turned the water on, it splashed playfully against my legs. I immediately felt lighter as the warm water thrummed against my back and cascaded down. The bottom of the shower changed a brownish-red color. It dawned on me that most of what I had thought initially was mud, was dried blood. I snatched some soap and started scrubbing.

I washed my hair several times until the bottom of the shower was no longer brown. I even scrubbed the blood and dirt from Artemis. The water cooled, and I turned the valve all the way left so it grew hot again. The hot water eased my tired muscles, but when the water became cool again I let it hit my face, letting my tears wash down the drain. *Plumbing. Glorious plumbing. How I missed you.*

I stepped out of the shower, feeling more energized than I had felt in a long time. My shoulders were less tense. The throbbing in my skull subsided. They really needed showers in the realm, not just tubs. My fingers and toes wrinkled from the water, but it made me smile. Not a true smile, but a small one. Home felt nice and safe. Wrapping the big, fluffy blue towel around me, I stepped cautiously in front of the mirror but kept my eyes down. I found a toothbrush and toothpaste and my old hairbrush. I would never take modern plumbing for granted again.

My eyes rose from the sink to the faucet and slowly, very slowly, rose until I looked at my reflection. I had to look in the mirror at some point. This time, the blue eyes staring back were more at ease. Her eyes, my eyes, were more self-assured like I was ready for anything else thrown my way. At least I hoped so.

My brown hair was lighter. Was it changing to white? The hair around my face was much lighter than it had ever been. I wrapped a long piece around my finger. Strands had lost their color. It was almost translucent. That was weird. I frowned.

Leaning in closer to look at my face, the bright, bathroom light showed every line and scar. White lines marred my skin. What were those?

They looked like scars... tiny white lines were on my jaw, forehead, across my nose, and one thicker line curved around the top of my left eye. The lines weren't clean and smooth, but jagged, reminding me of the creature's sharp claws tearing into my chest. What I imagined was bad but this was much worse. I lifted Artemis away from my neck. A thick and jagged white half-moon line marked the spot directly over my heart, reminding me of how the creature's claws slid into my chest and tried to scoop it out. My fingertips ran across the bumpy surface. The air, coming out of my mouth, shook as it left my body. Tears threatened to pour out of me again.

I was not crying for the thousandth time. Instead, I snatched my boots and blade from the floor and stomped back into my room. Rummaging through my bureau, I found a pair of faded jeans with matching holes in both knees that threatened to rip more. I pulled a dark blue, short-sleeved, V-neck shirt over my head. I slapped on a new pair of socks and tugged my leather boots on up to my knees, and tied Masada back on. Things were definitely out of whack. How did I get here? Should I wait for mom to get home? Should I be sitting at the kitchen table and saying, "Hi!" when she walks in the door?

I gathered up my dirty clothes and took them to the trash can. My stomach made a noise again, and I looked at the clock. It read 11:43 a.m. Wow, time flew by rather quickly. I shuffled to the fridge and peered inside. Mom changed some things. The fridge barely had anything in it. The cabinets were usually stocked, so I opened one of the doors. Some bread, cereal, chips, and other amounts of junk stared back at me. I grabbed a bag of chips and some bread, along with peanut butter and grape jelly. I made four sandwiches. And ate them all. Needless to say, I was slightly sick after eating so much. The clock now said 12:13 p.m.

What was I going to do? I looked around the room, trying to decide.

I needed to be doing something. My friends were stuck in the Realm with those creatures. I wasn't a huge help — I was probably a bigger hindrance than anything — but they had to be worried.

I picked Artemis up. "Artemis, where's Ashlen?" I hoped she would answer.

Artemis started spinning, my heart pounded with hope, but she slowed and continued to spin lazily around. My heart sank. It was worth a try, should have known she wouldn't work in this realm.

I cleared the table and washed my hands, not because they were dirty, but because I missed regular faucets. Funny, how I missed something so mundane and simple.

Walking slowly to my room, I wanted to stay home to see mom, but I kept thinking about the Realm. Pictures of my mom and me stared back in their never straight frames. Us together during birthdays. Us on a trip to Disney. My mom laughed while eating popcorn in a theater. Guilt washed over me. Things had been a whirlwind over in the other realm, and I hadn't thought about her as much. *Was that part of the magic? It made you forget about the normal world, so you wouldn't want to leave?*

The lights in my room were off, and the sun outside heated the space. I pulled the chain for the fan. As I sat down on the edge of the bed, my laptop's power light started flashing. I pushed the top up. The screen blinked on, and the fan started humming. It was eerie being back in my room and in the house without mom. My bedsheets were a mess. The blood, dirt, and black goo looked as if it had solidified. Mom was going to have a heart attack.

The computer's welcome music sounded, and I sat in the desk chair to stare at the screen. There at the bottom, I clicked the calendar. Eight months. It had been eight months since my birthday, and I went to the Realm. It seemed like a shockingly long time, but endless nights, foot travel, training, and everything else that went on in the realm, mentally it felt right. Guilt struck through me again. I hadn't thought much about this world in eight months. *What kind of person did that make me?* With that on my mind, I knew I had to stay and wait for mom to get home. I had to at least tell her goodbye. If she came home and found bloody, gooey sheets and prints, she might fall over with worry. I couldn't just leave a crime scene with no explanation.

I could research while I waited. I opened up the internet browser, but I didn't even bother checking my email. What could I do? My eyes flitted across the wall and out the window. My fingers drummed on the desktop.

Where had Ashlen said the Norm Defense was located? Is there a chance it would even be on the internet?

I moved the cursor to the search box, typed in Norm Defense, and waited. The loading symbol popped up at the bottom, and only one website was listed. My eyes locked onto the site that simply read: normdefense.org.

Well, aren't they crafty? Who would have thought to list a secret society on the internet under its real name... I mentally eye-rolled and chuckled to myself.

Moving the mouse, I clicked on the site. A black screen with a gold government seal located in the middle filled the page. The designs on the seal looked similar to the designs I had found in the books and on the wooden box my mom had. I clicked on the seal and waited. The screen blinked and a small text box appeared in the middle of the page:

Due to the numerous messages we receive, we ask that you please not contact us unless it is an absolute emergency. If you are inquiring only for information, please email us, and we will respond within 24 hours. Thank you for your interest and understanding.

The phone number was listed along with an email.

Guess I'll try that number. On the desk corner, sat my pink cordless phone. I picked it up, dialed the number, and waited to hear someone answer. It took an excruciating amount of time. The phone rang twenty times before someone answered.

"Yes?" It was a woman, who answered breathlessly. She sounded as if she had been running to catch the phone.

"Umm... hi. Is this the Norm Defense?"

3

Sloane

WHEN THE PHONE OPERATOR RESPONDED, SHE DID IN A SLIGHTLY annoyed and bored tone, "Yes, it is. I'm sorry, but I'm not at liberty to disclose any information about the agency. I'm guessing you looked at the web page?" She didn't wait for me to answer. "Just email us with any questions you have, and we *might* respond."

"Wait! I'm part of the Realm. Somehow I was sent back to the Norm, but now I need to find a way to get back!" the words tumbled in a rushed garble.

Silence.

"Hello? Are you there?" I waited, holding my breath. My tattered computer chair squeaked as I fidgeted nervously.

"You're part of the Realm?" she asked cautiously. What sounded like chewing smacked through the phone. Was she chewing gum?

"Yes," I said. I practically heard her thinking. "I am. I'm not lying," I waited some more.

"How'd you get back to the Norm?"

"I don't know, but I need to get back. The Nightlins attacked Kingston."

More silence.

She replied slowly, "Yes, we know. We sent people to help."

"Oh, good. Listen, I need to get back. Can you please help?" I tried the sweetest tone of influence that I stored away on rainy days.

"What is your title?"

Her question caught me off guard, and my mind raced to find an answer, "I'm a Watcher or will be soon." I knew that was the wrong answer.

This time her voice was smug, "I'm sorry." She didn't sound it. "But they definitely don't need a groundling."

I ground my teeth together. I held back from snapping, *and what's your title? If she was safe in the Norm answering phones, I doubt she was very useful.* "I'm asking if you will *please* give me your address, so I can use a portal to get back to the Realm." *More flies with honey, Sloane, I reminded myself and tried to sound sweet.*

"There's no need for you to go back..." Her tone sounded as if that was the last thing anyone needed or wanted. I was mentally ripping my hair out in frustration.

"Just tell someone Sloane Norwood is trying to get back to Kingston."

She grew quiet for a few moments. Clicking noises sounded in the background.

"There is no record of a Sloane Norwood."

"Then check, James Sullivan."

"James? How would you know him?"

A headache throbbed at the base of my skull and behind my ears.

"He's my father." *You idiot,* was implied.

She chuckled. "James never had a child."

"How would you know?"

"We have everyone listed in our database." She paused for what I guessed was for dramatic effect, "Everyone."

I massaged my temples. "Crap, what had Chuck told me to say?" I thumped my head trying to recall the code he had told me. What the hell had it been?? Ughhh. "Fuckity fuck. Why can't I think of it?"

"Excuse me, there is no need for that language."

"Nightlins fly, birds crow? Orrr..." I said ignoring her. I squeezed my eyes shut trying to cipher through all the useless knowledge stored in my brain.

She heaved a breath into the phone.

"Nightlins soar, birds fly?" I said hopefully.

She sighed, "All right, all right."

"Please, give me the address." I lunged for a pen and notepad next to my desk.

"It won't help you any. They'll just turn you away."

"I'll deal with it when I get there." I wet the end of the pen with my tongue and scribbled furiously, trying to get the ink to come out.

She sighed. "Okay, it's 2907 Hamilton Avenue, Oklahoma City."

Fumbling with an old pen, I scribbled the address down. The ink didn't work right away, and I scratched it furiously on the paper trying to activate the ink. My heart beat faster with each stroke of the pen.

"Oklahoma City?"

"Yes, that's what I said." She didn't try to explain.

"Okay, thanks."

A dial tone answered in return. I stared at the phone for a second before pushing end.

"Rude much?" I rolled my eyes. Some people had no class.

Since I didn't have my phone, I was having to go old school. I typed the address into Mapquest and printed out the directions. *God, please let me be able to do this.*

Okay, so Oklahoma City is six hours away. The clock said it was almost 1 p.m. Mom should be home from school a little after three, could I wait two more hours? No, I was too antsy, and I was dealing with life and death. I jumped up and grabbed my old denim book bag, stuffing a few extra clothes into it. I hurried down the hall to the bathroom, picking up my toothbrush, toothpaste, and shampoo.

Going into the kitchen, I spotted the coffee pot.

Money. I hadn't needed to use it in so long I'd forgotten about it. I was going to need some sort of means to pay for gas, food, and a place to stay. Like most parents, my mom had a hidden stash, but it wasn't where most people hid their mounds of cash. She kept hers in the coffee pot, which she never used. My father was the one who had liked coffee and after he disappeared, she used it as her piggy bank. Her reasoning was if a burglar came in, he would search in the likeliest places such as: behind the commode, under the mattress, in the cookie jar, or her sock drawer, so her extra cash was stored in our old, made in the 80s, coffee pot.

I got lucky. Apparently, she had been saving for a while. Usually, she spends it on shoes or a new outfit. A wad of tens and twenty-dollar bills was bound together with a hairband. It was a little over three hundred dollars. I felt awful taking it, but I was using it for a good reason, and isn't that why we have parents, to begin with? I left a hundred bucks and an I.O.U. I'd probably never pay her back, but it's the thought that counted? I went to the fridge and pulled out ingredients to make sandwiches for the road. Loading up on chips and cookies and several other kinds of foods that are bad for you. I had been deprived of junk food *since forever.*

I found a notepad in one of the junk drawers. I felt guilty writing a note to mom. She would throw a fit, but time was of the essence. I scratched out:

Mom,

Sorry, I didn't stay to see you... but there are some things that I need to take care of. I miss you and love you. Everything is going great. Try not to worry... I'll come back and see you in person again so I can get my hug.

Love always,

Sloane

P.S. I took some cash.

I frowned as I stared at my chicken scratch. Would mom be able to forgive me completely for this one? I stared a moment longer then left the note on the kitchen table.

Maybe I should stay around for a little bit and see if she comes home? But, she'll probably try and keep me from going back... I looked around the room at all of the familiar things. The worn, brown sofa where we'd sit and watch movies with bags of popcorn. Our silly photos were tacked on the fridge.

Longing to stay pulled at my heart. She was going to be so mad and hurt. But I needed to get back soon, somehow. Though it would be much easier to stay. I'd go back to school and work at the grocery store. I'd hang out with Mariah and mom. Days would be the same and predictable. Predictability was safe. No monsters would kill me. My cozy home was very tempting. I could quit the realm and go back to my normal life again. To the boring same ole, unsatisfying life where I never seemed to belong.

Despite the grim scene I left I couldn't help but think of my friends in the Realm and how each would miss me. Ashlen would surely kill me. Raleigh would beat me up. Harris would most likely laugh at me. And Callum, I wasn't sure what he would do if I didn't return. *Would he notice?* The small kiss we shared floated through my mind, soft and fleeting.

I made sure to turn off the lights and clean up my mess. My poor sheets were ruined and in the trash. Mom would have been more upset if I left a mess without seeing her. I slung my bag across the one shoulder that didn't hurt.

"Sloane!" My heart leapt to my throat. Mom stood in the doorway. Her bag fell to the floor as she pressed a hand over her mouth.

She ran to me and threw her arms around my neck. Her tiny frame trembled but her grip was tight as she held onto me. She cried and cried. My heart broke. I hadn't seen her breakdown since I'd catch her sniffling over dad leaving.

She wiped her face and pushed her black hair back. "Sloane, I can't believe it." She sniffed some more, tears threatened to pour again. She gripped my arms and squeezed.

"Hi, Mom. What are you doing home so early?" She glanced at my hands holding a bag.

An eyebrow rose. "Were you about to leave without seeing me?" Mascara slowly ran down her cheeks with her tears. She sniffled.

I glanced at my hand, the floor, then her face. "Uhh, I need to leave."

She shut the door and faced me. "I think you've got time to tell me what's been going on for the past eight months. I've been at a teaching conference the past two days. Now, where have you been?" She knew I was safe, and now she wanted to kick my ass for trying to leave without saying goodbye. No doubt I deserved it, it was nice to hear mom, even if she was using her teacher's voice that meant I was in trouble.

She placed a palm on each side of my face and pulled me closer to her level. "Sloane," she whispered. "What happened to your face?" Her eyes roamed over every scar and line. She tilted my head each way to get a better view.

"Umm. I was attacked by an animal." I couldn't very well tell her monsters had attacked me, right? Close enough.

She pushed me into the kitchen and pulled a chair out for me to sit. "Okay, *Musume*, start talking. Since you're in such a hurry I'll make some tea."

My embarrassment and guilt grew heavier with each pacing second, and each time my mom glared at me. Anytime she used Japanese and called me daughter, her emotions were running high.

What could I tell her about dad? What would make sense without her thinking I was a looney bin? I racked my brain for answers.

"I —" I paused, thinking. "I found some old notes from him." That was pretty safe.

"Oh? What did they say?" I knew I wouldn't need to clarify *him*.

"Well, he talked about you." I smiled gently.

She faced me. "Really?"

I nodded. "Yeah, he talked about how much he loved you and how he would do anything for you. He also told his dad to stick it up his ass. But his dad sent him on covert missions so he couldn't try to run off back to this world, to you. It was pretty messed up, and so many of the letters were him demanding to come back."

Her smile spread from ear to ear. "That sounds more like him." She set out two saucers and teacups. As she poured, she asked, "Anything else? What have you been doing?" She eyed me. "You look like you've been through a good bit."

I straightened in my seat, trying not to touch my scars and draw more attention to them. I picked up my Earl Grey tea, blowing on it so it'd cool faster. "I've been learning to fight mostly. I've made some new friends."

She brightened at that. "That's wonderful."

"Have you seen Mariah lately?"

"Yes, she has been by a few times to see me. I told her you won a scholarship to an overseas school so that's where you've been."

I frowned. "She believed that?"

"Eh, I'm not sure, but she stopped bothering me about it." She sipped some of her tea. "Anything else happen?"

I shuffled through my memory bank, trying to find something not too crazy to share. *Argh, who cares.* I'd tell her what she most would want to hear.

"I met a guy."

Her teacup clattered on her saucer as she hurried to set it down. "No! You did? You're not just telling me that?"

I smiled, a real one. "Yes, he's one of those quiet, brooding types."

Her eyes grew big along with her grin, and she clasped her hands together. "Oh, Sloane, I'm so happy. By the way, I'm purposely letting you change the subject because if I knew more about the *animal* that attacked you, I'd lock you up and never let you leave. But you are like your father and have a duty." She gave me a pointed look, and I nodded. She shook her head as if clearing it of all the pain and focused on the fun boy discussion. "Is he nice? What's his name?"

"Yes, he's very nice. He watches over me, and his name is Callum."

"Ooohh, Callum. I love that name." Her whole face lit up. At least I could make this one happy thing for her come true right now. There wasn't much more that made her happier than gossiping about boys.

I nodded. "I think you'd like him, though he is hard to figure out at first."

She waved a hand at me. "All guys are like that, especially when they like you." Her eyebrows wiggled.

This made it so much harder to leave, but I knew I had to. Time wasn't on my side. I needed to go. I drank in the moment of the happy crinkles around her eyes and mouth, the ease of her smile, and how her long, dark hair cascaded over her shoulders. Just in case something happened, and I didn't see her again.

I breathed in deep. "Okay, Mom, I have to go."

"Are you sure? You can stay. We can take a vacation?" she asked hopefully.

A vacation sounded like a dream. I frowned. The line between my eyes deepened, "I'm so close to finding Dad. To finding real answers."

She nodded and took a sip. "You think so?"

"Yes, besides my friends are there, and they need me. They need my help." I was sixty percent sure they needed my *specific* help.

Her shoulders and smile deflated but she nodded. She reached across the table and squeezed my hand, crunching my fingers between hers. She stirred her tea a few times. "All right, be safe. I'm so glad I saw you. And, if you find yourself at home again without me, you better pick up the phone and call since we do have a landline. " Her eyes met mine, and she smiled though it didn't reach her eyes.

"Okay. I'm glad I saw you too, Mom. I love you."

"I love you more, *Musume.*"

The corners of her lips ticked up slightly. I gathered my things and headed toward the door. My old car keys hung on the key rack. They felt weird in my hands like something foreign. I stopped and turned back to gaze across the space that was home. A heavy sigh escaped my lips.

Mom stood by the sofa. "Come back if you can?"

"Of course, Mom. You know I will."

She waved. Her eyes glistened with tears. "Will you call?"

I nodded again. "I will if I can. For a whole magical other realm, it's crazy to say, but there isn't much technology. Where I stayed we didn't have any electricity except for vitamin D lamps. I took my first shower in apparently eight months. Unless you walk for days and make it to a portal there isn't a way to get a hold of anyone on this side. I'll try to call from the Norm Defense before I cross over."

I pulled the door closed behind me, trying to hold my emotions at bay. Bright sunlight caused me to squint as I wound my way to my old car. I splayed my hands over my eyes, trying to block out the blinding rays. That was going to take some time to get used to again. I wasn't sure if I was happy for the sun or more disappointed.

My little Toyota sat in the carport awaiting my return. Dirt and grime had coated the windows long before I left for the Night Realm since the doctors had said I couldn't drive anymore. But since my days in the realm, I had been fine, mostly. A twinge of regret stung my heart, at the thought of leaving my friends again. *Come on, woman up.*

The keys clinked in my hands as my fingers toyed with the metal. It had been forever since I'd driven, much less been in a car. Months since I'd ridden with Mariah. Almost a year since I drove alone. At least I didn't have to worry about fainting at weird moments anymore. I frowned. Surely I didn't have to worry now that I'd been to the realm.

The driver's side was unlocked so I threw my bag into the passenger side. With my left hand on the door, little pinpricks, like when your hand falls asleep, started in my fingertips and traveled up my arm. I watched my skin move with the sensation. My mouth fell open and my eyes grew larger, threatening to fall out of their sockets. My skin stopped moving at the top of my shoulder, the tingling sensation dying with it.

Did that just happen?

I continued to stare at my arm, waiting for my skin to move again. What was happening to me...?

Fear crept back in, seeping into my bones as if it was home. I took a deep steadying breath and slid behind the wheel. I pulled my seat belt across me and fastened it. The car interior was hot and the air felt stale from not being used. I slid the keys into the ignition and turned it.

It didn't start. Dammit.

I tried it again. Still nothing. Tears welled, but I surprised myself by laughing instead. I wholeheartedly laughed. Mouth fully opened.

Tears streamed down my face. Snot ran from my nose. I was officially a waterworks.

I had lost my mind.

Laughter continued to flow out of me for a minute. I wiped the remnants of tears from my face with the edge of my shirt sleeve. I glanced in the rearview mirror and tried to make myself look a little better, which didn't help much. Today was a day, filled with deep breaths and tears. I took another inhale, exhaling slowly through my mouth.

One more time.

"Come on, motherfucker!" I slammed the steering wheel with my palm as I turned the key, and sure enough, the engine caught and started humming or more or less harrumphing. Relief flooded through my limbs. Hot air blew in my face. Well, at least my car was the same.

I pulled out of the driveway to see Mom standing at the doorway waving. Her long dark hair swirled around her face. My chest quivered. I lost it. Tears freely flowed as I drove away. My mom's tiny figure grew smaller. She continued to wave until I disappeared around the corner. I needed some tissues.

4

Callum

ALMOST A FULL DAY HAD PASSED SINCE THE FIGHT. THE SOUND OF Realmers trying to move out rubble and destruction echoed through our mountain. Hammers lifted, wheelbarrows were filled and litter hauled away. The reconstruction was underway. Now and then, something flew by, or the ground shook as someone used their powers to help. The fighting destroyed our crops to mulch. Glass from the Vitamin D bulbs littered the ground. Only a few survived. The hazy blue light lent an alien atmosphere, looking across all of the destruction.

Sloane was gone. The picture of her held by that creature wouldn't leave my mind. Her screams echoed in my ears. The terror scorched on her face as the creature tried to carve into her chest. It was terrifying. Now, my only thoughts of her being gone were because the creature had somehow taken her. I still had the fake Willow sword. It was hidden under my bed, away from prying eyes.

My fists tightened, and I squeezed my eyes shut, trying to abolish the horrific memory. No one found her. One second, she was a few feet from me, and the next, she was gone, as if a pit opened and swallowed her whole. I hadn't been able to save her. I was useless. Like usual.

After the battle, the remaining Nightlins ran off. The portals they used blinked out of existence. We were at a loss. I was lost. I felt useless like a broken rudder with no direction.

So far, we were missing thirteen people. Lucky thirteen. That number would rise.

The cleanup was underway, but I kept searching for Sloane. The creatures left so much destruction. How did they know how to get in? They were more aggressive and showed signs of intelligence that we had never seen before. Something changed amongst the Nightlins.

A ball of nerves sat in my stomach like a bomb about to detonate at any moment.

Things didn't make sense, and I questioned everyone around me. Not that I trusted people, to begin with, they always had a way of letting me down. Footsteps crunched the rubble behind me. I stiffened, not wanting to deal with anyone.

"Callum?" Irene approached. Her usually bright red hair was matted down with dust and swirled with sweat that made a pasty mud that stuck to her pale skin.

I nodded, signaling I heard her.

"We've searched everywhere. We can't find her. One other body was found, but that's it. Our missing numbers are now sixteen."

What the hell happened? How did those people disappear? I was sure the Nightlins were to blame, but the where and how completely confused me.

I drew in a ragged breath. "Okay, thanks for letting me know."

A corner of her mouth lifted. "Of course. And we found Harris under some rocks." She paused, "He isn't in great shape, but he should heal fine."

"Oh, okay. I'll go see him then."

She studied me for a moment and a flicker of what looked like pity creased her features. "Don't worry Callum. She'll turn up." She turned back the way she came and disappeared through once used to be a hallway.

The rough stone cut into my legs as I sat on the edge of the building. A vast hole from a blast lay beneath me. Sometimes, I felt like disappearing into the darkness. Sometimes, I wanted to be free of this place and all the burdens that fell on me. The wreckage reminded me even more of those burdens. Smoke rose from different burn piles, and rubble was strewn throughout the area. Realmers walked back and forth carrying debris or brushing paths off. My views on the Nightlins were changing by the minute despite hundreds of years of history. This attack was more calculated like they knew exactly where to hit us.

Running my fingers through my shaggy dark hair, I grasped the roots and tugged. The pain eased the tension behind my eyes. It was a mess. My emotions were a mess. My heart heaved from the grief of losing so many. It would take time to rebuild, but we would do it. Somehow, we always made it back from despair.

In the darkest of times, I thought of my sister and parents. *Would my sister even like me now?* Her russet brown hair and sparkling blue eyes flashed in my memory. Now and then, Sloane reminded me of her. *Would my parents have been proud of what I had become?* Who knows, most days I wasn't sure Sloane even liked me.

A hazy breeze blew in from one of the ducts piping fresh air into the mountain. It carried the scent of lavender and roses with it. The sound of crickets tuning their instruments barely reached me even with my enhanced hearing. This dark, bleak world chapped my ass sometimes.

"Sloane," I murmured. "You better be out there. You better come back." I rubbed the center of my chest, trying to ease the tension and pain. Another loss would break me.

Time to find Harris, Ashlen, and Raleigh. I had a mission to focus on, for now. I stood ready to find those crazy people I called friends. We needed to talk.

5

Sloane

THE NORM DEFENSE building was nondescript, with a lot of browns. I had driven by it several times before I finally realized where it was. It didn't help that it was dark out, and only street lights illuminated the signs. I'm sure that was part of their scheme. I parked in a nearby garage then walked to the street.

I stood outside the front door sizing it up. The office building was nestled between other boring office buildings. I think one held a few law firms while the other housed a software company. At least, that's what I made out from the signage. Unlike the other offices, the Norm Defense had no prominent signs or decorative features to call attention to it. A small gold-plated plaque was mounted onto the brick by the door. The address was nowhere to be found. I tried to peer inside the glass doors, but they were that annoying mirrored glass. *They better not be closed.* The only thing reflected was my rumpled disgruntled self staring hotly at the door.

Someone or something watched me, and I knew they were waiting for me to make a decision. My foot tapped impatiently on the cement sidewalk. *All right, let's do this.* I stood a little straighter and pushed my way through the double doors.

Cool air saved me from the Oklahoma heat. It didn't matter that the sun had set. It was still stifling.

As my eyes adjusted to the interior lights, I found a large, wooden reception desk centered in the open room. A large wall with what looked like gold leafing was positioned behind the desk. A small round woman waddled out from behind the wall. Thin bright-blue rimmed glasses perched on the tip of her nose, threatening to slip off. She smiled brightly but only with her mouth. Her eyes scrutinized every inch of me.

I scanned the rest of the room, there were no other exits except the front door and the way the lady had entered. I spotted a couple cameras perched in the corners, but nothing else stood out.

"Yes, may I help you?" Her voice was squeakier than I had imagined.

I smiled slightly to try to put her at ease. "Yes, thank you. This is the Norm Defense, right?"

I reached the desk and stopped right in front of her. I kept my hands down by my side and tried to look innocent, which was usually easy for me.

Her head tilted slightly like I had said something peculiar. "Yes, it is. Can I help you with something?"

"Well, you see I need to use a portal so I can get back to the Realm..."

Her eyebrows shot up, and her hand snapped out and hit something out of view. I looked around for a flashing light or men in security outfits to come running. She looked around the room like she was searching for something. Her small eyes had grown a size or two. "There is no reason for you to be here."

I pressed my lips together to keep from smarting off to her. "Why not?"

She crossed her arms tightly across her large chest. "You are a groundling and therefore have no importance in this office. Your self-value is not fitting to one who is allowed admittance back into the Realm," while she talked, she leaned closer toward me; her voice getting lower just in case someone overheard.

"Judy, that is no way to talk to one of ours." A tall, thin regal man walked out from behind the wall. He looked to be between forty and sixty. His features ran together in a way I couldn't tell his age. That was an issue with the realm. Time was different and those who went there aged differently. His salt and pepper hair had more pepper than salt. His jawline was square and strong. Light grey eyes smiled from beneath scraggly eyebrows. I didn't feel afraid of him, but he held a lot of power. The air surrounding him gave off small waves of electricity, which I had never experienced.

His hands were behind him, and he smiled slightly when he spoke, "Hi, I'm Adam Stephenson, the Director of the Norm Defense."

My eyes grew a little larger.

"Why don't you follow me, so we can speak more easily and be comfortable?"

He stood to the side and held out a hand, waiting for me to walk before him. I glanced at the lady. She looked more stunned than me; her cheeks tinted a slight pink when she had been reprimanded. Her attention was fixed on the Director as if horrified to have brought his attention. I peered behind me one last time at the double doors.

Adam chuckled. "You can leave anytime. I have a feeling though you'll want to stay." His eyes crinkled with a smile; they were kind and honest looking.

Now or never.

I took a deep breath and stepped around the desk. A regular wooden door blocked our way. I stopped and looked back at the Director. He smiled at the lady and tipped an imaginary hat at her.

"Thank you, Judy, for bringing my attention to our guest." He winked at me and strolled to the door.

Judy peered around the wall; her eyes staring unbelieving at us. I couldn't help but smile and wave as we walked through the doorway. We stepped into the middle of a grey hallway that had several closed doors located down the side of the hall and stark white floors that looked as if no one ever walked on them. The Director turned down the right side of the hall and stopped at a door with the number five painted a midnight black in the center.

This door led us into what looked like a normal executive office. Where the hallway had been bland, this room was rich and warm. Bookcases lined the walls. Each shelf was packed with books of every size and color. Large picture windows filled the main wall. A heavy wooden desk sat in front. Two comfy cranberry red upholstered chairs were paired in front of the desk. An enormous Oriental rug covered most of the cherry wood flooring.

The Director walked behind the desk and gestured for me to take a seat. He rested against his dark brown leather chair, folding his hands on top of the desk. His grey eyes sparkled with an unknown amusement.

"What can I do for you?"

I sat on the edge of my seat, ready to bolt at any moment. I scanned the room looking for any sort of threat.

"I can tell you're a fighter. Your eyes haven't been steady since we met." He seemed pleased with his observation, as he shifted in his fancy chair.

I ignored his comment and replied, "I need a portal to get to the Realm. Somehow, I was teleported back here, but my friends were in the middle of a battle. I need to get back to them."

He nodded as I spoke.

"Yes, we heard from Chuck. We lost many Realmers in that attack."

"You spoke to Chuck?" My heart hammered against my ribs.

He nodded solemnly. "He isn't sure of how many casualties yet, but he's certain at least twenty are missing. We sent over more help to regain order and rebuild Kingston. It's been a couple of days since we last heard from him. Our next contact is scheduled for tomorrow."

My mind stalled. "A couple days?"

He nodded, looking at me questioningly. I tallied up the hours from my time waking up, and it had been at most ten hours. Where had I been? Had I been knocked out on my bed for a day? Mom wouldn't have known since she was out of town. Another piece of the ever-growing puzzle.

"So, will you be able to send me back?" I asked hopefully.

He studied me for a moment before answering, "You are a

groundling. It is not customary to send over someone of your level out of the usual time frame. I understand how you might want to help your friends, but you must take into counsel the fact that it might be better for you to stay here."

My fingers clenched in my lap, digging into my legs. I fought the urge to roll my eyes. I settled for grinding my teeth.

"Listen, I need to go back. Please, let me go. I won't be a hindrance. They need me, and I need them." Tears pooled at the corners of my eyes. I was mad at them for appearing. *Don't be a cry baby in front of this idiot. Keep your shit together for a little longer for god's sake.*

The Director studied me. His fingertips pressed together forming a narrow triangle against his thin lips. He peered over the tips of his fingers, examining me. His chest and shoulders rose as he took a deep breath then gazed out the window into darkness mixed with city lights. His conflicting feelings were evident.

"Chuck did mention, you had certain abilities." He stared in thought. "The best answer I can give you is that the journey is up to you."

My heart sank slightly, but I fought to keep some hope.

He glanced at me. "For now, we can provide you with a place to stay and some food. I will make a call about finding a chaperone for you when you crossover. It might take some time to find someone, but I'll let you know."

I nodded slowly like I had a clue what he was talking about. "Okay."

He seemed to like my answer because he rose and opened the door. I stood quickly and tried to keep up with him.

Our shoes echoed as we made our way down the hall, passing the numbered doors. We passed the main door that led back to the lobby (I knew it was the lobby because of the black L painted on it) and stopped at the number twelve door. The hall was shorter and only had three doors to choose from. The director led me to the middle one, which led us into a large room with a magnificent staircase located in the center. The stairway traveled up. We mounted the stairs. The soft carpet muffled our steps.

The room we stepped into had windows that mirrored each other. Small beds, maybe thirty, were located in the center of the room. Two doors were positioned on one wall, each with either a figure of a boy or girl painted in the center. Probably the bathrooms.

"Pick up the phone and dial three to order food. Order anything you want. Someone will deliver it within a few minutes. Do you have any questions?"

My mind stuttered for a few seconds, rummaging through information. "Is there a Chris or Sam or Sarah here that would have known my dad? James?" He frowned in thought. I swear I saw a flicker of something, like annoyance, cross his face.

"No. Not that I'm aware."

"What about making calls out?"

"Dial nine first." He smiled and started down the grand staircase. Without turning around, he said, "If you yell for someone, no one will hear you, so make sure you pick up the phone." He disappeared.

That wasn't very nice of him to say. I looked around the space. Alone in a strange place once again. I picked a bed close to the bathroom but away from the windows. The springs in the mattress groaned when I sat, making me frown. I laid my bag on the floor beside me and examined my surroundings some more.

The room was comfortable and surprisingly cozy, despite its large size and dorm-style beds. Amber-colored walls would no doubt be gorgeous in the morning when they reflected the sunlight. Rich red drapes framed the massive wall of windows. The drapes touched the ceiling and pooled slightly on the floor. A rod stretched from one corner to the next, in case I wanted to block out the windows. The wood flooring was a mix of colors, but the planks were almost a foot wide. All of the cots had a grey-blue coverlet and a fluffy, white pillow along with crisp, white sheets that were amazingly soft when I ran my hand across it.

A glass railing encircled the staircase opening, so the space was uninterrupted. My eyes landed on the phone and my stomach instantly rumbled even though I had devoured all the snacks and sandwiches during the trip. I picked up the receiver. Sticking my finger in the number three spot I turned the dial and waited. The phone rang once and someone picked it up.

"Hello?" a boy asked.

"Hi, I'd like to order some food?"

"Sorry. Kitchen closed."

"Oh, I'm sorry. Is there maybe some—"

The boy snorted. "Just kidding. What ya need?"

I was slightly taken off guard, so I didn't respond right away.

"Hey, ya there?" he started mumbling.

"Yeah, sorry. I'm here. Ummm... what do you recommend?"

"Well, I can get you anything just name it."

"Umm... okay. Well..." I looked around the room for inspiration.

"Come on lady, I'm getting old." I heard him snort in the background. I don't think he communicated with very many people, or he was a more awkward teenager than me.

I looked at the phone. "Sorry, how about Italian?"

"I need more specifics than that."

My eyebrows knitted together, and I frowned at the phone.

"Well, how about vegetarian lasagna- no beef, with extra marinara sauce and breadsticks and a ginormous cup of lemonade. Oh, and some dark chocolate with maybe mint chocolate chip ice cream?"

No one replied.

"Uh, hello?"

"Yeah, lady I got it. I'm writing it down. I'll have it up in thirty." And he hung up.

I stared at the phone for a second longer then slowly replaced the receiver in the cradle. *What kind of place was I in?*

If the beds hadn't been in the room, the space could have been used as a dance floor. One set of windows looked onto the back of the building, a parking area, and a small park where a fish pond sat in the middle surrounded by benches and lights. A guy ran along the street on his evening run. Several cars drove out of the parking area. I reached the corner and pulled on the drapes. They glided easily along the rod, barely making a sound. I pulled them halfway across the view, blotting out part of the city's light.

I went to the opposite side of the room to look out those windows. Looking down, I saw the sidewalk, where I had entered the building. Small trees and planters were set into the ground intermittently along the sidewalk. More office buildings, apartments, and other parts of big city life stretched on for miles in both directions. Lights were on throughout some of the buildings and along the streets. Offices were empty, and people were already relaxing at home from a long day at work.

I grabbed the drapes in the corner and pulled them across. Footsteps echoed behind me and I spun around, readying myself for anything. A short, rounded boy stood by the staircase with a tray in his arms. Dressed in faded jeans that hung low, a worn red t-shirt, and a white apron with several stains, he visibly strained under the weight of the food.

"Where ya want it?"

I quickly walked toward him. "Can I help?"

He lifted his chin indignantly. "No, just tell me where to drop it."

I stopped and pointed to the bed I had chosen. His eyes narrowed as he concentrated on each step toward my spot. He made it without dropping anything if only for the sweat running down his forehead and neck. He panted a little. He nodded to me and turned to leave.

"Wait."

He stopped and peered over his shoulder at me. "What?"

"I was wondering about the place?"

One eyebrow rose and he faced me. "Oh? Like what?"

I shrugged. "Where are all the people? How does this place work? Have you been to the Realm?"

He studied me for a moment and glanced at the tray of towering food. "You better eat before it gets cold or melts."

I glanced at the food then back at him; he was watching me. I sat and pulled the tray into my lap, cutting a piece of steaming lasagna. I blew on it and took a bite.

"This is great."

"Well, of course, it is." He sat on one of the cots down from me, for some reason the bed didn't complain when he took his seat. I frowned again.

"Most of the people are located in the heart of the building working away on secret stuff. I have no clue what they do because everything is heavily guarded so I can't help you with that, and, no, I haven't been to the Realm, because I'm not of age yet." He stared at the floor as he talked, "I'm still in high school. I come here after school and on the weekends. My father works in a department that's too secret for me to know, and my mom helps out in the kitchen with me."

"What's your name?" I asked between bites.

His beady eyes regarded me before he answered, "I'm Andrew."

"Nice to meet you, I'm Sloane Sullivan." My father's last name popped out before I realized it. I liked the sound of it. "Hey, do you know if a Sam, or Sarah, or Chris works here?"

"Uh, I'm not sure but I can ask some of the people in the kitchen when I go back."

"Yes! That would be great. Thanks." I tried to keep my desperation to myself, but I was pretty sure I failed.

He smirked, got up, and turned away without saying anything.

"Um, thanks for the food and info."

He waved his hand back at me but didn't look back. "Yeah, whatever." He sauntered down the stairs.

People were so weird. Realmers were even weirder with their vague descriptions and everything being a damn secret. The secrecy ingrained into them even as kids was the reason I didn't know my father's real name, or that my mother didn't know she wasn't abandoned by the love of her life. I mean I get the need to protect the public. One stupid tweet and the whole world would be in chaos, sending nukes to a place they couldn't find, but seriously loved ones should know more.

Focusing my attention away from my anger and back to my glorious food, I quickly demolished it. Who knew when the next time I'd get such a great meal as lasagna. I laid the empty tray on one of the beds and grabbed my bag. I went into the bathroom and got ready for sleep. The shower I took was relaxing. Super hot water sprayed across my back reminding me how much I loved indoor plumbing. I would miss the nice bathrooms on the other side.

So used to the dark, I quickly switched off every light and snuggled under the soft sheets, hoping for sweet, undisturbed dreams. It didn't happen. Every little noise woke me. Subconsciously I feared an attack. When would I feel safe again?

"Psst!" a head popped up at the stairs.

My heart nearly stopped. A woman, with short-cropped brown hair and wearing a big coat over her loungewear, quietly hurried to my bed. She pressed a finger to her lips, motioning for me to stay quiet.

I nodded. She waved for me to follow her and for some reason, I did. My mom taught me all about stranger danger, yet here I was following a stranger. Mom would be pissed.

The woman went to the patio door, opened it, and stepped through. Her rubber galoshes squeaked on the brick patio. She held the door open for me. The night air was humid and left my skin feeling sticky.

She closed the door behind us then faced me. "One second." She pulled out a small black box and set it on the rail. The box illuminated and a blue light shot up and enveloped us. She smiled. "There. This way, no one will be able to listen in. I feel much better. Andrew told me you were here." Her eyes softened as they traveled down to my toes then back to my face. "You have your father's eyes."

6

Sloane

My lips parted in surprise. "You knew my dad?"

The woman smiled and nodded. "Yes, we fought together." She thrust her hand out. "I'm Sarah."

Hope filled me. I smiled back and grasped her hand. She shook mine firmly. Her palms and fingers had calluses and were dry. "Oh, I'm so happy to meet you. I didn't have a lot of faith in Andrew, but I'm glad he found you."

Sarah chuckled, "He doesn't seem like much, but he's a good boy. He knows about keeping secrets." She looked around us as if she was making sure no one heard. "We don't have long. I know they were able to get a hold of someone to take you back over, and I think she'll be here soon."

I nodded having no idea where this was going but feeling like I was finally getting somewhere.

"When you go back, be careful who you talk to."

Oh no. "Uhh."

She waved a hand. "I know it's a lot for you especially since you don't know much, but we learned recently that there are others in our ranks that might not be pulling for our side." She grabbed both of my hands in hers. "Watch out for those that try to lead you astray or send you down a different path. Keep searching for your father. Don't give up. Your uncle was a real jackass and wanted all the power and recognition. He was the one who got your father caught by those creatures."

My mouth fell open. "What?"

She nodded. "Yeah, I was with Jacob when he disregarded orders and went after James. The Nightlin that attacked us on our mission was stronger and faster and tore us to shreds. I and another survived. Barely." She took a deep breath. "There are some in the realm that doesn't want the light to win. They want power too. But I hope they don't get it. I think they are being fed lies. We aren't sure but the creatures may feed off of our bodies." She paused, eyeing me. "Sloane, you have to be careful. There's only a handful of The Dirty Dozen left."

She rummaged in her coat pocket. "We all have one of these." She held out a compass. It looked similar to the one around my neck, except it was smaller and black. "It will help you find the others."

I tugged Artemis out from under my collar. Sarah smiled.

"Yes, that one belonged to James." She brought hers close to it and the needles swung around to meet. A blue glow emitted from the compasses. "If you find Morgan, Alvaro, or Jameson, they will help you."

My eyebrows rose. "Morgan? I've already met him."

Sarah nodded and tucked her compass back into her pocket. "Yes, Morgan is a funny one for sure. But he will help you. He's been helping you even when you didn't know it."

A knock sounded from below us.

"Crap, that's her. Sloane, be careful. They will try to mislead you. Don't let them. Find the others." She hugged me tightly and stepped back. Her honey-colored eyes looked shiny as if tears might fall. "Gosh, you do look like him."

She grabbed the little black box, punching the button off. The blue light dissipated. The sounds of the night filled my ears. She grabbed my hand.

"Come on, gotta go now." She pulled me inside and shut the glass door. "Don't forget okay?"

I nodded. My heart jumped into my throat. Anxiety gripped me.

Sarah raced to the opposite end of the room. She glanced back one more time giving me a thumbs up.

"You've got this. Good luck." She whispered then vanished through the door. It clicked shut softly behind her.

I scurried to my bed and pulled the covers across my middle. My heart thundered in my chest. I took slow methodical breaths to slow it.

A small light, like from a candle, glowed from the stairs and grew brighter as whoever carried it traveled up. Someone with long hair, several layers of clothes, and a big backpack stopped at the top tread. They gazed around the room. A woman walked toward me.

The candlelight made her skin glow. She was maybe the most beautiful woman I had ever seen, but there was a threat of danger hiding underneath her façade. Her long-full hair fell across her shoulders accentuating her long neck and strong jaw. She had high cheekbones and full lips. Her dark eyes were large and paired with perfectly shaped brows. The only thing that made her face less than perfect was her nose, which was slightly out of line, but it somehow made her seem more real.

She stopped and sat on the cot opposite me. She set the candle between us, releasing the handle; it hovered steadily in the air. I stared at it, slightly afraid it might jump on me. I sat up quickly, swinging my legs around and setting my feet on the floor. Neither of us said anything at first, we simply studied each other. I glanced at the candle now and then. Her elbows rested on her knees and her fingers laced together. Her lips were tight, and her large eyes narrowed.

Her tall, brown leather boots reached the top of her knees. Even though it was summer and in the middle of Oklahoma, she wore a thick jacket that fell to mid-calf. A collared shirt and vest rounded out her ensemble. Her oil black, wavy hair easily reached her waist.

"You must be the girl everyone is talking about." Her honeyed voice had a slight accent, maybe French?

"I am?" I was still slightly in awe of her.

She tilted her head and a corner of her mouth lifted slightly, "I assume you are. There aren't any other groundlings here trying to travel back to the Realm."

"Yeah, that's true." My cheeks reddened. I hoped she hadn't seen it in the dark. "Who are you?"

Her smile grew wider. I had a feeling she had a perfect smile too. I wanted to hate her but not yet.

"You may call me Celest. I am a Hunter, though it has been several years since I was in the Realm. I was called to escort you tomorrow."

My eyebrows shot up. "You were called specifically to go back with me?"

She nodded. "You have, in a sense, been put into my charge."

"Your charge?" I felt slightly offended. This time she smiled, and it was *perfect*. My anger threatened my mood.

"Do not take offense, rather you should feel special that they called me and that I answered." She's awfully high and mighty.

"What made you agree?"

She sighed, her eyes became a little sad and she lowered her head. "Your father saved my life a long time ago, and I never was able to repay him. This is my payment."

I studied her for a moment. "How old are you?"

She smiled again. "You are quick. They said you were. I am twenty-seven." Her eyes sparkled with amusement.

I folded my arms over my chest. "How long have you been twenty-seven?"

She leaned forward. "You need your rest. We have a big morning ahead of us." She raised her sleeve, a watch face illuminated. "It's a little after two. You have about five more hours."

I leaned back, resting my head on the pillow. "I don't know how I'm going to be able to go to sleep," I muttered.

Celest stood and pulled something out from inside her coat. A small leather bag with drawstrings. She slid her hand inside and pulled something out.

"This should help." She released whatever was in her hand over my face. It felt like sand.

"Is that…" My mind went blank. Sleep consumed me.

7

THE SUN'S MORNING RAYS BURNED MY EYES — SOMETHING TO GET USED to again. But I wasn't going to have the time. Someone had pulled the curtains back. A tray of food sat next to me. It was piled with toast, jam, fruit, O.J., sausage, and waffles floating in syrup. I ate most of it.

Celest came down the spiral staircase. She looked even more beautiful in the morning light. Her golden skin glowed in the soft rays, and her black hair shone. A tinge of jealousy sang through me.

"Morning, you have about thirty minutes before we need to go up."

I immediately finished my food, grabbed my bag, and headed for the bathroom. I scrubbed my face and brushed my hair. I was ready in about twenty minutes.

My mind drifted back to Sarah last night and her warning. Was this woman trustworthy? I already didn't like her. She was too pretty and too lofty for my tastes. I chastised myself for being jealous. *Come on, Sloane, be a big girl.*

Celest stared out the back windows when I came out of the bathroom. She glanced at me. She looked older in that one glance, then it was gone, and her youth smoothed the lines on her face.

"Are you ready?" Her accent seemed a little more pronounced this morning.

"Yes, I think so." I secured my bag across my shoulders and chest. Artemis was still safely resting on the chain around my neck. I had tucked her underneath my shirt. I patted my thigh and felt Masada. The only one missing was the fake Willow, the one that would lead us. I winced inwardly. Hopefully, Callum or someone I trusted picked it up for me.

Celest grabbed her bag from the floor, swinging it onto her shoulders. She made her way to the spiral staircase.

We climbed the stairs in silence. I was too busy worrying about how I was getting back to the Realm, and she seemed at ease with the quiet. The stairs led us into a small sitting room with a fireplace and T.V. I wish I had known about the T.V. She stopped in front of the fireplace and moved one of the candle holders on the mantel. The back of the fireplace moved to reveal a dark hallway. It felt as if I was in the midst of my very own Agatha Christie novel.

We stepped over the wood and ashes and into the dark hall. Right when we stepped inside, the rock slid back in place, and lights flickered on overhead. The end of the hall led us to more stairs. These stairs continued upward for a while. My legs and lungs burned by the time we reached the door at the top. Celest didn't seem troubled by the exertion even with her heavy clothing on. We stepped through the door onto the top of the building. She glanced at her watch.

"We have about five minutes."

We walked across the gravelly flat top and around the vents of the A.C. units. I spotted the director in the corner of the rooftop. He kneeled while meddling with something I couldn't see.

He looked over his shoulder at us. "Good, you made it." He glanced at his watch. "Not much longer now. Sloane, did you sleep well?"

I glanced at Celest, she had her attention fixed on the director. "Yes, I did actually."

"I'm glad." He had both hands in his pockets. The only thing different about his outfit was his tie; it was bright yellow silk. It contrasted nicely with his hair and grey eyes. He smiled and rubbed his hands together. "All right, it's time."

He walked to the edge of the building, peered over, and gestured for us to follow.

"It's ready." He smiled wide.

I peeked over the edge. People going about their day hurried by on the dirty sidewalk. Cars zoomed the streets up and down oblivious to us overhead. I looked at him, "Don't tell me. We're supposed to jump?"

Celest rested her hand on my shoulder, it tightened slightly. I faced her, a corner of her mouth quirked up.

"Shit." I exhaled.

The director's eyebrows raised a fraction. "Are you going to be okay?"

"How do you know where the portal is?" I wasn't one to be scared of heights but jumping with no rope terrified me. *Call me crazy.*

"We have markers that tell us where it is as long as we jump between that orange marker and that one you should be fine."

I spotted small orange triangular markers that had been placed on the edge of the building. They were spaced about ten feet apart.

"How do we know how far to jump?"

"As long as you're in the middle of those markers you'll be fine." He looked at his watch. "You need to go now if you're going to make it."

Celest watched me. She bent down, picked up a small white pebble, and tossed it between the markers. A popping noise sounded and something that looked like electricity cracked when the pebble hit the portal, but it vanished.

"I'll go after you. Don't think, just jump."

Ha, yeah sure, lady. I took a deep breath and tried not to think. I stepped up on the edge with my hands extended out to the side for balance.

"You have less than a minute." The director's eyes were glued to his watch. "Forty seconds. Thirty-five."

"Adam, you're making it worse." Celest glared at him.

"She needs to go now if she's going."

"Stop being so pushy. She's going to go." Celest shifted her dark eyes my way and nodded.

"Twenty-five seconds…"

This was it. I looked below me and took another deep breath. No problem, we can do this. I lifted my left foot into the air and fell forward. The air rushed by me and the street below grew closer. The buildings around me blurred. I screamed with every ounce in me.

My body stopped an inch from the ground. I hovered for an excruciatingly long second. The pavement melted into a black liquid and before I knew it, I was being submerged. I found myself choking. Liquid filled my senses. I only saw black. My ears were a void. It felt as if hours passed before I became aware of my surroundings. Sounds were too far away. I coughed and gagged. Something or someone landed beside me.

"Sloane?" It was Celest. She had followed me after all.

"I'm here. I just can't see anything."

We were in a small clearing with trees surrounding us and of course, it was pitch-black. I fished around in my bag for my Maglite and eventually found it.

"Shut that off." Celest had her hand shielding her face.

"Sorry," I muttered and immediately switched it off.

"You newbies never learn. Hasn't your night vision been acquired yet?"

"Yeah, I guess."

Her eyes narrowed as she studied me, "You guess? You should know if it had or not." She stood and dusted herself off. She twisted her hair and used something to keep it pulled back from her face. She looked beautiful once again. She focused her attention on the sky. She kept walking around the clearing, trying to find something up in the stars. She mumbled as she walked back and forth.

"That way." She spun around and pointed in a direction past me. "Come on, hopefully, we aren't too far away." She grabbed her bag from the ground and marched past.

I scrambled to catch her.

The moonlight provided us with a perfect guiding light.

"So, are you like my fairy godmother or personal bodyguard?"

Celest glanced at me, a small smile spread across her face. "You might say I'm a little bit of both."

I recognized the precipice that Graham had first led us to the first time we used a portal into the city. As we neared the edge, my heart almost stopped. The area was filled with deafening silence. Bodies littered the ground. Thankfully, no portals were hanging open above Kingston's mountain.

I looked at Celest, who had stopped at the edge surveying the damage as well. Her face was a mask. She turned toward the small path that led down the cliffside without saying a word. I followed her and did my best not to trip and fall down the mountain. Celest was agile and gracefully moved over the large rocks or gaps in the path. She kept checking to see that I had made it unscathed. We reached the bottom faster than I remembered the first time descending the cliff.

The small river gurgled and moved slowly. Our footsteps echoed on the wooden planks when we stepped on them. Celest grabbed the rope and pulled us to the other side. Before going to the edge where the portal was located, she picked up a small rock off the side of the bank.

"Wait." She tossed the rock into the center of the portal. The rock made a plopping noise as it hit the water.

Celest shook her head. "Great. They must have closed this one after the attack. We have to take the old route. I hope it's been kept up."

I had no idea what that meant. My anxiety traveled from my toes to my fingers. My muscles quivered with uncertainty.

"This way." She faced the mountain and ambled to the right where the largest of the mountain ranges met.

My heart thundered in my chest with each footfall. Of course, things wouldn't be going as they should.

We stepped through the underbrush, fighting the tall grass and pine needles. Celest walked up to the mountain wall and gently tapped it with her knuckles. She stopped, listened, and looked north and south then headed south along the wall. Her fingertips brushed the rough rock.

She abruptly stopped and tilted her head as if listening to something, and rapped again on the rock and waited. "Here it is." She faced the mountain wall, staring at it. Celest inhaled deep and slowly released the air.

The rock wall vibrated and shook underneath her fingertips.

I took a step back watching as she revealed one of her Hunter abilities. She was an earthmover.

Pebbles and dirt fell from the mountainside. Celest stood firm, unwavering. She pressed her fingers harder into the rock. Her knuckles turned white. The mountain face quivered. A rough rectangle appeared in the rock. Small gaps formed between the shape and the rest of the mountain mass. It was maybe six feet tall and two feet wide.

Celest called over her shoulder, "Ready?"

I only nodded. I would have never found this place without her. The idea sent my mind racing into the what-ifs that would have happened if my powers had dropped me back into the realm. She focused back on the wall. Placing her palm against the rectangular shape, she barely pushed it inward. Something groaned and the rock sounded like an old man protesting being moved. Inch by inch the door pushed in. It swung on a hidden hinge to the right. A depthless tunnel welcomed us, with no end in sight.

Celest pulled out a long stick, similar to Callum's, and a bright white light exuded from the tip. The tunnel indeed seemed to go on forever and traveled upward.

"All right, watch your step. Let's hurry." Celest stepped through the opening and strode onward.

I paused for a brief moment at the incredulous-ness my life had become. I followed.

"Make sure you close the door," she called out behind her.

Do what? I stared at the rock then back at her. I grabbed hold of the edge and pushed the rock door closed. It wasn't as heavy as I had imagined but still took some effort. The door made a *whoosh* as it closed, sealing shut once again.

We trudged through the dark soundless tunnel. My heavy breathing echoed off the walls. We were on a slow incline. The stale air hung heavy with humidity. I stepped through countless spider-webs and rat carcasses. With each step, I held back a cringe.

I felt the opening of the tunnel before I saw it. The air grew cooler and lighter. Celest's light reflected off the rock wall. She ran her fingers along the edge. Pressing her hand against the rock, she pushed again. Cracking and creaking echoed in the tunnel. Bits of rock fell to the ground while the walls around us quaked. I grew worried that it might fall in on us, but slowly the rock door pushed outward. Light filled the tunnel. The door swung open resting against the wall.

We stopped.

The city was destroyed. The Kingston that had welcomed me was gone.

The thick masonry walls had crumbled, and massive chunks were missing. Most of the buildings were either flattened or had massive holes in them. Smoke rose from small burn piles at the edge of the city. The gardens were a total mess. My heart and stomach mourned for the fresh fruit and veggies, and all of the time and dedication that went into creating food, to survive here. The main building barely stood, but the heart of it was barely touched. Torches lined the walls along with several guards, who were armed to the teeth.

We reached the dirt path that led to the main gate. My heart hammered faster with each step; eager to see my friends and Callum.

8

Callum

MY MIND TANGLED, TRYING TO FIGURE OUT THE FIRE. OF COURSE, I knew it was my new powers being acquired, but it was hard to accept. I could be a danger to others. Yesterday, I had gotten mad at one of the Watchers about something completely inconsequential, and my hands burst into flames. This morning I stubbed my toe on the bed frame, and I scorched the frame leaving black handprints in the wood. I needed to get a grip on the fire at some point. It wasn't the best time to be testing out new powers. Thankfully, Jess said he'd help me later with some private lessons.

I scanned the small group of people. They all reflected the way I felt: tired, annoyed, frustrated, and a little scared. We sat around a long wood table in a small room off the main dining room. Luckily, no Nightlins had touched it. Rory leaned back in his chair like his usual arrogant self. His shirt read, 'Sorry, ladies I only date models'. Raleigh and Irene sat closest to me.

Jess's voice rose as he tried to battle Chuck. "We needed supplies and more people yesterday. Thankfully, they rounded up some new groundlings and redirected them to one of the other cities, but time is running out."

Chuck's fists clenched and unclenched. "We need our defenses now. We might as well be waving our hands outside with our pants down."

Jess scoffed.

They both had a point. Kingston had to be rebuilt now. People were scared when the walls were crumbling. They were able to move a majority of the people into the underground system beneath the city, but that wouldn't last forever. The city needed some serious reconstruction and needed it fast.

What gnawed at the back of my mind the most was the fact that Sloane had disappeared. It had been two days since the attack and Sloane's disappearance. I remembered seeing her in the clutches of that Nightlin. Remembered hearing her screams of agony, which I won't ever be able to erase from my mind, and how I felt completely helpless.

I waited impatiently for the arguments and plans to be resolved. Duty had me here. But once a plan was set, and the city was on the mend, I was setting out to find Sloane. I zoned back into the conversation to hear Chuck griping.

"Those need to have been rebuilt yesterday. Our defense is at zero. That is my main concern right now, rebuilding our defense. The Nightlins will return; it's just a matter of when," Chuck replied a little sharply. He was locked in eternal middle age as the leader, but at this moment he looked twice his age. "The portals to the Norm are at risk. Above all, we can't let them use our portals against us."

"Everyone is pulling their weight, trying to get the defense of the city back up and running." Jess's forehead creased, and his eyes narrowed. His Russian accent grew stronger with his emotions.

"I didn't say they weren't," Chuck snapped.

"Do you think they're done measuring?" Raleigh whispered to Irene, who coughed trying to disguise her giggles.

"And I didn't say you did. I was just stating the fact." Jess sat with his head bowed and his hands folded in front of him. His man-bun flopped to the side and strands escaped. "Waiting to hear from the Norm Defense, is taking a toll on everyone. They sent some people, but... who knows what they were thinking."

"Guys, we all want the same things. We just need to prioritize." Irene tapped her fingers on the table.

"We have to protect the portals," Chuck said as if she hadn't spoken.

Jess's brows knitted together. "And we have to protect the people and our city."

The side door opened and an amazingly beautiful woman walked into the room. Her long wavy black hair framed her face perfectly. She smiled, and it was nearly breathtaking. The testosterone in the room lifted its head and came to attention.

She spread her arms wide and moved toward Chuck, "It has been such a long time stranger." Her accent was European, maybe French. It wasn't very strong, just enough to make you notice.

Chuck rose when she opened the door and instantly returned the hug. The lines of stress wiped from his face and replaced with his usual youthful glow.

"Hi, beautiful." That was an understatement. Everyone either gaped or stared at the pair.

The mystery woman pulled away, pushing her hair back from her face. She was slightly shorter than Chuck and tilted her head up to meet his eyes. Chuck seemed to be completely entranced with her, so was every other male and female in the room.

"Sloane?" Irene asked.

I spun abruptly to look at Irene. Her face held the look of complete surprise and happiness written across it. She smiled and moved toward the doorway, where a thin blonde-haired girl stood, looking somewhat lost. *That couldn't be Sloane.* My chest tightened. It felt like a dream.

Sloane's hair hung around her face and fell across her shoulders, it looked as if her hair had gotten wet and was in the middle of drying. White markings decorated around her eyes and one on her cheek. Several white scars were on her biceps and forearms. Her blue eyes were tired but relieved. Her hair looked lighter. White strands framed her face. She looked so different from when I had last seen her only a couple of days ago.

Irene rushed forward and enveloped her in her arms. Irene wasn't big for her size, but she dwarfed Sloane, which had never happened before. Sloane seemed more fragile, somehow.

Raleigh wrapped Sloane in a hug and wouldn't let go for a solid minute. They both laughed.

"Sloane, where were you? We were getting a search party together!"

"It's a story for sure," Sloane said. The sound of her voice melted some of the tension inside of me.

Tears dotted the corners of Raleigh's eyes. "I can't believe you're okay." She pressed her fingertips to her lips.

I stood like a statue, only watching. I was an idiot for staring, but she probably wasn't surprised.

The others immediately hugged or patted Sloane lovingly. All asking what had happened and how she had gotten back. Sloane mostly kept quiet, only smiling or offering a few words as a response. They formed a semi-circle around her, and I found myself positioned opposite from her. Sloane's eyes landed on me, and her mouth curled into her familiar smile. I felt myself return it. She cut across the circle to stand in front of me.

"Hi." Her ocean-blue eyes were bright and smiling as she looked up.

"Hi." It came out as a whisper, but I smiled back.

She merely took a step toward me, wrapping her arms around my waist and laying her head on my chest. I reacted slowly but my arms instinctively wrapped around her body. My chin rested on the top of her head. I breathed her in, barely moving. I was too afraid I might crush her. That she might not be real. I looked around the room at everyone. They smiled and watched us, but I didn't care.

She had found me again.

9

Sloane

"WHERE HAVE YOU BEEN?" CHUCK ASKED ME FOR ABOUT THE hundredth time.

I sat next to him with Celest on my left. It felt surreal being back in the Realm surrounded by these people like years had passed. The faces surrounding me looked older, especially Chuck's and Callum's. I kept glancing at Callum. His dark green eyes were always watching like usual. The moment I walked in and saw him, calm and relief washed over me. I hadn't realized how much I wanted to see him. Or maybe I had and didn't want to acknowledge it.

I wanted to ask him about that kiss, but that would come later. A warm gooeyness spread throughout my middle at the thought of him. *Gah, I was such a girl.*

I brought my attention back to Chuck, "I woke up in my bed at home in the Norm. I was covered in blood and gore, but it was like I had been dropped there. At first, I couldn't remember what happened. I was so confused as to why I was covered in blood. I cleaned up and found where the Norm Defense was located. Packed my few belongings into my car and drove about six hours to the Defense building. There, I met Director Adam and Celest." I looked around the room and saw how everyone was hanging onto every word. With a sigh, I continued.

"The next morning, I jumped into the portal with Celest. Which was scarier than any of the portals we have here." I glanced at Chuck. He smiled. "We found ourselves in the middle of a clearing, and we walked here, so it took me about a day and a half. I'm not sure what happened between the time of me disappearing from here and waking up in the Norm. I have these scars though from the Nightlins attacking me." I pointed to the scars on my face and arms.

Chuck leaned in closer to look at them and ran his finger over the scars on my right arm.

"Well, we already knew you were different. Maybe your body was healing in stasis?" A frown creased his smooth features. He shook his head. "I'm not sure we will ever find the reasons behind your differences, not that it matters." He smiled gently.

"When we walked in, I noticed you needed some help to rebuild the walls." Celest had her arms folded across her chest with a somewhat smug expression on her face.

Chuck's eyebrows rose a little. "How observant of you." His eyes narrowed. "What do you have in mind?"

Celest rolled her eyes. "Charles, don't tell me you've forgotten me completely, or maybe you never knew me." She clapped her hands together. "Oh, never mind. I can help, but I will need a lot of food to finish my task."

Chuck's eyebrows slammed together, and this time he leaned back in his chair, folding his arms across his chest. "Why will you need food to help us?"

She smiled coyly and flicked her hand out. Rory and his chair immediately lifted off the ground slowly rotating at the same time. Rory yelped and clung to his chair as if it was a life preserver. The floor beneath him had risen under one leg, then another, making it unbalanced, and rotated. The amusement on my face slipped through, and a laugh escaped my lips.

Chuck looked at the rotating Rory and back at Celest. "I guess I didn't know you."

Raleigh took me to see Ashlen and Harris first. Callum followed us a few steps behind— the ever-watching shadow.

"I can't believe you showed up! Ashlen will shit a brick." Raleigh laughed as we followed her through the tunnels.

"Did I miss anything?" I couldn't stop myself from glancing at Callum.

Raleigh replied, "Not really. We are still cleaning up, trying to figure out how the Nightlins made portals, and how they even knew where we were. There have been talks of us relocating, but I'm not sure how that will happen."

We were winding our way up to the apartment rooms. Raleigh had said Ashlen was most likely still in bed.

"I got a new tattoo!" Raleigh stopped in mid-stride to roll her sleeve up and show a thick script style W tattooed in her skin that mixed in with the other part of her tattoo sleeve. "I'm going to get a new letter each time I level up. I can feel the P coming soon." She said excitedly. The skin was still red from the new ink. We all looked at each other and snorted in laughter. Tears welled up from laughing so hard. In her excitement, Raleigh failed to listen to her own words. Within a second she smacked my arm, laughing. "Grow up."

"Wow, nice." I glanced at Callum. "What about you? Anything New?"

A sly smile slowly crossed his face. He shook his head. "Not really."

Raleigh hammered on the door with her fist.

Ashlen yelled through the door, "What?!"

"Ash, it's Raleigh. Can I come in? Are you decent?"

"I'm never decent!"

"Well, get decent! And open the door!" Raleigh flashed a grin and winked at me.

Stomping reverberated through the walls and floor, the door yanked open, and Ashlen stood in the doorway with her rumpled PJs and hair sticking every which way. Her green eyes sparked with anger. "What the hell! This is your room —" Her eyes bloomed larger, and her mouth fell open.

"Oh my god!" Tears welled in Ashlen's eyes. "Sloane!" I had no idea what she said as she grabbed me into a bone-crunching hug. She kept saying something over and over, but her words ran together. My shirt became wet from tears and probably snot.

"Hey, Ash, I made it back." I laughed.

She held me out at arm's length and laughed as tears ran down her face. "I thought you were gone forever!" She grabbed me again and squeezed tighter.

"Agh, Ashlen!"

"Sorry, come in and sit. Tell me what happened." She took my hand and pulled me inside the room. Our old room was still the same, if not messier. She pulled me down to sit on the bed next to her. Her fingers intertwined with mine.

"Where's Harris?" I asked.

"Oh, I bet he's in the kitchen. I'll run and grab him." Raleigh jumped up and rushed out the door. Yelling for Harris as she went.

Callum sat in a chair closest to the door. He leaned back with his arms crossed over his chest. Had his arms gotten bigger? I smiled slightly at him. A rush of heat flooded my body as I thought about the kiss he had given me the night of the battle. Oh man, I was going to need a cold bath. I focused my attention back on Ashlen.

Ashlen still had tears running down her cheeks and snot bubbles blowing out her nose.

"OhmygodSloane. Ohmygod. Ijustdidntknow. Where. You were." Hiccups kept interrupting her breaths making her words run together.

"Ashlen, I'm sorry. It's okay. I'm okay. We are all okay." I patted her hand.

She burst into tears again, throwing her arms around my neck. More hiccups followed. "We're all going to die!"

I frowned and glanced at Callum. He only shrugged. I rolled my eyes.

"What are you talking about?"

She wiped at her eyes and nose. "The Nightlins can make portals. They can pop in here whenever they want." She breathed in deep and let it out slowly. What the hell?

Harris stumbled through the door.

"Thank the Lord! Sloane, you're okay!" His long legs crossed the room in two strides, and he picked me up in a big hug. "Girl, we were so worried. Ash hasn't been able to sleep at all." His southern drawl immediately made me feel warm and cozy. He set me back down beside Ashlen and patted my shoulder. "Hey, Callum, how was the meetin'?"

Callum focused his attention on Harris. "Not a lot happened today after Sloane came in."

Ashlen shook my arm to get my attention. "Okay, what happened? Where'd you go?"

I told her the same story I had told the others. How I woke up at home and made my way to the Norm Defense. Her eyes were so big by the time I finished. At least, her tears and nose had stopped running.

"We found the meeting room and walked in. I didn't realize how friendly Chuck and Celest would be. It was odd." I frowned.

"Wow, that's incredible." Ashlen took another deep breath. "What should we do now?"

We shifted toward everyone else in the room. Raleigh fiddled with a pillow. Harris had his eyes closed. Callum lifted a shoulder in response.

I only thought of one thing. "We need to find Willow. We had to abandon our search because of the attack, so we need to go back."

Ashlen frowned. "I was almost killed. We had to go through the snake pit. Idk."

"Ash, it's the only thing left to do. We need that sword. Speaking of which, where is the fake Willow?"

Callum spoke up, "I've got it in my room."

Heat crawled up my neck. My mind needed to get out of the gutter.

"Great, thanks. I was afraid that I had lost it somewhere." I said, not meeting his gaze.

He nodded. "I've got it when you're ready."

"Hey, do you need some food?" Raleigh asked.

"Yes, that would be wonderful." I smiled. Even if I had eaten more than my weight back at the Norm, I was starving after our travels.

She jumped up. "All right, let's go eat. We can plan our attack."

We filed out and down the hall. Ashlen had her arm wrapped through mine as if she was afraid I might disappear again. Callum, of course, was faithfully behind me. At some point, I needed to tell Ashlen about mine and Callum's kiss. She was going to die and probably be upset that it had taken so long to tell her. Granted an attack had occurred, and I was magically transported, but still, she was going to be pissed it took this long. Her priorities were a little different.

It made me happy to think about it.

A large, round table was empty in the dining hall. Harris took off for the kitchen. He came back with two trays laid out with bread, smoked meats, and steamed veggies. He even had some mead brought out. The ease of being around my friends combined with good food and mead, which was essentially as potent as a glass of sweet wine, helped calm my nerves. The long, bluish-white Vitamin-D bulbs swayed slightly.

I spotted Celest in the corner of the room with Chuck. They seemed to be in a deep conversation. Their bodies leaned in toward each other. I watched them for a moment trying to spot anything to shed some light on their relationship.

"Ready to go back to the room and sleep?" Ashlen asked.

I nodded. "Yeah, let's go."

She smiled and took my arm. As we walked along the corridors and up the stairs, the mead had us swaying slightly.

"Ash, I need to tell you something." I giggled.

"Oh? Some good gossip?" she poked my side.

"Hey, Sloane!" Callum yelled as he hurried down the hall toward us.

Ashlen and I swayed, breaking apart. She squeezed my elbow and winked at me, mouthing, 'Have fun.'

I shook my head at her and rolled my eyes.

She giggled as she headed for our room.

Callum stopped right before he got to me and paused. Silence fell over us for a moment.

I raised an eyebrow.

"Uh, do you want your sword now?" He gestured at the door to his room just a few feet away.

The little bit of alcohol in my system made my stomach swirl even more, and heat rushed up to my neck and cheeks. I nodded.

Callum opened the door to his room, leaving it open for me. My heart pounded like galloping horses as my feet carried me into the room.

His room was dark with only two lamps lighting the corners. Three beds lined the walls. It was a mirror of mine and the girls' room. A kitchen and a wood stove were against the opposite wall. They had no windows, which made me feel a tad sad for them.

Callum walked to the farthest bed and knelt. He swiftly pulled out a bulky item wrapped in blankets. He laid it on the bed.

I stepped forward and removed the blankets. The sword gleamed in the lamplight.

"Thank you for keeping it safe." I picked the sword up. My hand grazed his, and a jolt of electricity shot up my arm. Our eyes locked. *Whatever you do, don't start giggling like an idiot. Don't giggle.* My chest tightened from me stuffing my awkward giggles down.

The sword's weight settled in my hands. I backed away toward the door. I locked eyes with his dark green ones.

Callum shifted his weight from one foot to the other. "Sloane, I'm — I was so relieved to see you. We all were."

I paused almost at the door. My eyebrows rose in surprise, and I smiled slightly. "Thank you. I don't know what happened."

Why was his hair messy? My fingers itched with the want to fix the strands sticking out, instead I rubbed my sweaty palm on my jeans. The smell of my sweat and the gritty dirt all over my clothes made me more embarrassed. I backed closer to the door. His eyes roved over my face, searching for something.

"We have to figure something out. Why did you disappear? Why do you have different anomalies?"

I giggled. Damnit. I pushed my stringy hair from my face.

"One of these days things will come to light." I smiled nervously. The memory of our quick kiss jumped into my mind. Oh, man. Had it meant something?

Callum stood in the center of the room, watching me. Flashes of emotions, I couldn't name, skipped across his face in quick succession. He reminded me of a lonely awkward boy in a schoolyard.

The corner of his mouth lifted. "Have a good night."

I let out a slow breath, trying not to let my disappointment show.

"Thanks, you too." I decided to press my luck.

I stepped closer to him and wrapped my free arm around him in an embrace. He stood motionless for a minute, then wrapped both of his arms around me. His heart thundered in my ear, and his strong arms squeezed me gently. The smell of leather and trees wafted from his t-shirt. I breathed him in, trying to hold it in my mind.

"Sloane?" he whispered.

I looked up at him and smiled softly. His eyes bored into me, moving across my face. He glanced at my mouth for a second, then focused on my eyes. I smiled wider. *Did he find me attractive?* Go figure.

The door flew open and banged against the wall. We both jolted and separated. Harris danced into the room, literally. Gyrating his hips like Elvis, and belting out Britney Spears 'Baby One More Time.'

"Oh! Hey guys!"

I was either going to kill him or maim him one day, who knows what would happen in the heat of the moment. Callum glared at Harris.

"Hey, Harris," I muttered.

Harris flew around the room completely oblivious to Callum and me being in a moment. I started to smile, out of total disbelief.

I took a deep breath. "Well, guess that's my cue to leave. I'll see you later Callum." I waved at Harris. "Bye, Harris, see you tomorrow."

Harris was still humming Britney's hit song to himself. He waved. "Bye, Sloane! See ya in the morn."

I shook my head and slipped out the door.

"Sloane." Callum caught my arm before the door closed behind me.

I turned with my face tilted up toward him. I melted into him. His hand, placed at the base of my back, pulled me tight against him.

Heat crawled up my neck.

"Well, well, well... Finally getting some action. Huh?" Raleigh sauntered down the hall.

We jumped apart. A corner of his mouth lifted slightly. He disappeared behind his door. My goofy grin spread across my face. Gone before anything else happened.

Heat flamed my cheeks.

"Raleigh," I said exasperated and half embarrassed.

She clapped my back. "About time you two got physical. I was going to lock you in a closet together until you sorted things out. We were getting tired of you eye-fucking each other all the time." She laughed as we walked into our room.

I was slightly shocked by her statement. Everyone knew we liked each other? How did they know before I did?

"What do you mean?"

Ashlen looked up from her book.

Raleigh glanced at me. "Oh, come on, you should know better than to ask that. Right, Ash?"

Ashlen nodded, "Right. What are you right about?"

Raleigh gestured at me. "She and Callum, finally hooking up."

Ashlen jolted up in bed. "What! Why am I just now learning this?" She asked me accusingly.

"I — uh — Raleigh caught us in the hallway. I was going to tell you."

Ashlen frowned. "Was that the only time? What happened?"

I chuckled as I sat on my bed. "Nothing happened. Raleigh interrupted before things got interesting." I narrowed my eyes in her direction. She only shrugged. "We've only kissed once. Nothing very exciting. You can thank your boyfriend and Raleigh for interrupting us this last time."

"What am I going to do with you?" she asked accusingly. "And Raleigh, how could you mess things up for Sloane? She's barely gotten to first base with a boy!"

My eyes bugged. "I've gotten to first base with a boy!" Sweat accumulated on my neck and under my arms. I'd die from embarrassment. What was first base again?

Ashlen pierced me with her green eyes saying, oh yeah?

I straightened the bed sheet and my clothes, not meeting her gaze. "I have," I muttered.

"Yeah, okay. That's not the point though. You didn't tell me." Ashlen folded her arms across her chest.

"Ash, things have been pretty crazy the past couple of days. I haven't had time."

Her eyebrow rose, judging. "Yeah? When did the first kiss happen?"

I smoothed the wrinkles on my pants leg. "It was right before we all headed out to fight the Nightlins. It lasted maybe two seconds."

She stayed silent for a minute. "Well, I'll give you this one pass. But next time I wanna be the first to know!"

I smiled. "Okay, okay, I'll tell you first next time. If there's a next time."

Raleigh spooned peanut butter into her mouth. "Oh, there will be a next time." And she winked.

I shook my head. These girls were crazy.

10

Callum

I HAD SOME TROUBLE GETTING TO SLEEP LAST NIGHT BECAUSE OF Sloane. Who was I kidding? The almost kiss. She kept surprising me. I, of course, wanted more time with her, but I knew at some point things needed to be explained. This world grew more and more complicated each day. Who knew when the dust settled, if she would still want me? But no reason to think about that now.

The next morning at 7 a.m., I met Jess outside on the training ground. Needless to say, I was exhausted.

Jess cleared a spot for us to train where the destroyed garden was situated. People milled around us cleaning things up. The ceiling lights had mostly been destroyed so we had moonlight streaming in through the ducts. Plus, Jess positioned pale blue lights around in a small circle. He sat on the dirt with his feet tucked under him in a prayer pose.

"Morning," he said, without opening his eyes.

"Hey, Jess."

"Ready for some burn?" He opened his eyes then. They sparkled with amusement.

I shook my head. A slight smile flitted across my face. "You know it."

He leapt up in one swift movement. "All right, let's get started." He stood in front of me. "Do you have any control at all over it?"

"Some, but not really." The last time flashed in my mind of being fully engulfed. "It takes me a few minutes to de-flame."

Jess nodded. "Okay, ground your feet and breathe through your belly. Let's start small with you only trying to light one finger."

I mentally eye-rolled but took a deep breath centering myself.

"Start with your pinky."

I held my hand in front of my face and closed my mind. I focused on lighting my small finger with flame.

Smoke rose from the tip but no flame.

Jess smiled. "Don't stress. I'm sure the other times the fire came from emotions?"

I nodded. "Yes."

"You know that's not reliable."

"Yeah, it wasn't my choice."

"Okay, center yourself, close your eyes, and think of your internal flame igniting. Picture the flame lighting slowly. Once you have it, move it to your finger."

I felt like an idiot doing all this, but Jess knew what he was doing, so I had to bear with it. I closed my eyes and thought of the flame inside me. It wasn't a match but more like an oil-soaked torch ready to be lit.

I thought of the heat inside my belly burning, engulfing the torch, and setting it ablaze. The torch flickered once then twice. It went out. My patience wore thin.

"Just breathe. Let it pour into you like water."

My brows knitted in concentration. Like water. Let the flame pour like water.

That was the key for it to consume the torch. It rushed in and engulfed the torch in a billowing flame. All heat and blue flame. The hottest part of a fire. Blue flame like the blue of Sloane's eyes.

I poured the flame down my arm and to my finger. The heat travelled happily. Ready to bend to my will.

"You got it!" Jess exclaimed.

My eyes popped open. A soft blue flame danced on my pinky finger. The fire swayed back and forth. I smiled wide.

"All right, move it to your middle finger."

I honed the fire, bidding it to move. It immediately jumped to my middle finger. I smiled again.

"Now, extinguish it on that hand and move it to your middle finger on the other hand."

Oh, man. I pulled the flame back inside and channeled it down my left arm. The heat rushed through me and down my arm. It took a second longer then the flame flickered to life on my middle finger.

"Nice." Jess nodded with approval. "Okay, now spread to your whole body."

"What? Already?"

"Yeah, go for it."

I chuckled. He never failed to surprise me. "I thought you were all about slow and steady."

Jess shrugged. "Sometimes you gotta fly before you can walk. I want to see what all we're working with."

"Do I need a catchphrase?"

Jess smirked. "Oh, the guy has jokes now. Come on big shot. I know we haven't seen a fire starter in a while but no need to rub it in."

I shook my head. My smile spread farther. I took another centering breath and pictured the torch fully lit. It burned hot and crackled. I seized it and pushed it out. Pushed it through my pores, and my whole body felt the heat.

The air sizzled and cracked. Smoke and steam rose from my skin. *Come on flame.* Light. Burn.

My eyes flashed open. The world around me was covered in white light. Flames licked across my hands and arms.

"Amazing. Now pull it from you. Make a ball hang in the air.

Uh, what. My concentration burrowed, diving deeper.

I pulled everything within me and focused on the space in front of me. Holding my hand out I pictured a ball of flame materializing. A small blue orb formed from my palm. It glowed hot and hollow. It sputtered out of life.

"That was a great start." Jess applauded me.

The fire died. Exhaustion settled on my shoulders like a massive weight. All that concentrating took its toll.

"Since the night of that attack at the training ground, we haven't had the trials. Let's sit for a moment. Let you rest." He sat in one fluid movement, tucking his feet underneath him.

I sat like a heavy stone. My body was ready to give out.

"Have there been any more sightings of the creatures?" I asked.

"Yeah, they spotted some of them to the west last night. They were on the move, but we couldn't tell where."

A shiver tickled my spine.

"There's got to be something we're missing."

Jess's mouth and jaw tightened. "Yeah, I'm afraid it's worse than we think."

We fell silent for a moment, lost in thought.

"How long do you think it'll take for me to master this?" I flexed my fingers.

"For me, it took a while for my powers to surface. I had to push myself every day. Push the water into being." He held his palm flat. A tiny bead of water formed on his skin and he rolled it back and forth. "For others, it comes too easily. Some, their emotions get the best of them." He pointedly looked at me. "Most of us it takes a lot of time. The time to focus and harness the power inside."

I studied the lines on my palms, knowing I was meant to be a Hunter. Meant to wield fire.

"What of your Czar?"

Jess's face smoothed and he smiled as if a happy thought crossed his mind. "She is part of me and so much more."

"How long did it take for her to appear?" I leaned forward in anticipation.

"Once I conquered my water, she came. I was able to open that part of me so I could pay more attention and know the signs. But it took months."

I folded my hands in my lap, thinking and wishing for the day my Czar would appear.

"Does she have a name?"

Jess smiled. "Yareakh. It means moon god."

"That seems fitting."

He chuckled. "Yeah, she's incredible. Wanna see her?" His eyes twinkled.

"Of course!"

He smiled wide. "All right, sit tight."

He closed his eyes and stilled. Spreading his arms wide, he tilted his face upward. Water spilled from the ground around us and pooled around his legs then ran up his core and chest, down his arms and hands. The water rushed from each palm and massed in front of us, forming a massive sphere. Light blossomed in the center then pulsed out. Jess pulled his arms together and the sphere of water moved and undulated, like fish churning the waves.

Bright blue wings unfurled and a delicate snout and face peaked out. Yareakh rose higher and higher. Jess's hands stilled and his muscles strained as if he held great weight. She dipped her head toward me. Her shiny scales shimmered and feathers ruffled. A gust of air blew across my face, carrying the smell of salt and exotic flowers. Her nose lightly touched mine. It was cold and wet, and a voice whispered in my mind, *Hi*. The wind roared, and the sound of waves crashing echoed in the cavern. And she was gone in a flash.

Jess bent over. His shoulders heaved as if he had just finished a huge race.

"What did you think?" he gasped.

My mouth hung open. "Uh, yeah, that was incredible."

He leaned back on his elbows, breathing in deep.

"I've never seen one up close before. At least not in the middle of a battle."

"I'm spent now." He eyed me. "Are you feeling better?"

I shrugged a shoulder. "For the most part."

"Okay, let's focus on the smaller things right now. We can build on it as we go." He sat up, sitting cross-legged. "Let's focus on the ball first, separating it from your body and moving it around. If you can master that, you can do anything."

I nodded, breathing in deep and focusing on the fire inside. Heating my core and lighting the torch in a blue, hot flame.

11

Sloane

I found myself in the library walking through the stacks looking for Clifford. I found him in the far corner hunched over piles of books with an ink pen dangling from his lips and ink stains covering his fingers.

My easy smile spread across my face. "Clifford, I'm so glad to see you."

His eyes magnified as he looked up in his coke rim glasses. "Miss Sloane, so good to see you."

I wanted to hug him but was afraid I'd scare him, so I contained myself. "I know. I'm sorry. A good bit has happened."

He nodded. His little cap moved with his head. "I heard a good bit during supper time."

"Oh? People talked about me?"

His bushy white eyebrows shot up. "Of course they did. Why would they not?"

I smiled. He was the sweetest, little guy. "Do you have any news for me?"

He straightened, playing with the pen in his mouth. A spark of thought lit his features, and he motioned for me to follow him. I had to stay with him since he moved so quickly for an older man. He always surprised me with his speed.

I followed him to a bookcase in the farthest corner.

He leaned in closer. "Miss, do not speak of this to anyone. Do you swear?" His tone was very serious, and his eyes stern.

I paused somewhat unsure. "What about Callum?"

Clifford straightened as if measuring me and my question. "That boy from last time?"

A smile tugged the corner of my lips. I nodded.

He shook his head. "That poor boy he's been moping ever since you were gone, Miss."

Air whooshed from my lungs. Callum was that upset about me missing?

Clifford's big eyes watched me. "Okay, you can tell him but only him." We wagged his finger under my nose.

"Of course." I pressed my lips together to keep a smile from slipping out.

He studied me a second longer then faced the bookcase. He drew his finger down the colorful spines, finally landing on an old maroon cover, *Gone with the Wind*. Margaret Mitchell would have been shocked to see her book here. Or had she been a Realmer? How funny was that? My breath nearly stopped as he pulled the book back, and the bookcase swung inward.

Clifford beckoned me as he walked inside the dark stone corridor. He motioned me to follow. Insects ran along the seam of the walls.

"Clifford?" I called.

He peered around the corner waving me forward. "Come on, Miss." He disappeared into the dark hall. "Hurry," he called.

Now or never. As I stepped inside, the bookcase swung close with a thud. What was I getting myself into? Could I trust Clifford? I mean in all sense and purposes I didn't know him. It could be a trap. I bit my bottom lip trying to figure out what to do. The only choice was to follow him.

I always had terrible luck though with these kinds of situations.

Clifford slipped around a corner. I felt comfortable in the dark but this was a whole other level with a secret bookcase and cobwebs hanging down. *To be perfectly honest, this was pretty amazing and had my inner nerd dancing.* It would have been a much easier experience if my Realmer night vision worked. However, mine would flicker on here and there. For some reason, it wouldn't stay on. My powers didn't make any sense. Adrenaline spiked as my heart thundered with each step. I knew Clifford wouldn't put me in danger, but he was so secretive, and the words, *don't trust anyone,* kept tumbling in my mind. I rounded the corner to find myself in a small room. It seemed to be Clifford's. Huh, oddest route to a bedroom, ever.

Books littered the floors, walls, and furniture. His small cot sat in a corner, unmade. The rumpled sheets and pillow looked old and needed a good wash. Papers were tacked all over the walls. One bare bulb hung from the ceiling. Pity rang through me. No one should be living in that room.

He rummaged through some books in a case seeming to find the one he had been looking for. He brought me a bound, navy book. The cover was threadbare and dirty.

"I can't let you take it, but you can read it here." His eyes bore into mine, making sure I understood.

I frowned. "Okay?"

"Just pull the case back to let yourself out." He nodded then scurried from the room.

I stared after him dumbstruck. Was I lucky that I hadn't become minced meat? I released the breath I had been holding then spotted a small, tattered stool. I sat with the book in hand. My curiosity was on high alert.

I opened the book to read the first page, 'The Tales of Kane.'

A line formed between my brows trying to think. Kane? One of the firsts? My lips formed a straight line. What was I about to read? Why wasn't this in the regular library?

The Tales of Kane as told from oral history -

After the murder of Kane's elder brother, Kane disappeared for a time. No one was sure for how long, but some said a hundred years. Many thought him dead or insane until the day he reappeared. Barely aging a day. They wondered if he had found the wells of youth, but he never spoke of his time away.

They noticed his dark eyes though. They said the black bled onto his skin, but only at times of great anger. People began to say the darkness had swallowed him. That the dark was after him for murdering his brother.

What the hell was I reading? Coldness settled over me. I felt as if I was reading something that I shouldn't, yet I couldn't stop. I glanced around the room to see if I spotted any paintings with eyes moving or anything else my imagination conjured from a horror movie, but only old books and leftover trash containers surrounded me. I might have regretted it but I continued. Clifford thought I should read it for a reason.

Kane took what he wanted with no thought for anyone else. He soon took everything he touched. The darkness moved through him. Anything he touched blackened with rot. The disease he carried passed from one being to the next. He seemed delighted by the chaos and death. People would run to warn the next village, and the story spread as Kane came for them too.

The villages were covered with an eerie blackness. It continued to spread on and on. The rot spread like an epidemic with no end in sight.

We had nowhere to escape. We had nowhere to go. We longed for solace but found none. A light appeared. A light that erased the disease that consumed it.

The pages were charred. A few words here and there peeked out on the worn pages.

I sat for a moment trying to digest what I had read. Light and darkness. A disease. What was Clifford saying? I set the book down and found my way down the tunnel and pulled the case back. I squeezed through the opening.

Clifford stood over one of the desks at the entrance of the library.

"Clifford, what was that book?" I whispered.

He pushed his glasses up his nose. His eyes roamed the library then scratched his head. "Well, miss, it's a book I found a while ago. With the new happenings occurring, I thought it best to show you. See if it might help with your travels."

I searched his face for any clues. "What was the dark and light?"

He didn't look at me as he flipped through the various loose pages on the table.

"In the darkness, we shall find a light so dim it cannot hide. A light so faint we cannot see without the help of those who seek. The darkness consumes all it finds except for the light deep inside."

A headache was on its way. All of these rhymes and tricks. I rubbed the space between my brows. I needed a vacation.

12

I found the girls in the dining hall. They were laughing and eating.

"Hey! Where did you go this morning?" Ashlen stuffed her face with a biscuit.

"I went to the library."

Raleigh raised a brow. "More research?"

"Yes, pretty much."

Ashlen and Raleigh glanced at each other.

"Girl, you're going to start smelling like those old books one day," Ashlen said between bites.

Raleigh rolled her eyes. "So, what did you learn?"

Two lines formed between my brows, as I tried to concentrate, trying to figure out what to say. "I read this book."

"Oh, a dirty book?" Ashlen giggled. "I should get you one of those."

Raleigh elbowed her. "Ash, she's being serious."

Ashlen looked at me. "Sorry, what did you read?"

I glanced between them then around the room to see if anyone was paying attention. My chest was tight with tension and stress. Why were things never easy?

"This book spoke of Kane. The beginning."

"Like Kane, Kane?"

I nodded. "At least, I think so. What have you heard?"

Ashlen leaned forward and glanced around before speaking. "He's a big baddie. He murdered like everyone and wanted nothing more than to be the ruler over all. The elders would say how darkness clung to him." Her eyes grew larger.

I scooted my chair forward to be closer and dropped my voice. "It spoke of a darkness that consumed him. It infected more people and entire villages."

"Darkness? Like the Nightlins?" Raleigh asked.

"That's what I'm trying to figure out. It also said the light was within all of us."

They were quiet for a moment.

"So, they're saying we're all connected? Sounds like some kumbaya bullshit." Raleigh rolled her eyes.

"Yeah, I don't know about that, Sloane. I mean it makes sense, but then it doesn't at the same time."

I shook my head. "Yeah, it was strange. How the darkness spread like a disease. It made me think of the Nightlins and how the world is today."

"They're monsters. Creatures from before time even started. I don't see how that connects us to them." Raleigh stated.

I nibbled on my bottom lip and lowered my voice, "What if they aren't that different from us? Or at least started out more like us?"

The girls looked at each other.

Ashlen spoke first, "What are you trying to say?"

"I don't know. I just get the feeling that there's more that we don't know and need to figure out." The monster clawing my heart out flashed in my mind. "That creature that tried to kill me?"

They nodded.

"The one that made you disappear?" Ashlen asked.

"Yes. It felt," I paused, trying to find the word, "familiar."

The looks on their faces were of complete disbelief.

"I know. I know. It's weird, but I think we've barely scratched the surface of what they are." I waited. Hoping they would understand or at least wanted to try to.

The girls glanced at each other as if silently communicating.

Raleigh shrugged her shoulders. "So, what should we do?"

I took a breath. "We need to find Willow. I know that for sure." I paused debating if I should tell them. They probably would argue or throw a fit. I scratched my nail on the wood table.

Ashlen nudged my arm. "And?"

Oh well. Might as well jump in. They'd find out either way. "Then we need to find more of the dirty dozen."

They blinked. They probably weren't sure if they had heard right.

Raleigh leaned in closer. "And how do we find them?"

Okay, I knew that was coming. Ashlen still wasn't saying anything.

"I met one of them in the Norm. She was a friend of my dad's. Sarah. She said I needed to find them. That they would help, and we can trust them.

"Ashlen, you can't be serious?" Raleigh glanced between us.

"Raleigh, it's the only way. It's the only thing to do," Ashlen said without breaking our gaze. "We have to help her. She needs us to locate that dumb sword and storm the metaphorical castle. There's nothing else to do but act."

"You're crazy." Raleigh hung her head. "We have nothing to go on except to find the sword."

Ashlen took my hand. "That's okay. We can do it."

I grasped Ashlen's hand and mouthed, thank you. She winked.

"Okay, now to plan our adventure."

Raleigh narrowed her eyes. "Adventure my ass. It's literally finding a needle in a haystack. Whatever." She scooted her chair away from the table and left.

"Don't worry about her. She'll come around before we leave."

"Ash, I need to warn you."

Her face grew serious. "What is it?"

"I was told to be careful of some of the people here. They might try to lead us astray."

She frowned. "How do you know?"

I dropped my voice lower, "Sarah told me that there are some here that don't want the Realmers to succeed. They want the Nightlins to take over."

Ashlen leaned away in surprise. "You can't be serious?"

I nodded. "She gave me the names of the others that are still left of the dozen and told me to find them; that they would help."

"Wow, you have been busy."

I shook my head. "You have no idea."

"Have you told Callum?"

"No, not yet. I haven't had a chance."

"Ha! Yeah, too busy sticking your tongue down his throat." She giggled uncontrollably.

My cheeks warmed. "Ash!"

She shrugged. "Hey, that's on you, girlfriend. Besides, I can't say much. I've been there too. I say we find him and Harris. Make a game plan."

"Yeah, we need to leave soon."

She pushed her chair back and rose. "All right, let's find the boys. Ask Arty so we won't waste time."

I chuckled. "Okay, might as well." I pulled Artemis out and asked, "Artemis?" The needles started swinging round and round. "Where is Callum?" The needles spun around frantically then stopped at the farthest door that led to outside.

Wonder what he's doing out there?

Ashlen shrugged. "Maybe training?" Her eyes were unfocused as she daydreamed. "Probably covered in glistening sweat and his muscles are—"

I shoved her forward. "Stop! Go on." I laughed. "Boycrazy girl."

She laughed and jabbed her fingers into my ribs. "You know you were thinking the same thing!"

My face instantly flushed red. The heat scalded my cheeks.

"Ash! You have a boyfriend."

We stumbled down the hallway giggling.

"Oh, Harris knows I love all aspects of males." Her eyebrows wiggled, and she laughed more. "Besides, you know we don't practice monogamy."

We burst through the door laughing and immediately spotted Callum and Jess sparring.

Ashlen grabbed my arm. "Oh my… god loves me." She fanned her face.

Just like she had said, Callum glistened with sweat and the muscles in his arms bulged.

She yanked my arm like an excited schoolgirl at a carnival. "I told you. I told you. Look at those arms."

I did. And she was right. I tried to calm my features and be cool. Just be cool. Not a goober.

I shook my head trying to clear it. "Come on, we're adults."

She scoffed. "Adults ogle each other all the time. I mean, I'm sure Callum would want to know how much we appreciate his hard, hard work." She fanned herself some more.

My gosh, she needed a cold bath. But again, she wasn't wrong. They both had their shirts off.

Okay, we had real issues to get through. No more gawking. Was it hotter outside? Somehow my body felt hotter.

I grabbed Ashlen's arm and tugged her toward the two men. "Get yourself together before we talk to them."

She pulled from my grasp and surged toward them like a bull charging a red flag. This wasn't going to go well. How were her hormones raging all the time? Didn't she ever get tired? I felt tired just being near her in these moments.

I hurried after her before she embarrassed me.

"Hey fellas!" Ashlen yelled.

Dear lord. "Ash!" I whispered-yelled.

She ignored me as she entered their training circle. Both men were breathing heavily. Callum's hair stuck to his face. Sweat ran in rivulets down his neck and chest. Their shirts were cast off to the side of the circle. Jess and Callum turned to see who was making all the noise. Callum waved tiredly at us. Jess's long hair was in a messy bun on top of his head. Any white girl wearing Ugg boots and drinking a pumpkin latte would have been proud.

I waved meekly. "Hey, guys. How's it going?"

Jess motioned to Callum. "He should answer that one." Jess's lips pulled back slightly in a small smile like Jess was making fun of him.

Callum grimaced and pushed his hair from his forehead. I definitely didn't notice his muscles flexing. Ashlen elbowed me and kept casting her eyes toward him. I rolled my eyes.

"Jess is putting me through the wringer today. I'm practicing with my fire."

Ohhh, no wonder it felt hotter out here. Now that we were closer to them, I saw the veins in Callum's arms. Not the usual hot veiny arms of men working out but they were darker like blue lines running from his fingertips up his biceps.

"Wow, that's so cool," Ashlen said breathlessly. "Sloane has something to tell you."

All eyes fixed on me. I was going to kill her.

"Uh, yeah, just some things that I found in the library while back home." I met Callum's gaze and immediately thought about our last kiss. Heat rushed through me. I was going to die before this day was over.

He nodded. "Okay, I think we're almost done?" He asked Jess for confirmation.

Jess shrugged. "Up to you. Or you can practice with Sloane some." He smiled.

Oh great, nothing like training with some fire.

13

Callum

Sloane's eyes widened as if afraid I might melt her. Hopefully, that won't happen... The blue light of the lamps around us reflected on her pale skin. The white strips in her hair stood out in the darkness surrounding us. Jess handed her a wooden sword and shield. She hastened to fasten the shield to her arm.

"You'll be fine, Sloane. Don't worry. Be fast," Jess replied from the sidelines.

"Ha, yeah, easy for you to say." She hid behind the large round shield that Jess had given her for some protection. It was wood, so not sure how well it would hold up.

I nodded toward her. "Ready?"

"No, but go ahead."

I smiled.

Heat spread from my core and down my fingers. Holding my hands up, I lit each finger in rapid succession. At least, I had that down pat.

"Oh, wow," Ashlen muttered, bolstering my confidence.

The fire built in my palms. Yellow, blue, and white flames bound into a ball. I didn't want to scare Sloane even more, so I gently tossed a fireball.

"Ohmygod." She easily deflected the fire with her shield. The fire-ball bounced off and immediately extinguished on the ground. Black spots dotted the ground around us. Her eyes shone with amusement.

"Come on, Sloane! Beat his ass!" Ashlen yelled.

"Ash, this isn't a competition!" Sloane yelled back.

"Of course it is. It's Callum! Stop being such a limp dick and charge him!"

Jess covered his mouth as he tried to hold his laughter back. Sloane's eyes grew wider. Who knew that was possible?

"What is wrong with you?" Sloane asked Ashlen with a genuine *WTF* expression on her face.

"I am perfect. Now, kick his butt and all that girl power shit."

Sloane's resolve kicked in. Steel settled in her eyes. Her shoulders squared and fingers tightened around the wooden sword.

Fire leapt to my fingers in a seconds call, at the same time Sloane charged. She faked to the right but I was ready. Fire raced up my arm as I swung my arm out to clothesline her, but she slid on her knees and out of my way. She easily leapt to her feet and counterattacked, swinging the shield at my head. The fire jumped from my arm to the wood sword, immediately engulfing it. I swung the sword around to meet her shield, and the shield erupted into splinters. Fire and ash fell around us.

Ashlen whooped, "Hells yes!"

Jess clapped. "Excellent, guys."

Sloane panted and brushed wood chips off of her shirt and hair. "That was something." She smiled. The kind that made my stomach flip. What had she thought of our almost kiss last night I wonder?

"Here, Sloane, take this. It'll hold up better to the heat." Jess held out a slim circular metal shield. "Continue with the wooden swords for now."

Sloane slid her arm through the back of the shield, fitting the leather straps snuggly to her forearm. She nodded to me.

I twirled the sword in my hand, changing it between each hand.

She shook her head. "Such a showoff, Callum."

Was it weird I loved it when she said my name?

I lunged at her, aiming for her middle. She deftly blocked me and hit my shoulder for good measure. She spun away with a half-smile curling her lips. She was so light on her feet. I'd have to cheat if I wanted to win.

This time, I called the fire to the surface, and as I charged, I let it take over. Flames licked down my arms. Fireballs formed easily in my hands. I launched each at Sloane only trying to distract her, while I moved closer. She jabbed left then right and spun away. She kept moving her feet, so I aimed for them. The fire hit the ground at her toes.

She yelped. "Hey!"

A grin spread across my face. "It's fair!" I called.

She spun, hitting me full force in the chest with her shield. Air whooshed from my lungs, catching me off-guard.

"Come on, Callum, stop messing around!" Jess antagonized from the sidelines. "Let's see the real power."

I chuckled and shook my head not wanting to get hotter, but also wanting the release of not having to keep the fire at bay any longer. The space felt hot and humid. It was sometimes hard to breathe. Sloane shifted from right to left and back to right like a boxer in the ring.

Then she surprised me by saying, "Yeah, Callum, let's see the power."

Where was this Sloane coming from? For some reason, she loved aggravating me, but can't say much. I did the same.

"All right, you asked for it."

A devilish smile spread over her face. Her eyes twinkled with mischief and excitement.

I welcomed the fire burning in my gut.

My vision burst into white relief, and I surged forward. Heat exploded from my center, as we parried back and forth. The fire burned hotter and hotter. Little spots of blue danced across my eyes. The flames on my body grew taller and wider. Sloane stopped in midswing. Her eyes were the size of saucers. Her mouth formed an O.

The heat within pulsed. It spread through every inch of me. Every inch of my mind and space. It was a beast satiating its hunger for release but wouldn't last for long. What would happen if I let it take over? Would I cease to exist?

Over the roar in my ears, Jess yelled for me to stop. But I wasn't sure how. I had let a beast out and now wasn't sure how to tame it.

"Callum, you've got to reel it in. Get control," Jess said.

"I don't know how," I ground out. Somehow, it hurt to speak.

"Like we talked about. Center yourself and breathe. Think of something calming."

Sloane watched me with careful hooded eyes. She had taken several steps back. I didn't blame her fear. Her eyes searched mine.

"Callum?"

I squeezed my eyes shut, hating the fear in her voice. Come on, get it together. Don't blow up. Literally.

The sword dropped from my grasp, only ash now. Relaxing my hands and muscles, I stood still and breathed in deep. Sloane floated through my mind. The way she always smelled like cinnamon and honey. The way we had first met. Her large blue eyes peered up at me. The way it felt to hold her in my arms while dancing.

"Whatever you're doing, it's working. The fire is dying," Jess stated.

The feel of Sloane's lips against mine. The taste of her.

"Whoa! Stop! It's not working! What the hell are you thinking about?" Ashlen yelled.

Bloody hell.

"Hey, it's okay. You'll figure this out." Sloane sounded closer. Her cool voice calmed me.

I opened my eyes to find her standing a foot away. Fear had disappeared. She looked at me adoringly. Maybe? Or was it pity?

Get a grip.

I pictured the fire in my gut. It raged on and on. I envisioned the fire being suffocated slowly. The fire grew smaller and smaller until it was the size of a nail.

"You got it." Jess had moved closer too. "That's it."

I dragged in a steadying breath of cool air, letting it fill me up.

The atmosphere around us cooled instantly. The humidity dried. Fear and worry dissipated.

Exhaustion weighed me down. I knelt on the blackened earth, trying not to panic. I shook my head in disbelief. I had come so far before. I had to do better.

They formed a half-circle around me, but at a safe distance.

"We need to practice more. That's all. Don't beat yourself up about it," Jess said.

"I bet I can guess what he was thinking about that one time." Ashlen chuckled.

"Ashlen, hush." Sloane elbowed her.

Ashlen rolled her eyes but winked at me.

"Water." My voice scratched out as if I hadn't drunk anything in days. I wanted to be alone at that moment. Get away from the suffocation of pity.

Sloane and Jess nodded.

"Let's go to the kitchens." Jess grabbed my arm and helped me to stand. He pushed a towel into my hands.

Sweat drenched my whole body. I needed a bath. I eyed the small spring in the corner of the cave.

"I'm going to rinse off then head up."

"All right, I'll get some water and food laid out for you." Jess turned to Sloane. "Will you watch out for him?"

Sloane nodded. "Yeah, no problem."

I had already started to make my way through the crops to the water when Jess and Ashlen headed back to the main building. I was so thankful they were leaving.

Sloane's soft footsteps followed me.

14

Sloane

A STORM OF EMOTIONS CLOUDED CALLUM'S FACE. EMBARRASSMENT, fear, anger, worry—weighed on his shoulders. Not to mention his skin was mottled with red blotches. Must have been from the heat. What in the world did that feel like?

I followed him at a safe, cautious distance.

He stumbled into the black waters as if he hadn't seen it in a long time. His body sank into the murky pool with such weariness that I was almost afraid he wouldn't resurface. Steamy tendrils rose from the black surface as his body sank farther and farther and disappeared. A minute passed. Little bubbles broke the water's stillness. Water fell from the side of the rock wall in a slow steady stream. The sound echoed through the cavern.

Of course, since there was little light in the corner, Callum's form was hazy. Only the pale outline of his naked skin showed. I knelt at the edge of the spring and waited. The coolness felt great on my clammy skin.

Several seconds later, Callum finally broke the surface. Water dripped from his skin. His unruly hair hung in his face. Even now, he looked good. I tried not to appreciate his half-naked body but what can I say I'm human, at least, for the most part.

He sank next to me, sprawling onto his back. His chest heaved with forced breath. A hand splayed on his stomach. We stayed there for a moment. Him laying beside me. Me, watching him, afraid to move. His hand slithered along the dirt until he found my fingers. Our hands intertwined. His eyes remained closed as he dragged my hand onto his chest. Our hands stayed like that for a few minutes.

I wasn't sure if I'd start breathing again at some point. Too afraid to break the spell, I sat silent.

His thumb brushed mine back and forth.

What was happening between us? I pressed my lips into a thin line, trying to think. Trying to reason things out.

Callum spoke first, "Sorry, if I scared you."

I jerked from surprise. Scared? "What? No, it's okay." My brain rummaged through words to say so as not to shut him down. My heart sputtered. "I. I know you're trying to figure this out."

A moment of pause. His eyes opened as he sought mine.

"I'll figure it out. It'll just take time." He propped up on one elbow. "I wish a fire starter was alive so they could teach me."

A corner of my mouth twitched. "Yeah, we don't want you to self-combust."

Doubt clouded his features. Dammit, I said the wrong thing.

I squeezed his hand. "Hey, it'll be fine. You'll be burning Nightlins up before we know it."

Callum chuckled. He sat up beside me. His long arms stretched over his legs. I felt more self-conscious as he moved closer. I studied the mud.

"So, what did you need to tell me?"

"What?" I croaked. I drew a line in the dirt, lost in thought.

He knocked his shoulder into mine, "Sloane? What did you want to tell me?"

"Umm." I made the mistake of looking into his eyes. Get yourself together, girl. His eyes roamed my face. Landed on my mouth. Jerked away then searched my eyes. Is this how Ashlen felt? Are her hormones going haywire all the bloody time? I shook my head and drew in a breath.

"Clifford showed me a book about Kane. From the beginning." I focused my attention on him. "It said the darkness engulfed entire villages. It spread like a disease, and the light is a part of the dark."

Callum lifted a shoulder. "And? What does that have to do with us?"

"I think it has to do with who and what the Nightlins are. Why they are the way they are."

A minute passed before we spoke.

"What do you think we should do?"

I frowned. "I think we need to get Willow then go to Nightlin mountain."

He swiveled his head to look at me. "Go to the mountain? Have you gone crazy?"

"No... that's why we should get Willow to help fight the creatures. We can check things out. See if we can get more info."

"Sloane, I know the sword is important but we don't even know what it can do. If it can even help us"

I sighed. "I know. But I think it's what we need to do."

A line formed between his brows. He wrapped his arms around his knees.

His gaze fixed on mine. "You know I'll help you."

Relief washed through me that I didn't know I had been waiting for. "Okay, thank you."

"But," he paused. "We need a solid plan. We can't go in guns blazing and hope for the best."

"Right. That's why I have you." I sheepishly smiled.

He raised a brow and shook his head. "Inconceivable." He gave me a sidelong glance.

I paused. Was he quoting *The Princess Bride*? He had said that was his favorite movie.

All right, time to play along. "I do not think that word means what you think it means."

Callum's face lit up like a Christmas tree, and he actually laughed. A full laugh. Had I heard his laugh before? His head tilted back, and the sound reverberated off the rocks. How often did it happen? It was nice, and I grew a little sad because of the rarity. This realm wasn't set up to be pleasurable.

I drew in a breath. "I'm planning on asking Chuck about it too." He nodded. The smile slowly faded from his face. "Maybe Chuck will have a better idea of how to get back to the falls?"

"Yeah, he should be able to help us out some. Do you think Clifford would let me see the book?"

Oh, that was an idea. But I knew how secretive Clifford was. "Uh, I'm not sure. You know how he is, but we can ask."

"All right. Let's start there."

Warmth spread through me. Ideas churned. It was nice having someone to bounce ideas off of and have him care.

"Thanks, Callum."

He smiled, "Of course." His focus shifted behind me. "Let's head back."

I nodded. "Okay."

Callum stood and extended his hand to help me. His large hand grasped mine, pulling me up. I was fully aware of his naked chest.

Instead of letting me go, his grip tightened. I slowly, inch by inch, looked up into his dark green eyes. Oh boy.

His eyes had grown darker. His lashes lowered. He tugged me against his body.

"Uhh, hi?" I squeaked.

The corners of his mouth twitched. His other hand brushed my hair from my face.

"Do you want to know what I was thinking about earlier?" His voice grew huskier and deeper.

My heart raced, and my lungs stopped working. Oh gosh.

"Sure?" I managed to say.

His hand brushed my arm and down my side. My breathing hitched.

"I thought about you."

Oh, gods above. Pretty sure I melted right there. I bit down on my lower lip, dragging it through my teeth. His eyes caught the movement and watched. His free hand wrapped around the base of my head and pulled me to him. His mouth drank me in as if I was the water, and he was the drought. I melted into him. His fingers dug into my hair. His lips were warm and soft and eager. His tongue teased.

Something inside me woke up. My arms tightened around him like a snake as I wrapped them around his neck. My legs scrambled to get higher. His hands quickly pulled me into his arms so my legs wrapped around his waist. My thighs squeezed his waist, trying not to slip.

We got lost in the moment. Hands roaming. Trying to pull the other closer.

Callum broke away first. He pushed me back, tearing me away from his body. I stumbled to catch myself from falling.

I hadn't noticed the heat rising again.

Steam rose from his skin. Tiny sparks danced across his arms.

Oh wow. My thoughts were racing, my hormones raging.

"Cal?"

His chest rose in quick, deep breaths. "One second Sloane. Let me get control." Small plumes of smoke escaped his mouth.

Oh man, this was going to suck. I glanced around to see if anyone was watching but saw no one. Only the corn stalks surrounded us.

"Sorry." He leaned over with his hands on his knees.

I smiled slightly. "No need to be sorry."

His eyes searched mine. He nodded. "Let's head back."

"Okay." I considered holding his hand but thought better of it. We climbed the hill back, slowly. Our arms brushed as we walked. Neither of us moved away, content in the moment.

15

I waited, somewhat patiently, for Callum to return from his room in the dining hall. When we had returned from the training area, he went to his room to grab appropriate clothing. I may have been disappointed.

He showed a few minutes later, as I dug the toe of my boot into the stone floor.

He frowned. "What are you doing? Did you get bored?"

"Well, yes. You take longer than a girl to get ready."

He smirked. I knew he didn't believe me.

The halls echoed with our footsteps as we made our way back to the library. Clifford was nowhere to be seen when we entered, but that was pretty normal. Callum and I split down the rows of books. I spotted the top of Clifford's grey head near one of the windows.

Clifford's bushy brows rose as he spotted me. "Back so soon?"

"Yes, I am, but I brought Callum back with me." I gestured to Callum as he appeared from behind a bookshelf.

Clifford nodded to him, and Callum returned it.

"I was telling him about the book you had shown me and hoped I could show him too?"

"Wait here. But," he pointed his finger at me, then jabbed it at Callum and said, "no telling."

Callum's eyebrows shot up disappearing under his hair. He nodded. The ghost of a smile played on his lips.

Clifford trundled down an aisle and was gone.

Callum whispered, "I'm not sure he likes me."

I smiled. "I'm pretty sure he doesn't."

"Hey." he moved closer to stand beside me, nudging me with his elbow.

I chuckled and shrugged. We didn't have to wait too long before Clifford huffed back into view. He carefully laid the tattered book in front of us.

"You cannot speak of this to no one." He backed away slowly with his eyes focused solely on the book.

What was with him? Or did he always act this strange, and I didn't see it?

Callum focused on the small blue book, tenderly lifting the cover to open to the first page. He began reading.

"Hmmm." Callum's brows fit together, like a caterpillar.

He turned a page.

Anxiety rose in my chest, and I wanted him to hurry. My foot tapped on the stone flooring.

Callum's eyes lifted to mine, "What's with you today?" His eyes roamed over my body. "You're all twitchy."

I stilled out of spite. "I'm just impatient."

"Hmm, I'll say."

"Rude." I narrowed my eyes.

"So, this says something like death will settle over the land and wipe everyone off the planet?"

I shrugged. "That's what I was trying to figure out."

Callum flipped through the burnt pages. A small scrap of folded, yellowed paper fluttered out. The edges burned and black. Callum carefully unfolded the note.

His eyelashes brushed his skin as he read,

The world is black. No light enters. We are few and no one else is to be found. The creatures stalk us. We hear the screams. One is sick. I don't think they have much time. Night consumes them.

"That doesn't sound good." I chewed on my bottom lip.

"Yeah, no." Callum's forehead wrinkled in concentration. He grabbed a notepad and started scribbling the words onto the page.

"What are you doing?"

"In case we need these on our trip."

"Good idea. So, what do you think?"

He paused, "Obviously, something was terrorizing them. Sounds like it may have been eating them."

Ugh. Yuck. I eyed the small book with distaste, shivering.

"I wish we had more information on Willow," Callum whispered.

"I know. We only have what my grandfather told me and what Morgan said."

He nodded. "Let's find Chuck. See what he says about a portal that can get us closer."

"All right."

We located Clifford and handed him the book back. He took it gingerly and scurried away.

Next, we headed to the dining hall. People were preparing for dinner so we asked them if they had seen Chuck. We finally were told that he was in his chambers.

I had no idea where his room was but Callum knew, so I followed.

We wound down and down through the halls. Why would someone, especially the leader, want to be near the catacombs? My heart quickened at the thought. I silently wished Raleigh were with us to point out any ghosts that might have risen.

Chuck exited a large, dark wood door at the end of a hall.

He waved. "Hey, guys. Need something?" Dark circles lined his eyes, and his messy hair hung in his face.

Callum took the lead. "We needed to ask you if there's a portal that can bring us closer to the Nightlin mountain."

Chuck stopped. His brows furrowed. "Uh, why would you want to go there?" He looked between us, calculating.

"We have found some clues that will help us locate her grandfather's sword, Willow."

"Willow?" Chuck's brows somehow drew closer and deep lines formed around his eyes. "Willow hasn't been seen since he died. What kind of clues?"

I frowned. Why all the questions?

I jumped in. "I've been reading up on some old letters that led us to believe it's near the mountain."

Chuck began walking again. "I'm not sure I feel confident enough to tell you about the portal there. You might get into trouble."

"We've been once. We just wanted to find a quicker route."

Callum stayed silent, watching us like a tennis match.

"It's not safe out there."

"This whole world isn't safe."

Chuck's eyes narrowed, and his lips thinned. "Why don't you tell me where you want to go?"

So quickly as if it hadn't happened, Callum's fingers brushed my elbow in a warning.

I licked my lips, thinking. "There are multiple areas that we think it might be, but now it's near the mountain, somewhere."

Chuck's eyes shifted between me and Callum. "We currently have one portal active near the Nightlin mountain."

I perked up. "Okay. When can we go?"

He glanced at the digital watch on his wrist. "It will be active in five hours."

"That's at 11 pm," Callum said.

Chuck nodded and faced a black door. "Yep." He pushed the door open.

Air and dust whooshed out.

"Come back here tonight. When you're ready."

I peered around him, trying to get a peek of the room, but he eased the door shut behind him without another word.

Callum and I stood still for a moment.

"That wasn't foreboding at all," Callum stated.

That night Callum, Ashlen, Harris, Raleigh, and I trundled down to the room with the black door.

"Guys, we are going to die or worse." Raleigh objects for the millionth time.

"What's worse than death?" Harris murmured.

"We could get captured. We could have our arms chopped off or our legs."

I frowned. "That's worse than death?"

She groaned. "You know what I mean."

"Raleigh, you know you can stay if you want," Ashlen called over her shoulder. Her brown bag was stuffed full of who knows what. A brush head poked out of the top.

"Ha, yeah, like I'd let you get all the glory."

"Glory? What kinda mission are we thinkin' here?" Harris asked. "Thought this was just a find and grab."

"It is, baby. Don't listen to Raleigh. It's her time of the month."

Raleigh spluttered behind me. "No, it is not!"

Ashlen only laughed.

"Guys, play nice," I said, chastising and pulling on my shoulder straps. My heavy bag dug into my skin. "Harris, we are going to get Willow, my grandfather's sword. For reals this time. We might poke around the Nightlin mountain to see what's there." I glanced back at him. "I'm hoping Morgan is still there to ask him about the dirty dozen again. Surely, the ones that are left will help us."

Harris' blue eyes grew larger. "So, a real easy trip this time."

Raleigh snorted. "Exactly."

The black door was cracked open when we arrived. Callum knocked, and we waited. A few seconds passed, enough to make us wonder if Chuck wasn't there, then he appeared in a rush.

"Come on." He waved us through the doors. "We have one minute before the portal opens."

We surged forward haphazardly. I knocked into Callum, who almost upended a chair.

The room we entered was lit by the long blue-white bulbs. The stones reflected the light. On the center of the opposite wall was a cherry red door. A small table and chair sat in one corner, otherwise, the room was empty. Chuck quickly shut the door behind us and locked it. I didn't like the sound of the lock turning.

"Are you all ready?"

Raleigh muttered, "I suppose."

Something hissed and light burst from behind the red door. We grew quiet. The light escaped between the door and frame.

"That's your cue. The portal will only be open for 5 minutes." Chuck moved toward the door and flung it open. White light hit us. I squeezed my eyes shut until it dissipated. When I reopened my eyes, the light from the door had dimmed. A swirl of black and blue liquid expanded in the doorway.

"I'll go first," Callum said to me.

I nodded.

He tightened his pack and stepped forward.

Chuck grabbed his arm. "This will bring you to the base of the mountain near the river on the northside."

Callum faced the portal; the black-blue liquid enveloped him. It latched onto every inch of his skin and absorbed him. He disappeared within seconds.

How did he face scary things so easily?

Harris and Ashlen went next, followed by Raleigh. I hung back to go last.

Chuck replied, glancing at his watch, "You have one minute left until it closes." He nodded once. "Better get going."

I drew in a deep breath, letting it fill me. Stepping up to the portal, I could almost see the other side, or at least what I thought was the other side. Figures moved beyond the black liquid haze. I poked a finger into the undulating mass. The liquid cold adhered to my finger. I wasn't sure it would let go.

"Sloane, go," Chuck said hurriedly. He paced behind me.

Someone said from beyond, "Come on, Sloane, we're waiting."

Before I stepped through, I breathed in deep and held my breath. The wet coldness that wrapped around me and my senses took over for what felt like a solid minute but may have been a few seconds. I broke the surface with a gasp of air filling my lungs. Ashlen caught me before I fell.

Moonlight broke through the trees. The full moon lit our path through the woods.

Callum was up ahead. He turned. "Can you hear it? The falls?"

We fell silent as the roar of rushing water filled the air.

We were close.

16

Sloane

MOONLIGHT SHIMMERED ON THE WATER'S SURFACE, PIERCING THROUGH the darkness showing a small, black cavern several feet below the surface. The waterfall disrupted stillness, making it hard to see much more in the inky blackness.

Callum stood on the edge of the pool staring into the depths. I wasn't sure if he was regretting his decision to join me or if I was completely crazy. Maybe both?

Ashlen and Harris whispered behind me, who knows what they were gossiping about.

"Are you ready?" Callum had stripped off all of his weapons, shirt, and shoes. If there had been more light, he would have seen my face turning red.

"Uh, I guess I'll take off some more things." I pulled off the sword and Masada along with my boots.

"You want to be as light as possible. We don't know what's waiting for us."

I shivered at his words. We didn't know what to expect, and knowing my grandfather, it wouldn't be fun.

I took a deep breath, trying to calm my nerves. At the last moment, I decided to take my pants off too. No one needs skin-tight pants while swimming. Besides, my boy short undies were fine. I made sure to not make eye contact with Callum as I slid my pants down.

"Yeah, girl! Take it off! WOOHOO!" Ashlen yelled.

I tried not to laugh as I shot daggers at her with my eyes. Harris promptly turned his back to me. Callum dutifully concentrated on the black pool in front of us. I took Masada's holder and strapped it around my bare thigh. Knives are always handy, no matter what.

Raleigh swatted at Ashlen. "You'll wake the dead with that noise."

Knowing Raleigh's ability with ghosts, I hoped that wouldn't be true. We didn't need more shit popping up trying to get us.

"Why aren't we going again?" Raleigh dug dirt out from under her nails with her knife, flicking it into the water.

Reflections from the water moved across Callum's taut skin. I tried not to stare again.

"Because, Raleigh, you have to be here in case the Nightlins show up. The other two are here for backup so they can get help if something happens," Callum said.

Raleigh pouted but Harris and Ashlen looked as if they hadn't even heard.

"What was Morgan's rhyme?" Callum asked.

I closed my eyes, turning my memories over for the right one. "The Willow you seek is buried. Buried deep inside the Willow. This Willow you will find deep in the pool, deep in the caverns. You will have to use all of your power and the things given to you to pry her from death's cold fingers." I tilted my head to study him. "Or something close to that."

He smirked. "Okay, come on."

My toes brushed the water's edge, still not sure what to do. I carefully made my way to the rock that jutted over the water to sit.

"We're going to have to go for it. Think about it later." Callum stood behind me.

I nodded. "All right." I took another deep breath and without much more thought, plopped into the cold water. "Argh! It's cold." My teeth clenched as the icy water squeezed me.

Callum slid in, trying not to make too much of a disturbance in the water. The water surrounding us warmed. Steam rose from his skin. "Come on, let's get this over with." His light stick disrupted the water as he dove for the black hole under us.

I swallowed all of my scared thoughts and followed.

The cold water enveloped me and pulled me under. The air in my lungs collapsed. Callum's light was a bright spot in all the darkness. He was already at the lip of the tunnel, waiting. His body glowed a soft orange as if the fire within him wanted to get out.

I tried not to panic as I flutter kicked toward him.

He tapped his wrist like he had a watch on. I nodded, knowing we didn't have much time. He nodded once and turned down the black tunnel. I pushed on after him.

The black hole was even colder. Callum's light barely lit the tunnel. The darkness seemed to swallow the light. My lungs started to protest, and I steeled my nerves. I couldn't think about us being stuck or what creatures lived down there. I had a mission, and I had to finish it.

Callum swam with ease. He powered through the water as if he were a frog. I felt like I was flailing. Another minute passed as we traveled through the tunnel. Tree roots hung down and snaked out from the muddy walls. I thought at any moment a grindylow would surely grab my foot. Were those even real in this realm?

Callum's form was outlined hazily by his light. I hoped he saw more.

He shot upward.

I followed. Our gasps broke the surface. I coughed, thankful for air. Callum held the light above but only rock surrounded us. We had a small reprieve from the tunnel but had to keep going.

"You doing okay?" Callum asked.

My teeth chattered. "Yessss, I'm - ok-ay. Yyy-you?"

He smiled slightly, "Yeah, I'm all right." He pointed his light along the rock walls, looking for anything.

Water ran in rivulets down his bare skin then evaporated as the heat from his body changed it to steam. Here I was freezing my tits off, and I still wanted to admire him. I shook my head.

"We better keep going. You probably can't tread in the cold for too long."

I nodded.

He squeezed my arm. "If it's too far we'll turn back and try again."

"We can do it." I smiled my best.

"All right." He sank below the surface, disappearing in the dark. Only his wand light appeared beneath me like a candle flame.

I took a deep, deep breath and plunged below. We kicked and pulled the water before us. I wanted to tell Callum we should turn back, but I knew it would take even more to reach that one reprieve. Callum's feet started kicking faster. The bubbles roared past my ears. I kicked harder to keep up.

Callum's feet disappeared, and my heart stopped. Where had the light gone?

A hand grabbed my hair, and I screamed. Probably not the smartest move since water rushed into my mouth. But the hand only tapped my head and tugged upward. I went with it.

I broke the surface choking. This time we were in a large cave. Callum stood on the side with his light aloft peering around every corner.

I heaved myself out of the cold water, thankful to be out of the scary, black depths. I hacked up more water. My skin prickled from the cold. Maybe I should have worn my pants after all. My throat hurt from all the coughing.

"Sloane! Over here!"

Callum rushed toward me. His bare feet slapped the rock. He grabbed my arm and jerked me up. I almost fell over from the rush.

"Okay, okay. What is it?" I rubbed my shoulder where he had pulled so hastily.

He rushed ahead of me and disappeared.

I hesitated. "Callum?" My eyes hurt from trying to see in front of me. Small hazy outlines of rocks and the water appeared before me.

Callum's wand light flickered around a corner.

"We need to train you on how to use your eyes more."

"Yeah, kinda hard to do that when the realm is going to pot."

He smiled with teeth showing. "Come on." He extended his hand to me, waiting for me to take it.

A tentative smile spread as I took his hand. Granted, it was wet and pruney from being in the water for so long, but it felt wonderful holding his hand. I never thought that would happen.

He tugged me along easily. The white light from his stick spread out on the path before us. Little lizards darted into the shadows, their little shiny bodies lighting with bioluminescence.

"Almost there," Callum whispered. "The sounds of the cavern change up ahead."

We went around a bend, and the cave opened into an immense cavern. Moonlight pierced the darkness from above. Tiny slots peeked through, shining onto the rocks around us and along more pools spaced throughout. But what took my breath was a huge willow-like tree in the center. Its branches looked heavy as some almost touched the ground. Red fruit hung from the large, thick branches.

I hadn't realized I had stopped with my mouth hanging open.

"Can you believe this is down here?" Callum asked.

I shook my head.

Our eyes met. Callum's eyes reflected wonder and disbelief.

We walked along the thin ridges that led to the tree, being careful not to fall into the black water. The tree grew larger the closer we got.

"What's that smell?" Callum asked.

I frowned. "What do you mean?"

He looked at me. "Something smells rotten."

My frown deepened. "I only smell sweetness, like flowers."

Callum shook his head. "Maybe your nose isn't working either."

I chuckled. "No, my smeller is fine."

By then, we were near one of the branches bearing fruit. I reached out intending to pluck one of the red fruits from the tree. Callum slapped my hand away.

"What the hell?" I jerked away from him.

"What do you think you're doing?"

"Why did you slap my hand?" My eyes were the size of saucers as I stared at him with my mouth open.

He studied me for a moment. "So you wouldn't touch the rotted fruit."

I looked at him, then back at the tree. The bright red fruit hung perilously close to the dirt. It was perfectly round, if not slightly oval. The red skin bulged with juice as if it might burst at any moment. No blemishes.

My eyebrows knit together in confusion.

"What are you talking about? I think you're the one whose eyesight might be going bad."

His eyebrow rose. "Sloane, I'm being serious. That fruit is rotten. I can almost see flies buzzing around it." He leaned in closer, covering his nose and mouth. "Oh man, maggots."

What was he talking about? Maybe he swallowed too much water or something. The fruit's skin had highlights from the light shining in. Without too much more thought, I pulled the fruit off the limb.

Callum spun away, covering his face. His eyes scrunched in disgust.

My fingers dug into the soft flesh, and juice ran down my arm.

"Ugh, it reeks." Callum stepped farther away.

I had no idea what he was talking about. The red fruit looked polished. The skin was ripe and ready to sink your teeth into.

"I think I need to eat it."

"I might barf if you do."

My eyes narrowed slightly. "Can't believe you're being such a baby about this."

"If you saw what I do, you'd feel the same."

I paused, studying the fruit. I breathed it in.

"Sloane, you can't be serious?"

I looked around us. "I'm not sure what else to do?"

"What makes you think this is a good idea?"

I shrugged. The smell of the fruit enticed me. It filled my lungs, making me feel drunk. "It smells so good." My eyes fluttered closed as I inhaled.

"Sloane, that's not a good reason."

My mouth went dry as cotton. If I drank a hundred gallons, I still would have been thirsty, as if I had crossed the Sahara and been dying of thirst. I knew the only thing to satiate my desire was the red, shiny fruit.

"Here we go." Inhaling slightly before I bit down, I took a small bite. My teeth pierced the skin easily. Sweet juice ran down my chin in rivulets. I smeared it across my mouth. A small giggle escaped my lips.

"Disgusting." Callum's lips curled.

Energy zipped through my limbs and veins. I felt alive. No. Fire followed on its heels. No, no. Involuntarily, I squeezed the fruit in my hand. The pulp plopped to the ground, and I fell to my knees. Pain lanced through my skull and whole body. I toppled over. Dammit why me?

The last thing I saw was Callum trying to catch me.

17

WHAT WAS WITH THE BRIGHT LIGHT ALWAYS BLINDING ME?

My eyes ached from the sunlight hitting my face. The pain that had been coursing through my veins subsided.

I squinted, trying to see what was in front of me.

A breeze lifted my hair.

"So, you listened and found it," a gruff, hardened voice stated.

Well, shit, my grandfather. I cupped my hands over my eyes, shielding the light from my eyes.

"You didn't make it easy."

"Ha, of course not. Any Tom, Dick, or Harry would show up."

I inwardly rolled my eyes.

"Open your eyes," he grumbled.

I faced the direction of his voice and slowly eased my eyelids open. The same white house with blue shutters stood before me, and Charles sat on the same step. Maybe the familiarity of the house made the tension in my shoulders ease. Wisps of clouds dotted the pale blue sky. Tall, tall grass swayed in the breeze. The sun's rays heated my back.

I looked so out of place in my black shirt and underwear.

"Wasn't sure you'd eat the fruit."

"Why not?"

His dark eyes surveyed me. "You don't seem like the daring type, though you are missing half your clothes."

Something burned inside me. "We had to lighten our load so we could find the tree."

He waved his hand in dismissal. "Never mind. We don't have time."

How could one man be so infuriating?

I sighed and folded my arms across my chest. "Okay, what is it?"

"This will be the last time we see each other." His eyes surveyed me, then narrowed. "You have several trials coming that you will face. First, get the sword from the tree then go to the mountain."

"What? That's suicide!"

"You're being a child."

My teeth ground together, and my jaw ached.

He continued, "You must warn the others. An eclipse is coming. It will be their chance to take over. They have more disciples and power than ever. You must be prepared."

"Wait — what? An eclipse? How can there be one here?"

"Not here. In the Norm. A solar eclipse that happens every 500 hundred years. The night will be at its fullest. Their portals will destroy the normal world."

Goosebumps sprung along my flesh. Sweat dotted my lip and armpits. What would we do?

"Sloane, they will take you if they get the chance."

"Wh—what?" A chill spread through my bones even with the sun beating down on me.

"He wants you to fill the power bond."

My mind was about to implode.

"Who? What are you talking about?" Tears filled my eyes.

He stared, unblinking. "Your father."

Why was everything going to hell? Why couldn't we just be happy?

Tears spilled down my cheeks. "Why? Why would he harm me?" He didn't even know me.

"It's the power he craves. The power that's taken him over." His gaze shifted behind me. "Our time is up. Good luck."

I whipped around to see what he did but saw nothing. I turned back, but he was gone. The white porch was empty. The breeze picked up in force. I grabbed the column, trying to hold on. My tear tracks dried on my cheeks. A voice, my grandfather's, echoed in my head, telling me to let go. I gasped in gobs of air, hoping not to break down right there.

With one last squeeze of the sturdy column, I let go at once. The wind spun me around and around like a tornado. Thoughts of Dorothy filled my head. I flew up and up into the stratosphere and landed with a plop on the hard rock floor in the cavern. The back of my head smacked the floor. Stars danced across my vision. Someone yelled my name. Hands grabbed my arms and face.

Callum's dark green eyes swam before me. I think I smiled.

"Sloane? Sloane? Answer me. Can you hear me?" He frantically looked around us. "Shit. Why does this keep happening?" His grip tightened around me. I found myself in his lap. It felt nice. His sturdy arms and chest against me. His warm breath on my cheek. A nap sounded nice.

He shook me. "Sloane, don't you dare go to sleep."

I closed my eyes anyway. "Cal, just wanna sleep."

"You're going to give me a heart attack one day."

My mouth curled slightly into a smile.

His chest rattled. "Yeah, you would be happy about that."

I nestled into his chest and laid my head on his heart. The low thumping reverberated.

"Sloane, I'm sorry, but you have to wake up. We can cuddle later."

Later? There could be a later? I chuckled then slowly sat up. Pain shot down my neck and behind my eyes.

"I think my grandfather was hoping to kill me."

Callum frowned. "Your grandfather? You saw him again?"

I tried to nod but grimaced. "Yeah. He was his usual chipper self."

Callum took my hands, pulling me to my feet. The room spun, and my stomach felt weak.

"Did he give any advice as to how to retrieve the sword?"

"Nope. Just that it's in the tree."

"Morgan said, 'You will have to use all of your power and things given to you to pry her out of the cold fingers of death.'"

The tree before us loomed over our heads like an overbearing mother. The bright red fruit pulled the limbs low. I moved closer studying its branches. There was an overly sweet smell like something had gone rotten.

"You only see bad fruit?"

Callum nodded. "Yeah, it looks awful."

"So, if the tree is the fingers of death, Does that mean the sword is inside the tree?"

Callum's eyes roamed across the tree, inspecting. "Maybe use Masada to carve into the trunk?"

The weight of this situation felt enormous. I unstrapped Masada from my leg and wove in and out of the branches until I reached the trunk. Callum wasn't far behind.

The bark was almost black. The bulbous texture reminded me of a witch's skin like they described in fairytales.

Callum's heat pushed against my back. I pressed the tip of Masada into the trunk.

"Masada, need some help here. Please."

The tree groaned in answer, and we involuntarily took a step back. From the tip of Masada's point, blue light spread across the trunk like veins searching for its life source. They ran across the entire tree's structures, lighting up the cavern. A small ball of white light formed in the center of the trunk and throbbed like a heartbeat, growing larger with every beat.

"Push it in further," Callum whispered.

I thought the metal wouldn't be able to drive farther into the trunk, but the knife slid into the wood as if the tree was butter. A loud *pop* echoed through the cavern. A large crack formed where the knife pierced. The white light grew brighter, almost blinding.

I looked away from the light for a few seconds to give my eyes a rest.

"Now, what?" I asked.

"Is anything else happening?"

I glanced at Callum. His eyes were shut.

"Is it too bright for you?"

"Uh, yeah. Can only look for a few seconds."

"Well, nothing else is happening." I frowned.

"Morgan said you'd have to use all of your power."

Frustration grew in my belly and tightened my chest. Damn rhymes.

"Callum, I don't know. I have no clue." I ground my teeth and drew in deep breaths. "I just don't know."

"Focus, Sloane. Focus on that light inside of you. Hold it in your center then slowly let it go."

I paused, slightly stunned by how Buddha-acting Callum just sounded.

"Sloane, we don't have time for you to think." He grabbed my hand and forced it onto the tree's bark. "Stop thinking so much and just do it."

I tried not to get too annoyed by how well he might have known me so I focused on my hand touching the trunk. I closed my eyes and breathed in through my nose, pulling the air up from my toes and letting it out through my mouth.

Something pulsed below the surface of the tree. It started far, far away. Slowly, it galloped toward me. A rushing light sped from the roots of the tree to the surface. I pulled everything into my center and held it there. A wound-up ball of white energy. It hummed and throbbed with life.

I placed both hands on the trunk, searching for the thing that called for me, what I knew had to be my family's sword. Without much thought, I wrenched Masada from the trunk and sliced my palm. The blood ran freely. The hot stickiness smelled sweet like honey. I pushed my cut palm onto the tree and let the ball of light held inside of me out. The white energy poured from my palm, mixing with my blood. It poured and poured like a neverending tap. As the energy left my body, so did my blood.

My knees hit the stone floor. My body sagged against the tree. I know I heard someone yelling my name, but I couldn't wrap my mind around it. I felt so tired, so drained of energy. A part of me welcomed the stillness left after the energy was expelled. Relief washed over me.

Hands grabbed and tore at me. They tried to pull me from the energy, but it was too late. I let go.

18

Callum

White light erupted from her. From her eyes. From her hands.

"Sloane! Don't!" Panic quaked my limbs. I had her in my arms, trying to tear her away from the stupid tree. The life-sucking tree. That's exactly what it was doing. I saw her soul being torn from her body as if the tree drank her soul into its depths.

Her blood ran from her hand. Light poured from her veins straight into the bark and roots.

I shook her for the millionth time. "Sloane!" My voice rasped as I called for her. The light from the tree pulsed and danced as it drank. The rotting fruit around me grew and grew. Some popped open from being so engorged. My eyes burned with the light, with her. My breathing hitched. I wasn't sure how much more I could endure.

I had to think of something.

I grappled for her knife, even if it's my blood maybe it would work. I slashed my palm and slammed it onto the tree. I waited. And waited. Nothing happened. I pulled Sloane harder as if to share my soul with her.

Think. Think. Come on, Idiot. You can't ever do shit when you need to. You're so fucking worthless. Come on, for god's sake think of what to do! There has to be something.

Something sparked.

Something hot and bright. Being surrounded by darkness, when the light sparked I sprinted toward it. I grabbed hold of it and let it burn itself out.

For once, I let the fire unabashedly run free. It happily complied.

My cut palm, still pressed against the rough bark, gave the fire the perfect exit. It erupted. The dry, scaly bark of the tree stood no chance, as my fire consumed and raged.

Something in the center of the tree stood still. The fire hadn't touched it. Couldn't reach it. The cold metal stood stoic and passive as my fire devoured everything else.

Sloane slumped into me. Her light going dark. Her head lolled to the side and both arms fell. She had been released. Thankfully, her heart pounded against mine, if only slowly. I breathed in a sigh of relief.

A sob tore from my throat. I tried to stuff it back in, but Sloane wasn't awake to see me break. I almost hadn't cared at that moment.

"Sloane?" I brushed her hair back. Her cheeks were sullen and ashen. Her lips cracked.

Around us, the tree's ashes covered the cavern's stone floor. The moonlight streaming in caught pieces of ash falling. Pieces of the ugly red fruit littered the stones.

I gently shook her. "Sloane? Please answer."

The vastness of the cave felt empty. The fire left an icy breath behind. Darkness settled around us, but not the kind I was so accustomed to. This darkness felt more lonely; as if we were the only two people in the realm.

I brushed my fingers across her face. Her cold skin looked more translucent than before.

Come on. I pulled her tighter to me, trying to let my body heat warm her. Come on.

"Sloane, fight. Fight it." I pressed my forehead against hers. Focusing on the heat inside of me, I willed it to heat my skin. It was getting easier to call forth, to control. The fire eagerly answered.

My skin warmed. Sweat formed on my temples and the middle of my back, as the fire burned just below my skin's surface.

"Cal?"

My heart jumped to my throat. "Sloane? You're okay. I'll get you out." I just didn't know how.

"Cal. Fruit." She gasped.

A line formed between my brows. What was she talking about? That fruit was disgusting. It may have started all this.

"Callum." Her eyes squeezed shut. Lines wrinkled her forehead. Her palm pressed onto my chest.

Around us ash laid in heaps on the stone floor. The fruit looked just as grey or black as the debris.

I knew we didn't have much time. Maybe it was something her grandfather had told her to do?

With the utmost care, I laid her on the stone. I sifted with my toes to find a not-so-damaged piece of fruit then carried it back to her.

I pulled the flesh apart expecting to see rot but was shocked to see - whole, pink pulp. The juice ran down my hand. I pushed it into her mouth.

The juice coated her lips and down her chin. She tensed then opened her mouth to get more. As the juice trickled down her throat and face. The greyness in her skin faded. Replaced with pink. Her cheeks filled out and the skin on her lips smoothed. It was as if death was being beaten back from its claim.

Sloane's eyes flashed open, and she drank more. Her face was ravenous. The fruit fell from her hand.

"More?"

I didn't think twice, only moved to find another piece. I wiped it off. The ash smeared with the juice, leaving brown-grey streaks, but I didn't think she noticed. She reminded me of vampires in movies, how they had to satiate their thirst for blood, only hers was for a weird fruit.

She ate two more before she stopped.

I was glad she was breathing and talking.

Her hazel eyes appeared bluer in the pale moonlight. The white strands of her hair stood out in contrast. Her eyes were locked onto me as if she hadn't known I was there. Her cold hand found mine and squeezed it.

"Sorry, I messed things up," she rasped.

I only chuckled. "You do have a habit of doing that." I brushed some of her hair away from her forehead. Her eyes fell shut for a moment.

"Well, now what will we do?"

Gazing around us, my eyes landed on the solid gleaming scabbard of a sword. It stood upright where the tree previously stood. It was unblemished. The silver, just as shiny as the day it was made. My lips automatically curled at the corners.

I motioned toward the sword. "At least we have that."

Sloane peered around me. Her eyes lit up and she smiled.

"I can't believe it."

"I bet you'll have to retrieve it." I looked at her. A frown fell across her face.

"Probably."

"Do you have the energy?" She looked fine, but I knew I'd be so tired after almost having my body drained of life.

She leaned forward propping her elbows on her knees. "Yeah, I feel pretty good, actually really good." She smiled again.

I stood and held my hand out to help her. She grabbed hold and pulled up easily. The top of her head barely brushed my chin.

Resolve settled over her shoulders, and she set off toward the sword. Her bare feet turned black as she stepped through the burned piles. The sword never wavered as she grew closer. She stopped right before it and moved around it, inspecting.

"There are barbs on the handle."

"Barbs?" Who would do that?

She nodded. "Probably my grandfather's idea." She murmured. Her eyes met mine. "What do you think? Is there a trap?"

I scoffed, "I think we just got through one."

She smirked slightly. Her gaze ran up and down the scabbard. She knelt, trying to look at every angle. She stood and rubbed her palms on her thighs.

"Okay, here we go." She wrapped her right hand around the hilt. The barbs dug into her flesh. She winced. "Bastard."

A whine filled the air, then the sword lit from within. White light burst and disappeared in a wave as she tugged the sword out.

"Hello, Willow." She smiled. The sword hummed as if in answer.

19

My hand hurt. The barbs stung my palm. Blood ran down the hilt. I was so over this blood crap.

I met Callum's eyes. "Let's get out of here."

The barbs on the handle vanished back into the metal as if never there.

"They're gone," I said surprised.

"Good. It'll be easier to carry."

I was too tired to think, so I followed him.

"How do you feel?"

"Exhausted. But that seems to be the new norm," I said, as I dragged the sword behind me.

Callum chuckled. "Here, I'll carry it." He held his hand out, waiting.

I sluggishly passed the sword to him. The metal touched his skin and light exploded in my eyes. Callum yelled.

Once the light abated, I spotted Callum a few feet away on his back.

The sword stood on the tip like we had found it before. Again, it hummed. What the hell? Was it possessed?

Callum sat up. Our eyes locked.

"What was that?" he asked.

"Hell if I know." The sword hummed as if to answer. "I guess I'm carrying it."

Callum stood. "Yeah, guess so. Do you need more fruit before we go?"

Mmmm, fruit. I scanned the ground for more. A few littered the ground near me. I snatched them up and knelt by a pool to wash off the dirt. I handed one to Callum. He reluctantly took it.

"I don't know how you eat these."

Energy spread through my limbs as the juice poured down my throat. Mmmm. My eyes closed with satisfaction.

Callum shook his head and took a bite.

"Not so bad."

I rolled my eyes then stepped in front of Willow. The metal gleamed. Energy pulsed around it. I poked it with a finger but it didn't budge. More and more it felt like I was part of a Sci-fi movie. I tugged on it, and the sword fell into my hand. So weird.

We gathered our things and threaded through the pools to the far tunnel that led us to where we had entered.

"We came through this pool over here." He gestured to a black pool that looked like all the others. How did he know this stuff?

"Ready?" Callum sat on the edge of the water.

"Sure." I made my way to him and knelt. The murky, black pool didn't look welcoming.

I wrapped my arm around Willow's hilt and scabbard, trying to be careful of the barbs just in case they popped out again. *Won't ever be able to trust that old man.* The cold metal didn't help with the water as I slipped in.

Callum slid in and the water instantly warmed. His skin turned pink. Steam rose from the water surrounding us.

"Does that help?"

I smiled. "Yeah, it does actually." I shook my head.

He smiled. "Let's go." He took a deep breath then plunged below the surface. His light stick held aloft.

I breathed in deep and took off after him.

The white light bobbed ahead of me. The bottoms of Callum's feet blinked as he kicked. We stopped at the same cave as before to catch our breath then dove back under, not wasting more time. The black water gave me the heebie-jeebies. My imagination swirled with images of creatures lurking in the shadows, just waiting to jump out and grab me.

I told my mind to shut up.

Reaching the tunnel's mouth leading to the waterfall, eased the tension in my shoulders. Moonlight pierced the shadows and my heart sang. I broke the surface with lots of spluttering. The weight of Willow felt as if it might pull me under. I kicked and pulled the water to get to the rocks.

I noticed Callum at the last second. Frozen. His back faced me. He was crouched on a rock.

"Callum?"

He held a hand up.

Oh no. I peered around the little inlet. The waterfall thundered behind us. Everything else was quiet. I churned the water around me, trying to stay afloat. I lifted Willow out of the water and carefully set her on the silt.

Callum stood, his face tilted to the sky. I swear I saw him sniff the air. I don't think I had asked him about his smell before.

"Cal? Can I get out?"

He nodded. I grabbed hold of a big rock and pulled. The rock gave away and splashed into the pool.

Callum spun around, his face stony.

I grimaced. "Sorry." Why was I such a klutz? I looked for a sturdier rock and pushed on it to make sure it wasn't budging then pulled myself out.

Callum stepped down to where I was. He held a finger to his lips. I nodded.

He whispered, "Something was here. The others are gone."

Cold seeped into my bones. Where had they gone? We hadn't been gone that long had we?

He took my hand. "Come on. Up here. We can put our clothes back on out of view."

I picked up Willow and took his hand as he led me over the rocks and to the small tunnel back to the snake pool.

He grabbed our clothes. I tugged my pants and long shirt back on. My boots and socks felt wonderful as I slid them over my cold feet. I strapped everything back over my back and stood ready to go.

"What are you thinking?" I whispered.

Callum indicated out of the cave, "Tracks lead that way but I only spotted one set." His jaw firmed. "I hope the others are okay. Follow me, but be as quiet as possible. I'm not sure what's out there."

I nodded. Where was Ashlen? Raleigh? Harris? Surely, they were okay?

Callum picked his way through the rocks and up the wall. He pointed at the dirt. Something had pooled. Blood?

I grabbed his arm. "Is that?"

His lips pressed together, and he nodded.

No.

My heart hammered in my chest and goosebumps prickled my skin.

Callum pointed to a rock. Red blood smeared across it. Someone or something had lost a lot of blood. No, no, no. Maybe it was from an animal?

I followed him into the trees. He pointed out different spots where the dirt had been disturbed. More red blood smeared a tree or dotted the ground. We came to a small hill, and Callum motioned for me to stop and wait.

He crouched at the top of the hill then jumped, disappearing.

My heart rose to my throat as I waited. Seconds ticked by then minutes.

Callum called to me and I leapt up. I veered around the hill to see a small cave had been cut into the base. Callum stood right outside.

"Sloane, it's Harris. He's hurt."

"Oh god."

"He's passed out right now, so let's grab some wood and make a fire inside. It should shield us enough."

I nodded hurriedly. "Okay." I took off to find some small limbs and pine needles. Thoughts rushed through my head. Images of Ashlen and Raleigh being hurt or taken. I hoped above all hopes they hadn't been taken. Please let them be okay. Please, please. My teeth ground together, and I chewed on the inside of my cheek.

I hurried back to the cave, my arms full of twigs and underbrush.

Callum knelt inside. A stack of wood next to him.

"It's pretty bad."

I nodded. Words failed me at that moment. My nerves were shot.

He held his light above our heads as he led me further into the cave. A small mound huddled in the corner. Harris.

His hair stuck in every direction and had been turned a muddy brown. His back rose up and down slowly as he breathed. A large gash ran from shoulder to hip. Blood oozed. Callum handed the light to me. He knelt beside Harris and rolled him over. One of Harris' eyes was swollen shut. A long tear started at his chin and ran down his chest.

Bile rose, but I swallowed it. I sank to my knees, barely able to breathe.

"What—what happened?" I whispered barely audible.

"Looks like Nightlins."

My hands pressed over my mouth, trying to keep the sob from tearing out of my throat. Tears sprang to my eyes. My chest tightened. Not Ashlen and Raleigh...

20

THE FLAMES OF THE FIRE HEATED OUR LITTLE SPACE QUICKLY. CALLUM stoked it every few minutes. Harris still hadn't budged in the last half hour. And for whatever reason, Callum and I had remained silent. He bent over the fire as he made a concoction to bind Harris' wounds.

I ate some of the dried food in my pack, letting the heat warm my body. Today had been a shit day. I rested my head on a rock. Sorrow filled my chest and mind. The thoughts of what my grandfather had said flooded me.

What could he have meant? Surely, my dad didn't want me dead. He was the whole reason I was in this world, hoping to find him. Hoping to find the reason why he left.

Harris moaned from the corner. Callum moved toward him.

"Harris? You okay?" Callum touched Harris' arm, gently tugging him to face us.

He moaned. Pain sliced his face.

"Callum?" he rasped.

Callum grabbed his hand and squeezed. "Yeah, it's me." He grabbed the smelly, green goo he had been stirring. "I made a poultice to put on your wounds. You okay with that?"

Harris' eyes fluttered open, and he looked around the cave. His eyes landed on me then closed. He nodded.

Carefully, Callum poured the goo over Harris' back and chest. Harris groaned but fell asleep.

"He won't wake for several hours so might as well get some sleep while you can."

Harris' face relaxed. The fire had died to mere embers.

"What do you think happened?" I whispered.

Callum poked the fire a few times with a long stick before answering, "I can only imagine Nightlins ambushed them and took the girls." My heart plummeted.

Ashlen and Raleigh...

He gestured to Harris. "But won't know for sure until he wakes up and tells us what happened." He leaned against the cave wall, digging into his pack for something. "Listen, no reason to stress about it now. Get some sleep. I'll take the first watch." He fished out a food pack and opened it.

I nodded, not sure if I could sleep in the middle of all this. I rolled my pack out and faced the fire. Callum tapped the bottom of the bag so the contents fell into his mouth. A smile flitted across my lips as I laid down.

Callum's eyes locked onto mine, "Sloane, we'll figure it out. I promise."

I smiled a tad more then closed my eyes. The warmth lulled me to sleep. My dreams filled with looming fruit, dead trees, and trails of ice followed me.

———

Sounds of fire crackling and Harris talking woke me. Along with the smell of smoke from whatever they were burning.

Harris sat propped against a boulder. The green goo had changed to a ruddy brown. His eyes were bright, and he smiled easily as he spooned some dried food into his big mouth.

"Hey, Harris. How are you?" I asked sleepily.

His eyes swung to me. "Sloane!" He grimaced. "I hurt and ache but I'm all right." His southern drawl dripped heavier than usual.

I eased up as my joints popped from laying on the hard ground. I looked at Callum. "Did you get any sleep?"

His eyes shifted between Harris and me. "Uh, maybe an hour."

My eyebrows shot up.

He shrugged. "I'm used to it."

Harris chuckled but stopped. "Argh, hurts to laugh." He nodded at Callum. "He's a soldier, he's used to it."

I frowned. "Soldiers still need sleep."

"Anyways, now that Sloane's awake, wanna tell us what happened last night?"

Harris shifted uncomfortably, and his face tightened with apprehension. His shoulders sank in defeat. He shook his head. "I had hoped it was a dream." He took a deep breath. "The two of you disappeared, and we sat around the pool talking and eating as we waited. We were having a great time. I don't know how much time passed, maybe thirty minutes? Then monsters dropped from the sky." His voice cracked. "The screams were terrifying. Raleigh fought her best, you know her, but they took her first. Ashlen ran and one of 'em snatched her up." He grimaced, hanging his head. A few seconds passed before he spoke, "I ran as fast as my legs allowed and somehow found this cave. But, as you can see, they marked me up pretty good. I passed out. Next thing I know I see Callum's ugly face." He chuckled as he met Callum's gaze.

Oh my gosh. They were gone. Taken by the creatures. I tried holding my tears back, but they ran down my cheeks, and snot trickled down my lip. Callum sank beside me, wrapping an arm around my shoulders.

We fell silent. The fire crackled, and noises from nearby birds cooed.

"What can we do?" I asked.

Callum's arm tightened around me. "We have two options."

I peered at him. Harris waited.

"We can go to the mountain and get them, or go back to Kingston and try to get more people to help." Callum poked the fire, "Though, most likely things wouldn't happen right away and right now, the girls are on a ticking clock steadily dropping."

Fear whispered through my mind. Sleep wanted to weigh me down. Hopelessness settled in my bones.

"How?" Harris asked.

I wasn't sure we could do either.

Callum shrugged one shoulder. "We got Willow. I think we need to head off. It's been six hours already. There's no telling how, what, or where they've gone, but they might already be dead." The sentence hung in the air between us. "I think it's all we've got."

"I might not be good in a fight, but I can at least get help when needed." Harris smiled slightly. "The poultice has helped a lot so might be able to do some damage."

"Callum, I feel like we might be walking into a trap."

"Can you think of anything else for us to do? The girls are gone. We can send Harris back to the city for more help, and we go on."

I nodded that seemed more practical. I gestured to Harris, "We can show him the portal, then head to the mountain?"

Callum nodded. "Yeah, let's do that. Pack up and head that way."

We trudged our way back up and over the small hill and through the woods to the set of trees marking the portal. Two black trees intertwined. Their large leaves were as big as my head. A number thirteen had been scratched into the trunk. Callum traced the number with his finger. He glanced at his watch.

"It's almost eleven, so should be active soon."

"Man, wish we had known this was here the last time," Harris stated.

"For reals. Would have saved some time," I answered.

Something buzzed in my ear. The portal took shape. Black liquid moved and spread across the portal's entrance.

"Better go now, Harris." Callum gave him a slight push.

Before he stepped through, Harris glanced back. "Guys, thanks for finding me. Get my girl back." He smiled, then vanished through the portal.

The portal sizzled and blinked out a minute later.

Callum hitched his pack higher on his shoulder. "All right, let's go. We have a ways to go before we can sleep."

I nodded. The thought of traipsing through the Nightlin Mountain sent shivers down my spine. We were probably going to die there; if Ashlen and Raleigh hadn't already succumbed to whatever those creatures did in that place.

We faced the large dark mountain range in the north and fell in step together. The moon back-lit the peaks, helping to guide our movement through the dense forest.

21

"He said I'd have more trials, my father was trying to kill me, and an eclipse is coming." I recited what my grandfather had told me in the cave to Callum. I ducked before a low limb slapped my face.

"An eclipse? Here?" Callum crunched dry leaves as he walked a few steps in front.

"No, he said in the Norm. It happens every five hundred years. When the dark is longer."

Callum looked over his shoulder incredulously. "You can't be serious."

I shrugged. "That's what he said. I'm just the messenger."

I thought again about my father. That scary creature had almost scooped my heart out. The trail of iciness filled my soul at his touch. How was someone so evil?

"And your father?"

I sighed. "My grandfather said that James is power-hungry. He thinks my heart will complete the power cycle, and he will inherit vast amounts of power."

"Doesn't sound real."

"Tell me about it." I shifted my bag on my shoulders. I shouldn't have packed so much.

"I wonder what kind of trials he was talking about."

"Beats me. He's all about the riddles too. Why can't people here just tell it like it is?"

Callum chuckled as he stepped over a fallen tree. "You certainly do."

I smiled. "Can't help it."

"I like it." He peered back at me, the corners of his lips tipping upward.

A silent moment passed as we walked through the underbrush. Our footsteps crunched on dried twigs and smushed leaves. The full moon lit up the sky like a beacon.

An eclipse was coming, and he hadn't told me how long we had. But first, we had to rescue Ashlen and Raleigh. I had zero thoughts about how we were going to do that.

"Sloane? Why don't you ask Artemis how to get to the mountain?"

Man, I was such an airhead sometimes. I pulled Arty from under my shirt. Her needles swung around and around lazily.

"Artemis," I whispered, "Lead us to Nightlin Mountain."

The needles sped around then slowed pointing slightly northeast.

I pointed my arm in the direction. "That way."

The mountain loomed far above us. My nerves were on edge the closer we got to it as if at any moment the creatures would drop from the sky and catch us.

We found a small cave at the base of the mountain where we made our home for the night. After trudging through the mud and trees for a little over three hours, we were ready to sleep. I hadn't felt awkward until we sat down and were so close in the cave alone together.

Of course, Callum easily made a fire, so we made some food. He only had to lay his hands on the wood we had gathered and the kindling burst into yellow-orange flames. We sat across from each other, spooning the chili into our mouths. We didn't say much until after we had finished.

"So, I've been thinking about the battle." I met Callum's green eyes. "I'm pretty sure the creature was my dad."

A line formed between his brows. "What makes you say that?"

I breathed in deep. "Because, from what my grandfather said. My dad's powers were ice. When he reached into my chest, ice filled the air and burned my skin. It has to be him."

Callum's lips formed a thin line. "How? How could he be one of them?"

I didn't say anything for a moment. "I don't know, but we need to find out. When we go in, we have to find anything that we can that will help us learn what the hell is going on."

Callum nodded. "Sloane, do you have any idea what this means if it's true?"

I bit my lip and nodded. "Realmers can be changed into Nightlins." My eyes grew larger. "Cal, we killed other Realmers." My stomach flipped, and bile ran up my throat. "We've eaten them..."

I pressed my hand to my mouth, but the bile and food came up anyways. I spun away and wretched everything up that I had just eaten. Sharp quick breaths flooded my lungs. Oh my god. Oh my god. We ate them! My thoughts crashed together.

Callum sat beside me, rubbing small circles on my back. "It's okay. Sloane? It's okay. It'll be okay." He wrapped both arms around me to keep me still.

Sobs tore from my throat, and tears streamed down my cheeks. What had we done? How was it possible? More bile threatened to rise. I bent over trying to get my breathing under control. The warmth of the fire made it hard to breathe. I jumped up and darted to the cave opening, to the fresh air.

The cool air hit my face. My tears cooled, then dried. I leaned over and puked what was left of whatever had been in my stomach. The heat from Callum let me know he was right behind me. I pressed my back to the stone wall and tilted my face to the bright moon.

Callum breathed in deep, then spoke, "Sloane, we didn't know. There's no reason to feel shame. We know now, so we can tell the others. Okay?"

I didn't look at him as I nodded.

"When we're out there battling, things happen. Things you don't expect or intend, especially here. It's the act of war. You get used to horrible things that happen every time you're on a mission. You just have to learn how to compartmentalize and don't let it bother you or rule your life." He squeezed my hand.

I looked at him. His face was still as if he was schooling his features to be immobile. His forest green eyes searched mine, looking for understanding. There's no telling what things he had seen in this realm. Probably much worse. I breathed in deep, quelling my tears.

I swallowed. The burn from the bile stung my throat. It still felt as if at any moment I might break down. I turned back toward our small haven.

Fingers slipped into mine, pulling me backward. Callum's arms wrapped around me tightly, pressing my body into his. His face was buried in my hair.

"I'm sorry, Sloane."

I smiled shakily and tightened my arms around his waist in answer. I pulled back slightly, "Thank you, Cal."

His eyes measured mine, scanning my face. Carefully, he wrapped my arm around his, then led me back to our fire. I rested against him.

"Are you too warm?"

I snuggled closer to him. "A little."

He held a hand out toward the flames. His skin flushed red. Flames leapt into his outstretched hand. The fire danced for a second then sank into his skin, disappearing. He continued until only a few flames lit the wood, but mostly the embers burned.

I chuckled. "You're getting good at handling it."

He smirked and shrugged. "I practice as much as I can. It gets easier and easier."

"That's amazing. Want to practice with me?"

"Thanks, but we're both so tired."

I elbowed him playfully, "Oh, come on."

He studied his rough dirty hands. "You're the one who should be practicing. We need to work on you obtaining your Protector powers."

"How do you know I'll become a Protector?"

He chuckled. "How could you not be? Besides, Patrice said you'd be a Hunter."

I smiled. "We can practice together. I want to see what your Czar will look like."

"All right, but only for a little bit. We need rest."

We faced each other. The embers now glowed, casting a small light onto the cave walls.

Callum held his hand out, palm up. "When I'm practicing, I picture the flame burning inside, and I crank it up until it forms in my palm. Like this." He closed his eyes, growing calm and peaceful. A tiny blue flame sparked in the center of his palm. It lazily flickered on his skin. He pressed both hands together, and the flame detached, forming a small glowing ball of fire. He flipped his hands over and under, letting the fire roll across his skin. The fire winked out.

"Okay, you go."

I held my palm out and closed my eyes.

"Breathe in deep and find the light inside. The one that calls forth whenever you need help."

I frowned slightly. It's not like I did it on purpose. I drew in a deep breath, letting the calmness wash over me. A small tendril of light appeared in my mind's eye. It glowed a ghostly white. I tried to pull it to me, but it dimmed. Frustration broiled.

"Be calm, let it come to you."

I silently fumed. Easy for him to say. I shook my head to kick out the negative thoughts. I returned to my empty mind, searching for that pale light. It took a little longer for me to find it the second time.

It hid behind my creative thoughts. Smaller and paler. That time I waited as if it were a scared dog, and I was the rescuer patiently waiting with an arm outstretched holding dog treats. I waited and waited. My patience was tested. Ever so slowly the light moved closer to my hand. The light grew taller and brighter. It paused, then moved into my hands. I pulled it in close, joy washing over me. I'd never let it go.

White light flooded my senses. It rolled through my limbs and out my eyes.

"Whoa! Pull it back. You'll alert everyone that we're here."

Crap. I eased the light down. It obeyed easily.

"You have to have control."

I nodded, still with my eyes closed.

"Let it form in your hand," Callum said.

Instead of letting the light run free, I channeled it down my arm to my right palm. I pushed the light into my palm, trying to make a small ball.

"There ya go. You've almost got it."

I peeked a look at my hand. It wasn't quite a ball, but more of a soft blob. A spark of hope and pride blossomed in my chest.

"Concentrate on forming a solid ball of light."

I focused on the light, hoping to bend it to my will. Ever so slowly, the light contained to the confines of a small ball. It rolled back and forth in my palm. I giggled and the light burst, blinking out.

Callum laughed. "Great way to burst a bubble."

I shook my head. "Oh wells. At least I got it to form."

"Here, watch."

His palm held out flat, a flicker of flame popped up on his palm, then formed a small marble-sized ball. It might as well have been made of glass. The flames inside still moved and licked the sides of its confines.

"Jess was trying to get me to work on forming my Czar, but I can't seem to get very far." He placed both hands together in front of us. His eyes closed. Light sparked between his palms. A small orb of yellow light formed. The light swirled within.

"I can make my shield," he dropped one hand and lifted the other as light erupted forming his long rectangular shield of light. "But haven't quite made it form into the other yet." He dropped his hand, and the shield disintegrated. "Okay, now you. Think about extending the light out. Picture a shield in front of you."

I sighed and breathed in deep, closing my eyes to concentrate. Okay, think of a shield of light. Think of it building brighter and brighter, forming a circle of hardened light. Swirls of light formed in my mind. Prickles of energy dotted my skin.

"Keep going," Callum said.

With both hands held out, I imagined the light spreading from my fingertips. Imagined the light growing and building a large shield of protection. Something crackled and popped. The air sizzled with life.

I opened one eye. Thin lines of light were spread taut between my fingers as if a spider had spun a dainty web.

"Wow," I whispered.

"Now, make it into a shield."

I breathed in deep, focusing all of my energy on the light. The lines grew thicker and thicker. Light moved from strand to strand, pulsing. I pictured the large round shield in my mind, trying to bend the light to my will.

The light crackled as it moved to form a shield. It pulsed and moved, hurrying to obey. It grew and grew. A two feet in diameter mass formed between us. Spinning slowly as the light moved around, I smiled. Excitement surged through me.

Callum smiled too. "You're doing it. Just hold it as long as you can." His green eyes sparkled in the pale light.

I focused harder, trying to make it as solid as Callum's shield. The energy poured out of me and into the waiting light. It popped and undulated with a hiss.

Callum squinted. "What's happening?"

The light changed between my fingers to a shimmering pool of grey. Light still moved around the circle.

"It looks like a portal," Callum whispered. His eyes moved to mine. Picking up a small pebble, he tossed it at my shield, instead of bouncing off, the shield absorbed it.

My breath caught. What the hell?

"Uh, that's not right," Callum said.

The light sputtered and died. Sweat formed on my lip and temples. I laid my head in my hands, breathing hard. My arms shook slightly. Of course, I wasn't normal.

"You just need more practice," he stated.

I pressed my lips together, feeling the dry skin, and nodded, "Yeah, I'm sure you're right."

Callum patted the ground beside him. "Let's sleep, so we can find the girls."

My body felt like mush after pushing so hard and after all the walking. I leaned against him. He wrapped an arm around me, leaning back onto the dirt walls.

Sleep came instantly, filling my dreams with light and murky waters.

22

Callum

THREE HOURS LATER I AWOKE. SLOANE'S HEAD LAY ON MY SHOULDER AS she slept soundly. I gently lifted her chin. Her eyelids fluttered. Blue peeked out.

"Sloane? Time to go."

She moaned and tried to burrow into me more. As much as I loved having her near, I knew time wasn't on our side. I shook her.

Both of her eyes popped open. Anger flashed across her features then smoothed when she realized it was me. I smiled.

I rolled our packs up and put dirt on the remnants of our fire. She stretched and stuffed her pack. I walked to the edge of the cave and looked out. The forest was quiet. The moon hung low in the sky; in its fourth phase.

To the left of the cave, a small clearing had been disturbed. A path carved through the underbrush, leading up the mountain. I stopped listening to any strange noises. A few hundred yards away, the sounds of deer making their way through the woods reached my ears. Squirrels scampered through the treetops. A few rabbits not too far away burrowed in their dens. Thankfully, the skies were clear.

Sloane's footsteps crunched on the rocks. We needed to work on her quiet steps.

I waved her forward. "This way."

She pulled on the straps of her backpack and started in my direction. Her head tilted back as she looked up the mountain in the direction we were heading. "Oh my god, I'm going to die."

I chuckled and kept going. Her breathing grew more labored the higher we traveled. As we reached the top, she cussed between gasps of breath.

"Callum — are we — almost — there?" She panted.

I stepped to the side so she could see the opening before us. Her mouth fell open. I didn't blame her.

The valley below us opened up to a large black lake. Mountain ranges surrounded us. The moonlight reflected off the still water. The skies were clear. No creatures obscured the moon.

"Can we rest a moment?"

"Yeah, that should be fine. Going down we will have to be careful, so we don't tear down the side at full speed and call attention to ourselves."

She nodded. "Where do you think we will go?"

I pointed to her necklace. "You'll have to ask her once we are at the bottom."

"Right."

"All right, you ready?"

She breathed in deep. "I love the smell of the trees and soil. But yes, let's go."

We headed down like mountain goats. Steadily descending. The mountainside was so steep. The rocks were sharp. We had to grab hold of the tree trunks as we went to help with balance.

Something moved in the water, and I stopped, grabbing Sloane and yanking her down out of sight. The water's surface rippled and a creature's head poked from the water. Its sleek black head slid out of the water silently. Its black eyes searched the area then shot out of the water. Water sprayed across the surface of the lake making large ripples. The creature soared into the sky. I was slightly jealous of its flight.

Sloane shivered beside me, recoiling. She grimaced as the creature flew around the valley then faded to the west.

I gestured for her to follow, and we began our descent. We stopped close to the water's edge, still hidden by the trees.

"What do you think?" she asked.

"Let's wait a minute and see if we see any more of them."

She nodded and knelt by the tree. We didn't have to wait long. The same water lapped, and I caught the movement of a head appearing in the water. The creature did the same maneuvers as the other. It leapt from the water, flying around the valley then headed off.

"See what Artemis has to say."

She pulled the necklace out and whispered, "Artemis, where is the Nightlin mountain entrance?"

The needles swung around and around, then stopped pointing straight ahead, then pointed at the water, then back to the mountain, and back to the water.

She frowned. "She's never done that before."

"So, we've got two points of entry."

Sloane eyed the water. "After our last adventure, I'd rather not try water again."

I tried not to smile. "I might agree with you there. Let's head to the far side. See where that leads us."

She nodded and stood, tightening the straps on her bag.

We followed the tree line as we made our way around to where Artemis had indicated. We stopped a few times when a creature broke the surface, then we headed on. On the far side, we neared what looked like a small creek that emptied into the lake. Artemis pointed south down the rocky creek bed. The dark trees loomed over us. The leaves and limbs blocked most of the moonlight.

I faced Sloane. "Are you ready for this?"

She grimaced. "Not really, but let's go."

"We will go in and see what we can find. If we need to get out, head back here. Understand?"

She nodded. The fear on her face made her eyes widen.

"No matter what, listen to me. Okay?"

She nodded, gripping the straps of her backpack. I didn't dare dig out my light stick. We stepped through the forest, following the creek. We ran to the mountainside; the creek snaked through a small dark opening made by water. It looked just big enough for me to crawl through.

"Are you claustrophobic?"

She blanched. "It's not my favorite."

I tightened the straps around my chest and middle. "Follow me." I turned to the opening, kneeling. I barely fit with my pack on but slid through on my hands and knees.

The darkness swallowed us and the size of the rocks above our heads weighed on my consciousness but I ignored it. We slid on our hands and knees in the water. Thankful there wasn't much to fight with.

23

Sloane

THE SOUND OF OUR BREATHING AND SLIDING ALONG THE ROCKS ECHOED in the small space. I grew nervous that the Nightlins would hear us and be waiting for us at the end. I had to shut out the thoughts in my head of the mountain collapsing on top of us or of snakes slithering toward us. We kept crawling and crawling. This night would never end. My anxiety grew heavier the farther we went.

By the end, we slid along on our bellies. The wet rock tugged my clothes and scraped my skin. My forehead hit the bottom of Callum's boot. I muffled my grunt.

He muttered, "Sorry. There is fire ahead, and I can hear cries."

My body chilled more, which I didn't think was even impossible. My wet clothes already made me shiver. Gooseflesh rose along my arms.

"What kind of cries?" I whispered.

"For help."

I felt like puking right there. I just knew at any moment a Nightlin would find us and grab us. They would pull our innards out and roast us over a fire.

"Sloane, stay hidden. I'll come back for you when I can get a look."

I opened my mouth to object, but he moved too quickly. He was gone, leaving me in the dark. I army-crawled through the small space. The rock above me seemed to get lower and lower. I cursed Callum in my head. Surely he wouldn't leave me in this tiny space, crawling toward monsters. Leave it to me to find a guy who left me in a dark crevice.

I knew Ashlen wouldn't have left me behind, but she probably wouldn't have tried to crawl in here in the first place. Surely, with Harris back at the capital, reinforcements would come soon.

A white light pierced the darkness. Callum's voice echoed to me, "Hurry, we don't have much time."

I crawled with more fervor. Happy to be near the end and out of this small, dark space. Callum's hand waited in the opening. He knelt on the rocks to help pull me out. His hand grabbed mine and tugged with such force that the rocks burned my skin as I skidded along. I burst from the hole with open arms, falling into Callum's lap.

He smiled slightly and shook his head like he couldn't believe how clumsy I was. He pressed a finger to his lips and pointed above us. The creekbed that we were in was covered in small rocks, but we were below the main level. Only yellow light from flames flickered on the cave ceiling. The creek disappeared further ahead under the rock wall. Moisture hung on everything around us, sparkling in the dim light.

Callum's hand still held mine as he led me along the rock wall to the far end. Small pockets, large enough for toes to fit into, led up along the wall. Muffled cries drifted to my ears, but the words were garbled.

Callum faced me, his eyes solid black. "We are in a part filled with dungeons. I'm not sure who or what is in the cells, but we need to find out in case they're Realmers."

I nodded. Of course, we had to rescue our own. Maybe Ashlen and Raleigh were down here amongst them.

"To the far right is a set of stairs leading up. They go up a ways before reaching another floor. I'm sure there is another set of stairs somewhere in here, but I didn't get to look very far."

I nodded.

"You have your knife. Use him to open the doors. Even letting the prisoners out will confuse and should help us to find the girls."

"Okay." I unsheathed Masada from my leg.

He started up the wall then looked back. "If you find Realmers, send them down this way so they can make it out."

"All right."

He winked then jumped over the edge of the wall and disappeared. I scurried up after him. His dark hair vanished to the right.

I looked left. Muddy cells lined the wall before me. Crying and muttering echoed off the walls. Twelve cells were before me. I ran to the farthest one to start there. The large black lock had small scratches and rust but otherwise had no other marks.

"Masada." The knife glowed a soft blue as it sliced through the metal like butter. The lock fell to the ground. I pushed the bar upward as quietly as I could muster. The heavy wooden door swung open revealing three pairs of eyes. Three small girls sat in the corner, shivering. The one in the center jerked upright when she met my gaze.

I beckoned them, whispering, "Come on. Hurry. We don't have much time."

The girls looked at each other before the center one asked, "Is this a trick?"

I shook my head. "No, hurry." I moved to the next door, leaving them to make their decision. It didn't take long for them to stumble out of the cell.

The one girl caught my arm, her eyes and hair dark like the night. "Where can we go?"

I pointed to the corner. "Go down that way into the creekbed. There is a way out there."

They didn't wait. They ran.

I sliced through the next lock. Five more huddled together. Both boys and girls. I told them the same then ran to the next cell. This cell had two locks. I stared at it thinking. Why would there be two? I looked up and down the path. The kids jumped into the creekbed. Their muffled voices echoed back to me.

Without too much more thought, I sliced through the two locks.

The door swung open. A large man sat in the corner, alone. I peered in at him, but I didn't see much.

"Hello? We are rescuing as many as we can."

A baritone of a voice reverberated in his empty cell, "Aye, I've been waiting for ya, lass."

My mouth fell open and the bundle of nerves in the center of my chest melted. I slapped my hand over my mouth to keep from crying out. Brand. I stumbled toward him. He caught me in his big arms and squeezed me. His thick frame was much smaller than before. They must have been starving him. Tears leaked from my eyes.

"Brand," my voice broke, "Is it you?"

He chuckled. "Yes, lass, it is."

I hugged him then remembered where we were. I grabbed his arm and pulled him out of the cell.

I pointed to the corner. "Go that way to get out. There is a small hole that will lead you out."

In the flame light, the toll of being captured reflected in his face and body. His eyes were sunken. The lines on his face were deeper. But his eyes still shone that mischief gleam.

He nodded and squeezed my hand. "Be careful, bonnie. They aren't ever far behind."

I wanted to cry and hug him but knew that had to wait. At least he was safe! A smile spread across my sweaty face. I nodded then went to the next cell before I forgot again.

The next two cells were filled with more Realmers. Watchers and groundlings from what I could tell.

A boy grabbed my arm before Masada sliced through the next lock. His eyes were haunted and face gaunt. "Don't free that one. They aren't normal." He took off without another word.

I stared at him for a moment. What did that mean? I studied the door. Only one lock. I stepped up to it and listened. No sound or shuffle. I tapped on the door. Something rammed the wood. The panels shook and hinges quaked. My eyes bulged. Would they have imprisoned one of their own?

I quickly moved to the next door. Inside, someone huddled in the corner.

"Hello?"

The face whipped to meet mine, and I gasped.

"Raleigh!" I fell on my knees as she scrambled to me. Her arms wrapped around my torso. Her small body shook as sobs tore from her. Mud and dirt streaked her face, but that wasn't the most concerning. Long black cuts raked down her arms. A long gash tore across her jaw and ear. Red blood caked along her wound.

"Raleigh," I whispered as I took in all of the cuts. Tears threatened to fall.

A black wound marred her chest. It ran from her shoulder down to her hip. She only shook her head and wiped her tears, smearing the dirt and blood more.

"I didn't think I'd ever see — see you again." Her hands shook, and her voice rattled. Shock had set in.

I gathered her hands in mine. "Where is Ash?"

"There are so many souls here. So many." Her eyes gazed around the cell. "They're everywhere." Her eyes were unfocused as if she saw something beyond. Spirits.

I glanced over my shoulder, hoping not to catch sight of any ghosts. A shiver ran down my neck. I gripped her hands. "Raleigh, where is Ashlen?"

Her eyes focused on mine for a second. "I haven't — seen her since."

Cold settled around me and my heart sank. "Okay, come on. Let's get you out." I pulled her up, sliding an arm around her shoulders. We walked out of the cell and stopped. Silence met us. The flames in the torches flickered back and forth.

Something was coming. I felt it in my bones. I squeezed Raleigh to my side and tugged her to the far corner. I hoped to see Callum but didn't glimpse him anywhere. I went down into the creek first and pointed out all the holds for her to use. Raleigh's legs shook as she climbed down to find purchase. We slid over the small smooth rocks, trying to hurry and be quiet at the same time. My pulse thundered in my ears.

Whatever monster was in that cell, rammed the door again. The sound reverberated in the cave. It bellowed. Crap. Crap. We were going to die.

I was sure whatever it was saying was a warning to the Nightlins.

"Come on, Raleigh." I bent down at the hole and pointed inside. "There. Go now."

She grabbed my hands, her eyes changing to black. "Aren't you coming?"

"No, Callum is somewhere."

Tears ran down her face, her teeth chattered. "Sss-Sloane. Ppp-please."

"I'll be right behind you. Hurry. It won't take long for you to be in the open. Brand will be there." I smiled encouragingly.

Her eyes locked onto mine. My face reflected in the black pools. She nodded then slid through the space. Her bare feet vanished in an instant.

A screech tore through the cave, piercing my eardrums. Nightlins were coming.

24

The Dark

THE CREATURE BELLOWED. THE STRUCTURE SHOOK AND THE HALLS echoed with the sound.

Her smell pierced his nostrils. It slid through the walls and slithered along the rock floor, under his door. She was close. But how? Why?

His claws scraped along the floor as he neared the door. He breathed in deeply. Among the smells of the dirt and rot within the walls, a tendril of her essence appeared. The smell of her — the honey, vanilla, and flowers rushed through his lungs. Then he felt it. The tug of light within her. The power. It pulsed with anticipation.

She hadn't accepted it yet. Hadn't let it in.

He breathed in deep, searching the halls for her. He would have that power even if it killed him. If it was the last thing he did. No matter what the others said. They didn't know.

He would squeeze the life from her as he drank in her power. He almost felt it. Almost felt it calling out to him, beckoning him to take it.

The creature ripped the door away and hunted.

25

Callum

I BOUNDED UP THE STONE STEPS, STICKING TO THE SHADOWS AND BARELY making a sound. Only a soft whoosh sounded as I padded upward. There weren't many torches lighting the way so I had to use my not-so-great night vision. The ghostly shapes of the walls loomed over me.

Claws scraping the stones reached my ears first. I braced myself against the stone wall and waited. The smell of the wet earth and stone permeated my senses. I had no idea where I was going or what I was heading into. Only that I was looking for the girls, and whatever else I could find about these creatures before I needed to get back to Sloane. I hoped she was okay. I buried that thought deep inside before it distracted me.

I peered around the corner of the next floor. Four hallways branched out. The ends were solid black. A torch flickered here and there. Doors were placed sporadically down each. No rhyme or reason to any. I listened, opening my ears to the smallest of noises.

Down the first hallway, only the sound of small scurrying feet like those of mice skittered about. In the second hall, claws clicked on stone along with growls and snarls. The third hall held fear. Metal clanked and chains rattled. Soft cries drifted from the doors. The fourth hall was quiet.

I eased down the third hall. Letting each foot fall heel to toe. The first door I pressed my ear against. Soft cries escaped through the cracks. A screech echoed through the halls, and I froze. Nothing else happened, so I moved on to the next door. Chains rattled and someone or something muttered behind the large wooden door.

A voice I recognized? I paused. Could it be him? I glanced behind me listening for any sound coming my way. Nothing.

The door was locked with a large metal padlock. I pulled, testing. Iron. Wrapping both hands around the cold metal, I pulled on the fire within then pushed it toward my palms. The lock instantly heated, glowing yellow then orange. The lock cracked, and I pulled. It broke in my hands.

Carefully, I pushed the door inward. Thankfully the hinges didn't protest. Inside was total darkness. The smell, like rotting flesh, hit me first as I stepped inside and closed the door behind me. I set the lock on the floor.

I scanned the room, seeing a hunched figure in the corner. It was chained so I moved slowly toward it. Nothing else was in the small space. The chains rattled as the figure realized I was in there with it. The head moved up; its face turned to me. Its eyes locked onto mine.

The pulse in my throat throbbed as I eased closer.

"Hello?" I whispered, hoping they answered.

A snarl rose. I paused.

"It's me, Callum."

The figure paused as if recollecting who I was.

"Don't come closer." A raspy voice spoke as if he hadn't spoken real words in a while.

"Graham?" I listened with every fiber.

He growled. "Don't come closer." His teeth ground. "I can't control whatever is inside me."

No. Not him too. "Graham, maybe we can help you. I've got Sloane with me. We can get you out."

"No, Callum. It's too late. Whatever they put in me is taking over." He growled. "You should go. Get out before they find you. Before — before they do the same to you."

Each word he spoke ended with a growl as if his tongue wasn't used to forming words.

I stepped closer. He growled. The chains moaned with tension.

Hair hung in his face. The golden strands were now dingy and matted. His muscles strained. Instead of the Greek god cast into marble, his skin was thinner. His large muscles lessened. Bones stuck out in relief. The tendons in his arms pulled with resistance.

"No," he growled.

The chains clinked. His muscles bulged. His eyes glowed a faint yellow in the dark, but I saw him wholly. Black streaks marred his skin, then I realized it was his veins. Every vein in his body was black. Trailing through his system showing the direction each ran. Even the veins in his eyes.

"Leave." He watched me fearfully. His large eyes pleading.

"Let me help you." I held a hand out toward him.

He shook his head. "I told you it's too late." He breathed in deep; the muscles in his chest rippled. "Leave!" he cried.

I stopped listening for other movements.

"Leave!!" he bellowed.

My mouth fell open and I stepped back.

"Graham."

He snarled then bellowed louder. The metal rattling.

I sped for the door, still not sure what to do, but knew I couldn't wait for the creatures to find me. I wrenched the door open and closed it. Sobs echoed behind me. My heart seized. I paused outside the door unsure, listening.

Then, from far above and below screeches echoed, and the sound of talons scraping the rocks reverberated through the halls. I ran. Ran as fast as my feet allowed.

Sloane would be waiting. Maybe she had already left and safely waited outside, but I knew that was the last thing she would do. I stumbled down the stairs, my feet trying to keep up with my fear and adrenaline. The creatures grew closer. I had to reach her first. I had caused this. If only I had grabbed him.

I burst through the cave entrance in a sprint. Each footfall pounded the stones. Sloane had her back against a cell door. Her knife, Masada, glowed in her outstretched hand. Her white eyes shone dimly in the dark.

A Nightlin stood a few feet away, its massive head craned down to look at her. Its black wings tucked behind it. The face made me stop on my heels. There were no eyes or nose, only large spiky teeth. They were long like needles. The head swung from side to side as if trying to smell her out. It let out a low hiss.

It was all going to hell.

I pulled on the flame within, calling it up and out. It answered gleefully. The blue flames licked down my arms to my hands, settling in my palms. I balled it up and threw it at the monster.

The fire happily engulfed the creature's rags hanging from its bones. Sloane whirled to me. Her features lit with relief and happiness as she saw me.

"Cal." She breathed.

The monster bellowed and spun toward Sloane. I let another fireball loose, hitting it squarely in its teeth. It reeled away, teetering on the edge of the wall. A flurry of motion, talons scraping, and roars echoed through the mountain. The whole of the Nightlin colony knew we were in their territory.

"Sloane, come on! We've gotta get out!" I yelled. I rushed to her side, my breaths coming in ragged from my sprinting.

Incredibly, she shook her head. "No, I didn't find Ashlen."

I wrapped a hand around her elbow. "We don't have time. We can come back."

"Ha, yeah right."

Even I knew that was a stretch. I frowned.

"Callum, we have to find her."

The echoes of the creatures grew closer. Their anger and feral energy rolled through the dungeons. The monster before us huddled on the floor, trying to collect itself for another attack. Orange and yellow embers glowed at its feet.

The roaring grew louder and the flapping of wings echoed

through the chamber. There was the door at the other end that we could try, or we had to leave immediately.

Creatures of various sizes appeared in the entrance, some flew or crawled, and some slithered along the floor. I called on the fire, readying it in my palms, then launched them at the encroaching figures. They scattered and roared.

White light erupted behind me and the creatures screamed. I shielded my eyes to see what it was. Sloane stood a few feet away with her hands held aloft, trying to ward off the monsters. White electrical currents spread between her fingers, alighting each one. It fizzled and popped. Her eyes were scrunched in concentration. Her teeth bared. The white current spread wider and wider as it took an oval shape. It spread and formed into a shield.

The creatures roared with anger and surged toward us. I easily opened my palms creating my shield of warm orange and flame. We backed away from the creek entrance and toward the small wooden door behind us. With each toss of the fireball, a new one appeared in my hand. The creatures scattered around us. The hunger on their faces was clear in their snarls.

"Sloane, the door behind us," I said through gritted teeth.

She glanced behind her shoulder and nodded.

"We can try to find her through there."

"Okay."

We were almost to the door when a deafening roar shook the whole chamber.

26

Sloane

MY HEART LEAPT TO MY THROAT. THE MONSTERS BEFORE US SPREAD wide to get out of the way for the beast heading our way. His wings spread to their full extent, seeming to fill the cave. A rush of icy air surrounded us.

It was him. I knew it. My father.

I felt like screaming and crying at the same time. Instead, I bolted for the small door behind me. What can I say? My fight or flight took hold, and I almost always fly when given the chance.

Callum yelled. He was close on my heels.

I wrenched the door open and threw myself into the darkness, knowing it had to be better than in the cavern with that *thing*. A set of rough stone stairs ran upward. I didn't think, just acted, as I bolted up. The sound of Callum slamming the door behind us echoed through the small space. Rocks littered the steps, and cobwebs stuck to me as I raced on. I shut the thoughts out of my father and the monsters. My only goal was to escape.

The stairs went up in a tight spiral. Each step was a slightly different height. I almost ran past a door then skidded to a stop. Callum bounced off of me.

"Sorry," I stammered.

"Wait." Callum touched my arm.

I paused. Callum pressed his ear to the doorjamb and waited. Seconds ticked by and my anxiety ramped up. My ears craned to hear if something followed us from below.

He nodded slowly. "Okay."

I carefully cracked the door.

A hall opened before us. Dim light lit the far end. Several doors lined the hallway. Callum stepped in front of me, pushing me slightly behind him. I rolled my eyes. He would always be the protector.

The walls and floor shook with each roar that reverberated through the mountain. They would find us. I knew it. He would find me. I tried not to think about my father, about him being trapped in that gruesome creature.

Callum stopped abruptly.

"What is it?" I whispered.

"Something is coming."

Fear tore through me as if my body was on fire. I tightened my grip on Masada as the knife glowed a faint blue.

He pushed me back toward the door. "Hurry, go back."

He didn't have to tell me twice. I spun around, back through the door, and pounded up the rock steps, engulfing more spiderwebs. My lungs burned for air. My legs grew numb the faster I pushed myself. Fear speared my soul.

We kept going, past more doors, pushing ourselves to the top. Callum labored behind me. Sweat covered every inch of me. Salt stung my eyes. Callum pressed his ear to the door again, waiting to hear for anything. Though I knew it wouldn't matter if they beat us there. It would be over.

He slowly pulled the door back, and another hallway welcomed us. We must have been on the outside of the mountain because large windows lined the left side of the wall. They were covered by heavy, thick shutters. I was sure it was to block out the light in the mornings. Specks of moonlight entered the hall through cracks. The vast windows were large enough for the creatures to get through. It must have been where they flew out.

The air felt heavier as I breathed it in, or maybe it was from all the exertion. Callum took his spot in front of me, leading me past the foreboding windows. I listened with all my might to see if I heard the monsters too, but only my and Callum's puffs of air disturbed the stillness.

Only a few doors lined the right side of the hall. I gestured to them. "Could Ashlen be in one of those?"

He shook his head. "I don't hear anyone in them."

Slight relief flooded me, but it didn't last. The walls shook as the creatures rampaged below us.

"Sloane, they'll find us." Callum craned his head back to me, his dark hair plastered to his head. His face was covered in dirt and sweat. "We're outnumbered."

A sob threatened to break from my mouth, but I gulped it down. I pressed my lips together hard, biting on my lower trying to think of anything to do.

"What about the windows?" I faced one and pushed on it. "Can we make it out?"

Callum sighed but focused on one. He rattled the shutters. He glanced behind down the dark hall.

"We don't have much time." He pushed me against the wall. "Stand back." Steam rose from his skin and his arms lit with the telltale orange glow that accompanied his fire. Fire blossomed in his palm, and he launched it at the shutters. A softball-sized hole blossomed in the thick wood.

"Oh, you got it. Keep going." I shook his arm, digging my short nails into his skin. A rumble sounded behind us.

He released them in rapid succession, making a hole the size of a large dog. He pushed on some of the ruined parts, breaking it off and making the hole slightly bigger.

A mist enveloped us.

Callum yelled, "No!" He disappeared. "Sloane!"

"Callum!" I screamed.

I was blind. I held my hands out in front of me, and they vanished in the mist. Rows of sharp teeth flashed on my left. A glint of a yellowed eye rose on my right. The spirits. I gasped. I hadn't ever seen one of those. Only fragments of what Graham had told me about them flitted through my mind. They could be killed though.

Blue flames sparked far ahead of me. Callum?

"Cal?" I squeaked.

The mist swirled around me, obscuring the flame. My hand shook as I held Masada out. The faint glow of the blade disappeared in the black mist. I pulled a breath in, centering myself then struck out. I started high, then drug the blade down. The creature screeched. Black mist thinned and swirled around me. Rows of teeth flashed before my face. I thrust Masada upward. Black blood sprayed my face. The mist disintegrated as what was left of the monster fell to the floor.

Its thin body looked hollow. Its arms and legs were bones. What had happened to it? I couldn't think too long because Callum was in the midst of a battle with a large beast. Its wings tucked behind. My father.

My heart dropped as I watched him. The memory of him sinking his claws into my chest and seizing my heart in his grasp stilled my blood. I stood frozen to that spot. My eyes were transfixed on the monster who used to be my dad. The dad I'd never met. Who didn't know I existed. It wasn't exactly how I imagined our meeting.

I thought I'd find him, and we'd embrace. We'd discuss all that he missed. All the things to do in the future. He'd reconnect with my mom, and they'd live happily ever after. But as I watched him fight Callum, watched his teeth gnash and claws rip, I knew the future I wanted was gone and would never be.

A small part of me died at that moment. The small part of my childhood and naivete, but I had no time to mourn. Callum was losing the battle.

I pulled Willow from my back and unsheathed the long sword. It hummed in my hands, sending a shiver up my arm. The cool metal pressed into my palm. It gleamed.

Callum had transformed into his human torch self, but it wasn't enough to fight the creature. They spun in the tight space, making it hard for me to attack and not hit Callum. The creature that was my dad sliced with his needle-like claws. His teeth snapped at anything.

I realized what the real problem was. My father's ice abilities were combating Callum's fire. Callum still didn't have a hold on his powers, and my father had many years. What I had thought were burn marks or part of Callum's fire, were instead ice patches on his skin. The kind that caused hypothermia. Patches of black and purple now mottled his smooth, olive skin. Pain and exertion tightly set his jaw. He tried to burn the monster, but my father only burned him with his ice.

Horror and helplessness filled me. I took a step forward, then another, trying to find an opening, but they kept grappling.

"Callum!" I called out, hoping he'd let me help him.

He glanced my way, but so did my father. And then the unthinkable happened. My father charged Callum, pushing him into the already damaged shutter. The wood splintered away and the two of them fell out.

I rushed to the window. They fell down and down, then my father took hold of Callum and shot upward. Breath caught in my throat.

"No, no!" My fingers dug into the window sill hoping my fears wouldn't come true.

They rose higher and higher and higher. Tears pricked the corners of my eyes as I watched them suspended in the sky, outlined by the moon, then the creature released Callum and he fell.

27

Callum

THE CREATURE AND I SOARED HIGHER AND HIGHER, AND THE FEELING OF impending doom rose in my throat. The full moon seemed to cheer us on as it lit our way up into the night sky. All of the stars were out. We were giving them a show, and they were all out for us.

The creature snarled in my face, "You won't ever have her." Its claws tore through my shirt and skin, then it let me go.

My thoughts screamed, and my heart pounded my ribs. The wind buffeted my body, filling my ears with a roar. I fell facing the sky with the stars and moon watching. I hadn't wanted to see the ground reaching for me. Memories flashed in my mind's eye. My family that was now gone. The battles I had fought. Sloane. The girl to break through my heart and mind. I wasn't giving up yet.

I was a fucking Hunter. It was about damn time I acted like one.

I pulled on that flame inside of me. I called to it, hoping I had enough energy in reserve. The small spark inside of me flickered. *Come on. I need you this time. I need you to burn. Answer.*

I beckoned it with an outstretched hand. *You can take all of me. Consume me.*

It was as if the fire had been waiting the whole time for my permission. My vision exploded with red hot flames. And from those flames, a creature grew with large wings and a long snout. Smoke and fire poured from its mouth. It bellowed with power.

My czar.

It swooped under me to break my fall. Its wings blasted the air, and we sailed above the trees. The wind cooled my skin. I wrapped my arms around its strong neck and fitted my legs under its wings so it had better aerodynamics. Its ethereal body shimmered with light and flame, holding a faint yellow glow.

Sloane was far above me, but my energy depleted by the second. My thoughts escaped me. The lake glimmered beneath us, and I pushed the czar toward it.

It flew in a tight circle around the lake. I caught sight of people at the far corner. It was the Realmers from the dungeons. Their skinny frames and small coverings made them stand out from the terrain. My czar touched down on the grassy bank, like a boat mooring on land. The Realmers ran toward us. Their smiling faces greeted me.

I all but fell off the czar's back. The dirt and grass kissed my face with a loud thunk. I groaned. My body had spent all of its resources, on top of the injuries I had; I needed a nap. Hands gently rolled me over to my back. Pain lanced through every inch of me.

"Dear lord, it's Callum," someone murmured.

"I thought he didn't burn?"

"Not sure what those are, but it's not from fire."

Be well small one. I shall be here when you rise. My czar nudged me with its head, then shimmered and disintegrated. Orange light fell like ash, absorbing into the ground.

"Let's get him out of sight."

"We need to get him away from this mountain. Back to Kingston."

"How will we do that?"

"Hell, if I know. I'm just glad to be alive right now."

More murmuring and arguing ensued.

"Sloane," I whispered.

Silence fell.

"What did he say?"

Someone knelt closer to me. "What was that Callum?" a thick Scottish accent asked.

"Sloane."

"She isn't here. Has anyone seen her?"

"She must still be in there."

I had to get her out. I had to find her. I just needed some rest. With one last big conscious breath, the darkness covered me. I sank.

28

A PIT FORMED IN MY STOMACH AS CALLUM FELL OUT OF VIEW. THE creatures behind me moved to attack as soon as they had gone out the window.

I swirled to face them, Willow in hand, ready to cut them down. I arced the blade across the black, oily creatures, taking out three instantly. More replaced them. They kept coming with each fell stroke. Soon, carcasses surrounded me. The stench of rot filled the air. Wind blew in from the open window. Moonlight gave me enough light to see the creatures hiding in the shadows.

Ice filled the space, and I knew my father would be there soon. He landed on the sill. His large talons dug into the stone. The monsters stopped their advance, seeming to take a step back and see what my father did.

A chill raced up my spine. Would he try to remove my heart again? How could he think that he needed it for power?

I held Willow aloft with as much strength as I mustered. The holes where his eyes should have been, watched me. His head tilted slightly my way.

"So, we meet again." His voice was raspy and garbled.

I didn't respond, only watched, waiting for him to pounce.

He flicked his arm at the other creatures in a gesture to leave. They immediately dispersed. He stepped one leg onto the stone floor then the other. His legs bent in the other direction. He stood beside the window, not moving.

"Brother, I know you don't mean to take all the power for yourself." A voice said out of the shadows. Jacob. My uncle, or what was left of him. He looked the same as before. The spikes along his back and arms looked painful. Pieces of cloth covered him. When he spoke, his needle-like teeth moved in and out of the holes in his mouth.

I wasn't sure if his presence was a good or bad thing. I assumed it was bad.

"No, of course not, Brother," my father said. He turned to address me, "If you drop your sword, we can move on."

I eyed Willow, "I don't feel comfortable with that."

My uncle coughed raggedly, and I realized it was supposed to be a laugh. I tightened my grip.

"If you don't then you'll pay."

I looked between the both of them, "I'll take my chances."

Before I moved, ice bloomed on the floor, anchoring me to the stone. It raced up my legs. The cold bit my flesh as it ran to the top of my head. My lips sealed shut, and Willow clambered to the floor.

"Much better." My father stalked toward me. Tendrils of smoke bloomed in the air from where each foot fell. "We have much to discuss, girl."

One claw drug across my jaw then over my exposed neck. A threat that he could easily rip my throat out. I wanted to shiver but I was frozen because of his hold on me. Only my eyes followed his progression.

"Jake put her with the other one." My father growled.

My uncle nodded. He stood in front of me and raised one arm. The ice cementing my limbs lessened but my vision went black. Razor-like claws gripped my arm and lifted me. My sight was gone but at least my ears worked. Of course, maybe that was more terrifying.

We traveled through halls and up some stairs for several minutes before he stopped and the sounds of metal scraping and what had to be a lock opened. He dropped me onto a rough wood floor. His claws clicking on the floor moved away from me. The door shut, and the darkness covering my eyes melted away.

I was in a small cell in the dark. My ears strained to hear anything around me. A minute passed then something rustled in the corner.

A small voice broke the stillness, "Hello?"

I faced the voice. "Yes? Who are you?"

My eyes tried so hard to flip over to night vision but they wouldn't work. A small form moved closer to me. At least, my blue eyes were slowly adjusting to the dark.

"Sloane?" the voice cried.

"Ash?" Happiness and sorrow filled me.

She scurried closer and embraced me tightly. Sobs tore through her and soon my shirt was wet with tears. I squeezed her tightly and rubbed circles on her back.

"It's okay Ash. I'm here. We'll get out."

She only cried harder.

"Ash, calm down. You're going to start panicking."

Between breaths, she said, "Too — late." Her breathing was labored, and she was hyperventilating. I patted her back some more.

"Come on. Don't do that." Although, I had no idea how to get out, and my tears spilled down my cheeks. I racked my brain. "We found Harris. He's okay. And I got Raleigh out."

She gasped for air. "You — you did?"

I nodded then remembered she couldn't see me. "Yes," I answered.

She wrapped her arms around me and cried some more.

"Ashlen, what have you seen?" Hoping to distract her.

She paused, catching her breath. She grasped my hands. "Not much." She blew out a breath. "They took me to another room and tried to question me about things, but I didn't understand them. They made me drink this black liquid. It was horrible."

A chill swept over me. Was that how they changed them?

I hadn't wanted to frighten her, but I needed to know. "Have you been feeling okay since?"

"I've just been so tired and cold, but that's it. Why?" Her voice grew more steady.

"Just wanted to make sure they hadn't poisoned you or something." I waited, hoping that would be enough to pass.

"Oh, no. I don't think so."

I sighed inwardly, surely she would be okay.

29

Callum

My head throbbed, and my eyes felt stale. I was being carried on a makeshift gurney made from what felt like branches and leaves. The stars above me twinkled through the trees. My memory before I blacked out was still fuzzy.

"Hey, he's awake." They immediately set me on the ground.

Brand's gaunt face swam before me. My heart leapt when I saw him, and I tried to grab his hand.

"Hello, Cal, glad you could make it." His gruff Scottish accent warmed my ears, and I shut my eyes. He touched my arm, shaking gently. "We are almost back to the portal. Can yous tell us anything we need to know before we get back?"

My mind hurt to think, but I shook my head.

"Sloane?" My voice croaked.

Brand shook his head, "Sorry, lad. I saw her once but not since."

I tried to roll to my side but my body hurt to move. My skin felt like rough paper. The creature's face and claws flashed in my mind. That's why I was hurt. He had burned me with ice. But my czar had finally come. Wait, it spoke to me? What had it said? My thoughts swirled as they picked me back up and carried on through the woods.

"Sloane."

"Not much further, lad," Brand said. He walked beside me. "Can't believe yous came to get us. We will forever be thankful."

I couldn't respond. I couldn't think. Words escaped me.

The trees above swayed with a breeze. The moon was a waning crescent tonight. I wasn't sure if I wanted my skin to be cool or hot. Heat was my natural tendency, but maybe that wouldn't help with ice burns?

A few minutes later we stopped, and voices murmured not too far away. All my power and energy were used in the fight and for my czar. Where was he or she anyways? Shouldn't I be able to hear them?

"All right, we're going through. Hold on." Brand patted my knee.

A sleepy stillness settled over me as they carried me through the portal. It had to have been the weirdest feeling yet. The glow of the soft blue lights disrupted the darkness. All the rescued realmers surrounded my gurney. Raleigh's small face appeared above me.

"Is she okay?" Her dark eyes were so large. Her lip trembled.

I could barely talk, but I answered honestly, "I don't know."

Her eyes fell, and her jaw set. She nodded once then moved away. She looked more and more like a ghost every day. Her usually brown skin had turned grey in her captivity.

I needed food.

"Here, let me through." Chuck pushed through the people to get to me. He knelt. "Callum, what happened?"

His eyes moved from my face down my body. Horror spread across his features.

"Never mind." He stood. "Get him to Medic, and someone grab some food."

Everyone moved into action. I was lifted and carried down the hall to the medics. I closed my eyes to keep my head from swimming.

We entered the small room. The petite nurse sat in the corner with a romance novel perched on her knee. She dropped it on the table and jumped to her feet.

What was her name again? Something old.

"Ethel, Callum needs immediate attention."

Oh, yes, Ethel. The healer. I tried to close my eyes but couldn't as she bustled around the room.

"Oh gosh, oh gosh." Her voice was high and wispy just like her. Her bright white hair had a blue tinge. She kept darting back and forth to me and then back to the cabinets. "Haven't seen skin this bad in a while." She tsked.

The stove clicked on, and smells of herbs rushed into the room as she boiled water and made her concoction.

"Oh dear, oh dear. Callum, you can't be hurt. You're like one of the men in my romance books."

I had no idea what she was saying and wasn't sure if that was a good thing or not. My eyes fluttered closed anyways.

"Need some help?" A voice asked from the doorway.

Ethel spun around in surprise. "Oh Jess, yes that would be great."

Jess walked into my view. A small smile lit his face. He kept his eyes trained on mine.

"Well, got yourself into some trouble I see." His Russian accent was slightly stronger at the moment.

I sighed. "Yeah, you know how it goes."

"We thought you might be dead."

"Almost."

"Here, cut his clothes off so I can put this poultice on him." Ethel handed Jess some scissors.

He turned to me. "Ready?"

I nodded.

He started cutting slowly at my sleeves and working up to my neck. The ice had burned my clothes to my skin.

I watched his face as he cut, but he didn't give anything away. Not until he got to my chest. His skin paled, and his lips thinned. He flicked his gaze to mine then focused back on what was left of my clothes.

Ethel came into view. "Here are some wet cloths to help remove the fabric from his skin." She had a bowl filled with water and rags cradled in her arms. "We have to act fast before his skin starts healing.

Jess took it from her and set it on the table next to us. He didn't speak for a long moment then he broke the silence.

"Here, take some of these." Ethel thrust two white pills in my face. "For pain."

I wanted to laugh but couldn't, so I opened my mouth obligingly. She popped them in then poked a straw into my mouth. The water felt so good going down.

She held a bowl up for me to see. "I'm going to slather this on to help with the nerves and pain too."

I nodded once. She got to work.

"Did I ever tell you how my partner died?"

My thoughts cleared as I focused on Jess. I shook my head.

He nodded. His accent became more pronounced as he spoke, "It's been ten years now. But he died in a fire. We had been together for ten years before that."

That was saying something since the majority of the Realmers didn't stay with one person.

He continued, "We were out on a hunt. There were about fifteen of us. Only three stayed up on watch. I was one of them that night. He had crawled into our tent to sleep. The other two had spread out like we usually do."

I nodded slowly to affirm.

"The Nightlins came out of nowhere like they usually seem to do. Half of them were spirits."

Those were one of the worst. I shuddered.

Ethel worked fast and the gel she spread across me felt cool and numbing, thank the gods.

"The other two guards were killed. I was lucky and only have an ugly scar on my leg. Then the fire spread throughout the whole camp. I couldn't find him. Everyone ran to take cover, or they were taken by the creatures. But he had been asleep and didn't hear the alarm before the fire engulfed our tent." He took a steadying breath. "I should have been in there with him, but had been asked by another guy if I would take his place for that time. I said yes without thinking anything else about it."

Jess's hands were methodical as he carefully placed the wet rags on my burns. The cold from the rags sent a shock through my body. A small remembrance of what had happened with the ice. He picked up some tongs then began to lift the rags off.

"I should have died with him, but I didn't, and I didn't know he was in the tent until too late." He gingerly tugged at a part of my burnt clothes.

I gasped as part of my skin went with it.

"Sorry." He paused then tugged a little bit more. "I saw him after we doused the fire. I saw his burned body still laying on the cot. At least, it happened fast, so he didn't suffer."

The realization of my burned skin, and what I must look like to him hit me.

"Jess."

He shook his head, "I told you so you'd know why I reacted. It's not your fault nor mine. Just thought I'd share. I've been there and have seen it. Though I haven't seen frostbite like this since I was home in Mother Russia." His lips curled slightly.

I breathed in deep through my nose then slowly let it out through my parted lips. I closed my eyes, trying to keep the pain from taking over.

Jess was almost done with one arm and was working his way across my chest.

"I'm sorry Jess. I didn't know," I said once Ethel had hurried off.

He smiled sadly. "It's fine. He was a great soul. I was lucky to have the time I had with him."

Scents of lavender, dandelion root, and some other scent I couldn't place flooded the tiny space.

"Okay, it's ready!" Ethel squeaked. Her little round body rushed back and forth with more rags then brought the stew to the table. "You finish up on that side and I'll start covering this side." She gestured to Jess.

His smile broadened. "Yes, madam."

I settled my head back on the flat pillow and closed my swollen eyes. Having two people crowded over me made my anxiety rise. The heat from the poultice eased some of the tension. My tight skin welcomed the gooeyness as Ethel spread it across my arm. Lavender filled my senses, and I drifted off.

30

The Dark

SHE WAS HERE, FINALLY, AFTER SO LONG. *WE WOULD HAVE OUR CHANCE.* He could feel her not too far away. The power rolled off her in waves.

The others were getting the tools and materials together, so we could fix her. So we could use her power to open the other side. The other had said it would be perfect. That she was the key to the realm's undoing. We would break the realm apart and storm through the norm, killing and feeding off the humans. We would be able to satiate the hunger that never died. It would be a buffet of people lined up for us, and we would take it all.

He barely contained his excitement. He threw the shutters open and roared. The room shook from his power.

The door opened, and Jake appeared. "James, it's time."

He nodded. Time for medicine. Time for power. We would have it all.

31

Callum

I AWOKE TO SILENCE AND MOONLIGHT. I WAS IN THE ROOM THAT I shared with Harris. The pipes filtering in the moonlight lit the room with an eerie white haze along with our pale vitamin D bulbs. I was alone. Where was Harris now? Surely, they had patched him up by now.

I tried to sit up but stopped. My flesh felt like a drum skin pulled too tight. A moan escaped from my lips. I was mostly naked but covered in poultice and cloth strips.

A soft knock disrupted my quiet. I wasn't ready for reality just yet. Maybe they'd go away. The door crept open, and Irene's pale face and bright red hair peeked around the door.

"Are you awake?" She pulled the door open further and stepped inside.

"Yeah." I breathed. Even that hurt.

She pushed the big door closed and padded over to my bed. She peered around then grabbed a chair in the corner, plopping it next to me.

"How are you feeling?"

"Ugh."

She chuckled. "That good, huh?"

"Yeah, I can barely move." Even my lips hurt. I needed some chapstick.

She frowned. "What happened exactly?"

I sighed then replied, "One of the creatures burned me with his ice powers."

"Uhh, how is that possible?"

How much could I tell Irene? I felt she was trustworthy, but I wasn't so sure. Everything seemed messed up now. I took a chance. Someone had to know at some point.

"Is there some water?"

She glanced around. "Let me see. I'm sure you'd know better than me." Knowing I was putting her off, her eyebrow rose. She got up anyway and hunted for a cup, retrieving water from the faucet. "Here," She handed me the small cup and I greedily slurped it down, spilling a good bit on the sheets and soaking the cloth around my neck.

"Thanks."

She smiled. "So, what did you mean?"

"Sloane and I think the Nightlins are actually Realmers."

Irene stared. Her mouth parted slightly. She closed it then opened it. "Why would you think that?"

"We are sure that one of the main creatures is her dad. That's why he has ice powers."

She frowned then rubbed her hands over her thighs. She gulped. "But, Callum, we've eaten them."

I only nodded. "Yeahhh. So, people need to know, so we don't keep cannibalizing."

She shivered. "How are they doing it?"

"That we don't know." I drank more water and handed her the cup. She rose, lost in thought, and poured more water then brought it back. "Irene?"

She met my gaze. "Yes?"

"Have you seen Harris?"

Her gaze shifted away in thought. "I saw him yesterday, I think, but haven't seen him since."

"Did he not tell everyone that we needed help?"

Her eyes grew larger. "Not that I know of."

I pressed my lips together, thinking. I needed to ask Chuck if he spoke to Harris and, if so, what he said. Surely, he would have met him at the portal. Something felt off.

"When you see Chuck will you tell him I want to see him?"

She nodded. "Of course. Want me to bring you some food?"

My stomach rumbled in answer.

She laughed. "All right I'm going. I'll be back in a few."

Irene shut the door behind her. A few minutes passed until a heavier knock sounded on the wood door. This time Chuck appeared.

"Hey, Cal, how are you doing?" He sauntered in and sat in the chair Irene had left.

"I could be better, but I could be worse."

Chuck smiled and nodded. "So true." He didn't waste any more time. "Irene said you wanted to see me?"

Another knock disrupted. Irene walked in with a tray covered in foods of all kinds. Meats, cheeses, fruit, and what looked like chocolate? My stomach made some very protesting noises as she brought it closer. I wasn't sure what I could eat fast enough. I sandwiched the meat between two pieces of cheese then wolfed it all down. Irene pulled another chair up on the opposite of Chuck.

Irene asked, "Chuck, have you seen Harris lately?"

"Not lately, no."

Irene gestured to me. "Harris was supposed to have come back and gotten reinforcements."

Chuck glanced at me. His eyebrows rose in surprise. "This is the first I'm hearing of that."

"Were you there when he came through?" I asked.

"Not right when he came back but I found him in the hall. Looked like he had been attacked."

I nodded. "Yeah, the Nightlins attacked him when they took the girls."

"What happened there?"

I told him about Sloane and me finding the sword and coming out to find Ashlen and Raleigh gone and Harris injured.

"Ashlen and Sloane are still gone?"

Irene nodded. "As far as we know, sir."

"One of the creatures attacked me and I fell. My czar appeared, and I was able to escape, but yes, Sloane was left behind, and Ashlen we never found."

The skin around my throat and jaw burned from use, so I ate some fruit and drank more water.

Chuck folded his hands on his lap and leaned forward. "Okay, so we need to send out some others to get them."

"Sir, I want to go."

He looked at me incredulously. "Cal, look at you. You can barely move."

"I know I just need more time. A few more days."

"I think we both know they won't have that much time."

My heart sank knowing he was right. Irene seemed just as hopeless.

"If you find Harris let me know."

Chuck nodded. "I will." He glanced at Irene. "Is there anything else I can get you?"

"I think we're good for now," Irene said measuredly.

Chuck rose from his seat and headed for the door. "I'll get some Hunters together to scout things out and report back."

"Okay."

Chuck walked out. The door thudded shut behind him.

Irene spoke, "I'll ask around about Harris. If I find him, I'll bring him here."

I exhaled slowly. "Thanks."

"Also, how about I have Jess come stay with you, so you won't be alone? I don't know about you, Cal, but things seem off."

I tried to stretch my neck, but it hurt too much, so I settled with turning my head each way.

"I feel the same. If you can find a way to heal me faster that would be great."

"Ha, yeah, I'll try. I'll send Jess up for the night."

"Irene," I said as she stopped on her way to the door, "thanks again." I didn't have to say what, she knew.

She winked. "Anytime."

I laid back trying to sleep again. Thoughts of Harris crowded my mind. Where had he gone? Why hadn't he told anyone that we needed help? Had he been taken somehow? I'd get answers somehow, and someone would pay for them.

32

Sloane

ASHLEN AND I HUDDLED TOGETHER FOR WARMTH UNTIL WE FELL ASLEEP. There was nothing in our cell for us to lay on or cover with. It was one of the worst nights of sleep I had ever had.

She kept moving in her sleep and randomly talking. Of course, my sense of time was out of whack even more now that we were being held, and there were no clocks anywhere. I remembered in history class that prisoners of war were sometimes punished by not letting them see what time it was or know the days. Everything ran together and made your mind more muddled.

Our door slammed open, rattling the walls and scaring the crap out of us. A creature that looked similar to a hunched dog, scuttled in. I held my scream in. Its eyes were gone, only rows of teeth gnashed. Its long claws clicked on the floorboards. Two other Nightlins barred the doorway to keep us from escaping, though I wasn't sure how we would have done it anyway. The creature grabbed me. Its razor claws sliced my arm.

I tried to stand, but it didn't give me the chance, instead of dragging me out on the floor. I cried out, and the creature spun, bearing its teeth in my face. I shrunk. Pain rippled down my arm as it pulled me after it. It slung me into a slightly larger room, then slammed the door shut.

I cradled my arm against my chest, then studied the room. A small shuttered window sat in the center wall. Rays of moonlight cast shadows across the stones. Large bolts were anchored to the rock floor. Chains hung from the ceiling. It looked like a torture room. Odd stains covered the floor around the bolts. The room had a metallic and rotten smell hanging in the air.

The door opened, and my uncle stood in the frame. Jacob. My heart sputtered. He was a thing of nightmares. He stooped as he walked into the room. The bones and nodules on his back scraped the door jamb. Instinctively, I moved away.

He ignored me at first. A small table next to the door held different vials and instruments. He rifled through some, selecting the ones he wanted, placing them separately.

"Stand there." He pointed at the bolts on the floor.

I stared then back at him. I wasn't about to volunteer to chain myself.

"I will make you," his voice ground out. Each word clipped and gravelly. I was sure the rows of teeth sticking out of his face hindered his speech.

When I didn't move, he turned on me. My back hit the wall as he made his way to me. I pressed against the stone as if I could melt into it and escape. My teeth chattered as his claws wrapped around my arm and yanked me forward. The room spun as he placed me over the bolts. Slowly, he grabbed each lock and fastened it to my ankles, then he grabbed the ones above me, snapping them on each wrist.

I locked my thoughts away, not letting me dwell on what was about to happen. What were they planning on doing with me? I wasn't one for fighting or combat, but I had learned once I got to this realm. Now, I was going to have to deal with torture? It wasn't how I imagined things to go.

Jacob paced in front of me for several seconds. Maybe he was trying to decide the best way to kill me? I didn't have information, so I didn't see how they would torture me for information.

He stopped and faced me. The holes where his eyes should have been scared the shit out of me. I wanted to be strong, but staring at those twin holes made my heart scream in terror.

He sniffed the air, and what had to be a smile spread across what was left of his features. His needle-like teeth flashed in the dark.

"What do you know about our world?"

I paused before answering, trying to think of any sort of trick to his question. "Not much," I whispered, not meaning to, but I was so terrified that I might puke.

He picked a small vial containing black liquid. It swirled and lapped up the sides of the glass tube.

"We are made. Sometimes we are chosen." He held the vial up to my eyes so I could see it more clearly. "I was chosen." He said almost reverently. He focused on me. "You have been chosen now. Will you join us?"

What kind of drugs was he on? He thought I would join their tribe without much thought? My lips parted in surprise.

"I think you know my answer," I said slowly, still not quite sure where he was going with all this.

He nodded his big head. "It would be easier for you if you'd accept it."

"I don't see how I can."

He shrugged. "Just allow it to take over."

I pressed my lips into a thin line then tightened my jaw. "I won't ever be like you." Spittle sprayed as I ground each word out. The disgust over what he said churned my stomach.

"Have it your way. It will hurt, and the transition will take much longer, but you can't fight it." He unstoppered the vial and a sweet smell rolled out of it. "Just accept and it will be much easier for you."

My brain rushed with thoughts, trying to stop him. "I thought you wanted me dead?"

He shifted slightly. "Yes, eventually. My brother does, but I get my fun first."

Ice filled my veins. I scanned the room, hoping to see some way out. There was nothing. Nothing for me to do. I craned my body as far away from him as I could, but there was no use. He practically filled the whole room.

His mouth stretched open, and various clicking noises poured out. The door opened, and one of the creatures came in. It slinked toward me, moving behind me. Its long claws slid across my throat. Panic set in. The room became a blur, and sweat dotted my upper lip.

The creature behind tightened its grip on my throat, lifting my jaw so I'd be exposed. Jacob moved within an inch of my face. The vial tipped above my mouth.

"Open wide."

I pressed my lips together and tried to move my head. The claws gripped tighter. Something wet ran down my neck. Jacob pinched my nose until I gasped for air. He emptied the vial into my mouth. I coughed and wheezed as it went down. Whatever it was stung. It had a metallic taste, something like raw vinegar.

Jacob chuckled. "Take her back. She'll be useless for a while."

The chains around my limbs opened. My knees buckled, and I hit the floor, gasping for air. My lungs felt as if they were about to rip from my rib cage, and my heart beat radically. Sweat dampened my hair, shirt, and pants. The room continued to spin as the creature dragged me from the room and down the hall. If I had ever taken acid before, I think that's what it would have felt like. Colors blossomed across my vision. Walls and floors melted together in a swirl of grey and brown. Stars blinked in and out on the ceiling.

The creature tossed me into the cell with Ashlen. She crawled to my side. Her voice sounded garbled, so I heard snippets.

"Sloane? What — they do — you okay?" She mumbled some more, but I had no idea what she was trying to say.

My mind couldn't make heads or tails of anything that had happened. I think I tried to speak, but my insides felt as if a fire had been poured throughout. Maybe Callum had set me on fire by accident? I rolled and writhed on the cold stone floor. I cried out. Tears ran freely down my face. The salt stung my eyes.

I gave up and relented to the pain.

175

33

Callum

JESS CAME IN WITH HIS LONG HAIR TIED UP IN A MAN BUN, WEARING some furry boots, a long cardigan. A large mug filled with coffee and whipped cream was clutched between his hands. Mostly whipped cream though. It always made me smile to see the juxtaposition of his lean muscles wrapped up in fur and baggy floral pants. Somehow, he made it all look good though, especially with his Russian accent.

"Can I take this one?" He pointed to the bed closest to the door.

"Yeah, go for it."

He threw his things down. "Can I get you something?"

I nodded slightly. "Water would be great."

Jess smiled one of his rare smiles. "Food?"

"Yeah, if they have anything around."

"All right. I'll be back." He spun back for the door and slipped through. His man bun flopped back and forth as he walked.

I eased back onto my pillow, trying my best not to move an inch. My skin was still a mottled red and purple. It looked as if it was scabbing over though, so that was good. Maybe my healing was starting to rev up. I focused my attention on the stone ceiling. The cracks raced from one corner to the next. The vitamin bulbs glowed a soft blue in the far corner.

My eyes shuttered slowly. I was so tired. Maybe Sloane and I could take a vacation one day.

Static popped around my ears. I jumped. The bulb in the corner sputtered then popped. Glass shards hit the floor. What the hell?

"You look like literal shit," a voice stated from the darkened corner. The accent had a thick Spanish flair.

I tried to sit up but failed. "Who's there?"

"No one of importance. How long until your friend gets back?"

I glanced at the door. "Maybe a few minutes."

"Okay, I'll be brief. You already know the danger, that's obvious from your current state. But there are things that you don't know, and I don't have the time to fill you in."

I tried to focus on the dark corner, but my exhaustion made it hard for my eyes to fill in what was there. Static sizzled loud near my ears.

"I know you've read about us in some journals, and most of us are dead. So understandably, we are a little cautious with who we speak to."

My mind rifled through my memories of what I read. Was he a part of Sloane's family?

"I understand." Though I didn't.

His voice held amusement when he spoke. "Sloane spoke to Sarah at the defense, so I know what she has been told. Maybe you can fill me in with what you know about the dirty dozen."

Ohhh. So, not family really but part of it. My thoughts crashed together as it tried to piece together all the info I had stored about the dozen.

"I don't know much." My mouth worked to try and replenish the saliva that had since evaporated. Needed the water Jess was bringing. "Sloane's father was a part of it and her uncle. We met Morgan when we were trying to find the sword."

"Yeah, he mentioned that run-in. Five of us are left, including me. Charles used us as his ragtag team. The ones who cleaned up the mess. Even after his death, there are messes to clean up."

I frowned, having no clue where this was going.

"After everything, most of us went into hiding. More than a couple went missing, though I'm sure you will hear a different tale. There are three of us in the realm right now. The other two are at the Defense. So, if you find yourself needing help, we can be there."

A bulb slowly lit in my mind.

"I need to heal faster."

"Si, si, I've got that covered." He stood then. Static currents crackled around him as he moved closer. Blue and white sparks popped. Tall didn't cover his height. He was massive, like a giant. His black eyes sparkled in the faint moonlight that entered the room, and thick, black hair hung past his shoulders. A five o'clock shadow skimmed his face. What made him stand out though, was the long white scar that ran from his forehead down his neck and disappeared under his collar, marring his tan skin.

He opened a satchel hanging from his side and rifled through it. Out came something wrapped in brown paper. He unfolded it, and a piece of fruit sat in the middle. A piece of fruit from the tree.

I instantly made a disgusted face.

"I know, it smells bad, but I think you already know it'll help."

I knew but hated the stench.

"How did you find more?" I asked.

"More grew in the place of the one you burned."

If my cheeks could have reddened at that moment, they would have. "Sorry."

He chuckled. "You made it better. There are more trees. We should have done it a long time ago. Who would have thought."

He set the rotten fruit in my lap. The air around him crackled. Bits of energy zipped past us. I hadn't heard of power like his.

I picked up the piece of fruit and eyed it. It still had blemishes on the skin. The flesh had a putrid smell to it, but I obeyed him and pushed it into my mouth, and swallowed without thinking too much more about it. The juice rushed over my tongue, at once rotten but then turning sweet like a mango.

It hit my stomach, a tingling started in my middle, then ebbed through my limbs. The small tinder flame in my gut roared to life. It rolled and broiled. My skin grew hot and steam rose from my pores. The man beside me stepped back. My chest constricted as if a vice grip had wrapped around me. Fire erupted along my body. Black smoke furled to the ceiling. I felt as if I was choking. The heat tingled and prickled my skin. The fire died as fast as it had started. My bed was ash and splinters. I wheezed and coughed trying to clear my throat.

"Yep, that helped the healing process," the stranger muttered. A small smile tugged at one side of his lopsided mouth.

I was butt-ass naked. Everything had burned. But my skin was no longer red and purple but shiny like a newborn's. Except for the ash that covered me. Nothing hurt. I felt as if I had had the longest rest and ate and drank my fill.

The man threw me a towel that I covered my lap with.

He set something down on the table. "It's like Sloane's. You can use it to find us. Its name is Mercury." He moved toward the door and stopped. "I'll be back later with some recruits so be on the lookout. We'll get her out of there. Don't worry." He winked, opening the door.

"Hey, what's your name?"

He stopped midstep. "Alvaro." The space where he stood crackled and popped. He zapped out of existence, and the door shut.

A moment later, Jess walked in with a tray ladened with drinks, fruit, cheeses, and dried meats.

He halted seeing me naked on the floor. His eyes scanned the room.

"Uhhh, I missed something, didn't I?" His eyes roamed over my new skin.

34

DEATH KNOCKED ON MY DOOR, AND I KNEW IT.

Whatever they had given me was changing me from the inside out. My soul would die, and I would become one of them. I wallowed then. The first time in a long while. Pain lacerated my body as if something tried to eat its way through. My control was gone. I vomited over and over. My bowels emptied on the floor, trying to eradicate what they had given me.

Now and then, Ashlen's voice echoed in the void. Tiny snippets of her calling my name or hoping I'd wake up.

I was so tired. That was an understatement.

Once the monster took over, would I be gone forever? Or could I still be rescued?

Claws scratched my insides, and I cried out. When would this be over?

"Sloane? Can you hear me? I think they're coming back."

Fear gripped me. I burrowed deeper in myself, closing and bolting the door. They might take my body, but that's all they'd get. The thick, black haze surrounding me evaporated, leaving me feeling somewhat disoriented.

Ashlen leaned over me. Her eyes were scared and dark. The black orbs reflected my ashen face.

"Sloane? Can you move?"

I smelled awful like days-old trash left in the sun.

"Have they taken you yet?" I asked huskily.

"They took me once but only measured me for something. I don't know what." Her eyes shifted to the door. A key scraped in the lock, and the door swung inward.

One of the creatures slithered into the cell. Its wings were tucked behind it. It was much smaller than my father. This one looked more like it had once been a person. The vestiges of its human form hadn't been erased yet.

Involuntarily, we both shuffled away from the creature. Panic gripped my chest again.

The creature pointed a talon at Ashlen and beckoned her to it.

Ashlen whimpered. "No." She gripped my hand and buried her face in my shoulder.

The creature moved closer to us still beckoning for her to go with it.

She screamed, "No! No, I won't go."

A shiver ran through me. I knew what they were going to do and I knew what the outcome would be for her. I didn't want to see her like that, like me.

I shifted forward. "Take me."

"What? No, you can't go again." Ashlen gripped my arm and pulled me back.

My head hit the wall, making me dazed.

"Take me instead."

The creature looked at me and shook its big skeletal head. It pointed to Ashlen. "She must go."

Ashlen cried harder. I pushed myself up against the wall, trying to stand.

"Take me instead."

The creature shook its head then swiftly gripped Ashlen's arm. She cried. It yanked her toward the door, and she fell, grappling at its claws to release her.

"Please, stop. Don't." I reached out with my left arm, meaning to grab the creature's rags, but instead, my arm became translucent and it went through the thing. I blanched. My arm solidified once more. Had I truly lost my mind?

The creature yanked Ashlen through the door then slammed it in my face. Ashlen screamed and sobbed as it pulled her down the hall.

35

Callum

I was so thankful for that fruit, yet I wasn't sure what I could tell others about it. Jess was a real friend so I filled him in on what happened with the stranger into the morning.

"Alvaro?" Jess asked for the hundredth time.

"Yes."

"A fruit made you whole?"

"Yes, it's from that tree I told you about. The one Sloane and I found. Somehow, it gives you strength and heals."

A small crease formed between his brows.

"Have you heard of a power that uses energy?"

Jess frowned. "Energy?"

"Yeah, that's the only thing I can think of. The air sizzled and popped while he was here, then when he left it was as if he disappeared."

He nodded in thought. "There have been those that bend light around them to make it seem as if they disappeared. That could be it."

"He said he would be back with recruits, but not sure when."

"Chuck will be coming sometime today. How will we explain your miraculous recovery?" Jess asked.

I gestured to what had once been my bed. "Well, can we tell a half-truth? Somehow in the night, my fire consumed me, and like with forest fires, with fire comes new growth?"

Jess blinked, then smiled, shaking his head. "You're pretty good at this lying thing."

I shrugged. "This place makes you get used to it." I started moving. I snatched my bag from the floor, and opened my dresser drawers, stuffing clothes inside.

"What are you doing?" Jess stood over me.

"I've gotta get my things together to get Sloane," I said without much thought.

He pulled me back. "Whoa, whoa. You just came back from there nearly dead. And you're already planning to go back?" His dark eyes stared at me incredulously.

I didn't meet his gaze but continued to grab up materials around the room. "Of course, I've got to get Sloane. She's probably having who knows what done to her. We don't have time to talk and strategize."

Jess caught my arm. "Listen, I get it, but you can't. It's suicide."

I shook my head and pulled my arm from his grip. "Jess. I have to help her."

"I'm not saying not to, but we can't go in there with no plan and no help." He searched my face. "Cal, we will get her back, but we have to think this through. We need that guy's help. We need lots of help. There is so much more at play here." He took a step toward me with his hands splayed. "Give us time to plan. See what this guy says. Let's be smart about it instead of trying to scale the tower and kill the dragon to rescue the princess."

I sighed, shaking my head. Between going and fighting with everyone or waiting and planning, I was torn. Would I almost die again trying to save her? Probably. I shoved a shirt in my pack, zipped it up, and let it drop to the floor, hoping it wasn't making a mistake.

"All right. Now what?"

Jess's face cracked slightly with a smile, and he slung an arm over my shoulders. "Let's go eat, so we won't be wishing later for real food."

I let him tug me out of the room and down to the dining hall.

A couple of hours later after we ate, Chuck knocked on the door. I made sure to hide the compass Alvaro had left in a drawer. When he walked in, the shock on his face was priceless.

"Callum, wow, I thought you had a few more days to recoup but guess not."

"Yeah, my fire helped me out on this one but as you can see my bed didn't fare as well."

He chuckled, and Jess smiled as he played along.

"Have you tracked Harris?" Jess asked Chuck.

"Not yet. I'm sorry. I don't know where he could have gone. But they're still looking for him."

"Thanks." My thoughts drifted to the small black compass, Mercury, in the drawer. I'd have to see if it would locate Harris.

"All right, let me know if you need anything else from me, and I'll keep you updated with news about Harris." Chuck stood and moved toward the door.

"Yeah, sounds good." My brain was already in overdrive with figuring out what to do.

The door clicked shut behind him, and I faced Jess. "Let's go hunting for Harris."

"How do you plan on us doing that?"

I pulled Mercury from the drawer, holding it out. "With this."

We stepped outside the city walls and into the oversized garden before I pulled Mercury from my pocket. We were decked out in our gear along with a pack of food just in case. Who knew where this adventure would take us. I glanced around to make sure no one was nearby.

"How sure are you that this will work?" Jess asked skeptically.

"I'm hoping but not too sure. If it works like Sloane's, then it should lead us to him." I held the small compass to my lips and whispered, "Mercury, lead us to Harris?" The small white needles spun around and around then slowly stopped pointing east. A tiny white light burst from the needle and shot through the dark. "Artemis doesn't do that." I glanced at Jess, he only shrugged. "Come on."

We followed the faint white streak.

It led us to the edge then dropped down into the entrance of the tombs. I should have known. It was a perfect spot to hide. The white light ended at the big iron doors. Jess unsheathed his Russian Kindjal sword.

The tomb hadn't changed from the time before. It was still dark and scary. We didn't light the torches this time though. Instead, I lit a ball of fire and pushed it out of me so it would hover right above our heads to give us plenty of light to see.

The orange glow bounced off the stone walls as we descended. I tried not to think about the ghosts Raleigh spoke to last time. We walked through the walnut doors and the invisible shield. It tugged on us as we passed through.

We came to a fork, and we investigated one side then went down the other branch, making sure to look in every dark crevice and hole. It continued like that for a while. It took time, but we couldn't make a mistake and miss him.

A yellow flame flickered around a corner. Jess signaled to me, and we eased around the corner. Harris hadn't expected people to find him in the tombs. He had set up camp, with a nice fire in the middle, with his food splayed out on the ridges. His sleep roll was out by the fire, and Harris was draped across, snoring like a bear in hibernation.

Jess and I looked at each other. *Unbelievable.*

"Guess we aren't working with a mastermind," Jess said as he sheathed his sword.

I shook my head and couldn't help the smile that tugged at my lips.

I knelt beside Harris' head and jabbed him in the arm. He didn't move. I rolled my eyes. If I remembered right, it took a while for him to wake up. I ran my hand over my face then jabbed him again, this time much harder. He groaned and rolled to his side.

"Harris!" I snatched his arm, jerking upward.

He yelped and rolled toward the fire. I yanked him back just out of reach of the flames.

"Arghh!"

Jess and I stood back but blocked the exits. Harris gawked at his surroundings before realizing where he was.

"Callum? Jess? What are y'all doin' down here?"

"We were going to ask you the same thing."

His eyes swiveled between us and the exit. A good ole country boy just trying to take a nap. My jaw clenched.

"Oh, ya know just, uh, needed to get away from everyone, but I'm so glad you made it back, Callum." He stood and brushed his pants off.

Jess took a fighter's stance at the exit, slowly pulling his sword from the scabbard. I called the fire to my gut and eased it into my palms. I didn't want to frighten Harris just yet.

"Yeah, weren't you supposed to tell everyone to send help?"

Harris' eyes grew. "I did. I did."

I shook my head. "That's not what we heard. Chuck said he never saw you again."

Harris rubbed his palms on his pants then wiped his mouth. "I swear I told him that you needed help."

"We can't figure out why you wouldn't tell them. Are you working with the Nightlins?" Jess asked.

Harris grew visibly paler. "I, uh, I would never."

I moved a step closer. "Is there something you want to tell us?"

Harris rubbed his arm as he shifted from one foot to the next. His eyes continually darted around the space, trying to find a way out. "I, uh," he couldn't seem to come up with any sort of explanation, and he deflated. "They have my parents and said if I helped them they would give them back."

Jess and I glanced at each other. I hadn't expected that answer.

"All right, you're coming with us. We'll see what Chuck says."

Harris stepped back, shaking his head. "No, you can't."

Jess held his hands up. "Harris, don't worry about it. We'll figure it out."

He shook his head and wiped the sweat from his face on his sleeve. "No, you don't understand. Chuck knows."

36

TIME PASSED LIKE A SNAIL AS I WAITED FOR ASHLEN TO COME BACK. I huddled in the corner trying to quiet my mind and the restless thoughts nagging that we were going to die. The smell in our cell made me feel sick, but there was nothing to do about it. I had to wait. I didn't hear any screams or cries for help so I took that as good news.

Seconds ticked by then the door slot opened and something was dumped inside. I waited for a beat then crawled toward the dark mass at the door. My eyes adjusted some to the dark and I could see it was a small cloth bag. Inside were scraps of food. I felt annoyed, speechless, and hungry all at the same time.

I smelled each piece before putting it in my mouth. What had my life come to? Surely, Callum would rescue me soon before I became some nameless monster. I munched on what had to be a potato until the door swung open, and Ashlen was tossed in.

Tears streaked her face. Dirt covered her clothes. She hiccuped from crying too much and probably having a panic attack. She scrambled for me. Her nails bit into my skin, and her body shook as she sobbed.

"Ash, you're okay. You're back now." I patted her hair. "What happened? Did they make you swallow that stuff?"

She nodded her head then promptly puked beside us.

I sighed. We were going to die from dehydration if we didn't die from whatever they were giving us first.

"They brought us some food if you think you can eat?" I asked her.

She groaned and shook her head.

A minute passed and another creature opened the door. There was no time for me to react when it snatched my wrist and yanked me through the door. Ashlen yelled behind me.

I gave up and went limp as it dragged me through the hall. We ended up in the same room before. The chains hung from the ceiling and bolted to the floor. I wanted to cry but nothing came out.

Two creatures chained me up. My arms above my head and my ankles shackled to the floor. My clothes were a mess. My hair hung in my face. I felt small. The moonlight entered through a tiny crack in the barred window.

The door swung open, and my uncle stood there. He ambled in on his haunches and opened the shutters slightly. Cool air washed in, bathing me in the scents of the forest. If I strained hard enough, the sound of a waterfall not too far away trickled in the opened window. I breathed in deep, trying to hold the clean air in. The moonlight washed over the small space. My uncle had produced his tools again on the tiny table. Vials of dark liquid were laid out. Dread covered me and sweat broke on my scalp and neck. It trickled down my back. I clenched my teeth. A sharp pain lanced through my jaw.

When would this all be over? Tears found me that time. They fell onto the floor below me.

"You reek of fear." My uncle grabbed a vial and unstoppered it before facing me. "Maybe we should hose you off." He cackled.

One of his minions hunkered against the wall waiting for its orders. The tears flowed. It was as if I couldn't stop the tide. I didn't want to become one of those scary things that shrunk and hollowed. Where was my light? Why didn't it answer my pleas? I had tried so often to call it to me, but it wouldn't stir. It felt so far away as if I had miles to go to find it. Where was Callum?

"Hold her," he said, his voice barely discernible.

The smaller creature lurched toward me. Its razor claws sliced my thin pale skin. Its grip tightened on my throat. I just knew one slip, and its claws would cut my aorta, and I'd bleed out on this stinky floor.

"We have five vials to try this time. Next time, it'll be ten."

I held the sob that wanted to rip from me. Five? Next, it would be ten? My mind couldn't fathom it. Surely, I wasn't about to go out like that. Whatever my story said, it hadn't said I'd become a monster. Patrice would have told me. She was one of the most honest people I knew.

Something inside me reared its head, and I clapped for joy, begging it to answer. My uncle had the vial at my lips when my arm fell to my side. The chain rattled as it fell uselessly. We stared at each other for a second. Both of us were stunned. Then, I acted and swung my loose arm at him. The vial went soaring through the open window.

"How'd she do that?!" My uncle screamed.

The creature latched onto me, grasping my freed arm. The other chains weren't letting go. I didn't have much of a chance but I fought as hard as I could in that minute than I had ever fought in my life. *Please help!* I screamed in my head at whatever power hid inside me. But it never came again. They wrapped the chain around my arm once more. He made sure it snapped in place.

My soul was crushed in that moment, of feeling a second of freedom, of having the open window right there, but not having the way to get to it. The sobs came that time.

"Noooo!" I sobbed ugly tears. Panic clawed my throat. My heart thrashed in my chest. I pulled and fought the chains holding me.

He tipped a vial in my mouth. The inky blackness scorched my insides as it ran down, burning the rest of my hope away with it.

37

The Dark

THINGS WEREN'T GOING HIS WAY. HIS BROTHER HAD CONVINCED HIM IT would be better to change her instead of consuming her, and he regretted it. The whole time he had pictured eating her heart and tasting her power. Letting the power ravage his body.

But now, she would become one of them. Jacob said she would make them go farther. But who knew? He just knew he wasn't getting her raw powers.

It was probably because Jacob didn't want him to become more powerful, so they would stay equals. Jacob had always been jealous.

He stood against the window frame watching the creatures below. If it didn't work, he'd been promised her heart. He guessed that would work for now. The other agreed with Jacob, so he had been overruled. One day, he would rule alone with all the power.

His day was coming; he felt it.

38

Callum

WE LEFT HARRIS WHERE HE WAS IN THE TOMB, PROMISING TO BE BACK later to grab him. My mind still reeled from the bomb he had just dropped on us.

"Do you think he was being honest?" Jess asked again.

"Yeah, I'm pretty sure he was." My stomach churned with butterflies. What would we do?

We traveled through the dining hall without seeing Chuck, thankfully. I had no idea how I'd handle seeing him. We got back to the room.

"Any ideas?" I paced the room.

Jess sat on the bed. "If he's a part of the Nightlin attack, then we have a whole other set of problems."

I nodded.

"If he is a part of it, then we're on our own. Or have a very limited amount of help."

I stopped pacing for a moment, thinking. "What about Alvaro?"

Jess shrugged. "What about him? Do you think we can trust him?"

"Who knows, but I don't think he's working for Chuck."

"Do you have any idea when he'll be back?"

"No, zero."

"Okay, so until then, what to do?"

I started pacing again. Jess wrung his hands.

"If we keep Harris in the tombs, for now, we can try to pick up some more people. I bet some of those taken would side with us. But then what?" Sloane would have been able to think more clearly about this.

Jess's head hung between his shoulders. "We need to wait it out. Until you hear from that guy."

I crossed my arms over my chest. "Ask Alvaro what he thinks? He said something about others in another city. Maybe we will go there?"

Jess nodded. "Yeah, see what he says. If we can trust him."

I pulled Mercury out of my pocket. "Alvaro, we're ready when you are." The needles spun around and around, not stopping. It blinked white once. What was that? He had said it could find him. Was that what he meant?

I stuffed it back in my pocket. Now, we just had to wait.

Later that night, we took turns going to the dining hall and grabbing food. Jess came back with a tray full, saying all had gone well. We thought it would seem less obvious if we took turns. I'd slip Mercury from my pocket and say Alvaro's name, hoping that was doing something. But so far nothing.

I left the room, trying to staunch my nerves. Around every corner, I tensed thinking I was about to run into Chuck. I reached the bottom and skirted the edge of the bustling dining room, keeping my eyes peeled for him.

Instead, I ran into Brand.

"Aye, lad, where yous hurrying to?" He asked warmly as he elbowed me. His face had filled in some, but he still hadn't filled his clothes back in. But he seemed to be making up for it with the large plate heaped with food and a big beer mug.

"Brand, trying to grab food before you take it all." I tried to smile, but I was pretty sure it was a grimace.

He laughed, almost spilling his beer. "Aye, Callum, yous better hurry!"

A genuine smile spread across my face.

He grew somber then lowered his voice, "Yous look much better now than when we brought you back. We were worried for ya."

I patted his shoulder. "Thanks, Brand. Again, for bringing me back."

His eyes twinkled and nodded his head. He turned to make his way to a table.

"Uh, Brand?"

He stopped. "Aye?"

"I might need some help soon. Think you'd be willing to pitch in?"

"Aye! Of course, never no need to ask, just tell me when." He winked then.

I smiled and waved as he left. A large hand grasped my shoulder, and I turned without much attention. Chuck stood blocking my way to the table.

"What kind of help are you looking for?"

I paused. Oh, gods. "You know, with getting Sloane back. Once we can get enough people to help."

He nodded, and relief flooded me.

"We'll get her back, don't worry. Just waiting on more to fill in and for the extras from the defense, then we can scout out the Nightlin mountain."

I nodded. "Yeah, we'll be ready soon. I'm sure."

His grip tightened. "Of course." Someone called his name, and he waved in acknowledgment. "Don't go running off again without back-up," he said jokingly, but I knew he was serious.

I chuckled and made my way to the table, letting the tension ease from my shoulders. That had been close. I snatched up a tray and placed an assortment of meat on it then. I grabbed a beer mug and filled it too.

For a second, I thought about taking Harris some food, but he didn't deserve it, so I headed back up. As my foot hit the top step, Patrice rounded the corner.

What was with the day? I kept running into everyone.

"Hey, there mister. Don't be running old women over." She stood against the wall to let me pass.

"Sorry, Patrice, I didn't see you."

"Mmhmm." I thought I was safe, then her hand shot out and gripped my arm with surprising strength for an older woman.

Sadly, I gasped.

"Callum, something is coming for you." Her eyes glazed over as she stared unblinkingly at the ceiling. The long white scar on her face pulled taut as her eyes rolled back. "Someone will take you from here. Beware of the leader and watch the girl. You are the key to her survival." Her eyes closed, then blinked rapidly.

I stood rigid, my mouth slack.

"What did I say?" She eyed me, questioningly.

I stammered trying to find words, "You said to be careful someone was coming for me."

"Ah, okay. Good." She patted my arm, then descended the stairs.

What the hell? What had that meant? Slowly, I headed back to the room, careful not to spill my food or drink. What was coming for me? Beware of the leader was easy. Sloane had to be the girl.

I opened the door to our room to find Alvaro looming over Jess. His fist clenched, and Jess brandished his Kindjal. The space between them hummed and popped with bursts of light.

"Whoa! What's happening?" I set my tray and beer mug down on the table, out of harm's way.

Jess's eyes didn't move from Alvaro's. "Good, you're back. Tell him I'm on your side."

"Alvaro? What's going on?"

He gestured to Jess, "He's the one who pulled a sword on me."

I stepped forward with my arms out as if I held a white flag.

"Jess? How about you drop the sword?"

Jess muttered something in Russian, then lowered his sword slightly.

"Hey, I'm not a cocksucker." Alvaro pointed a finger at him and zips of light spurted from his fingertip.

Jess's sword lowered, and he smiled a true one, then said something else in Russian that I had zero clues about.

Alvaro laughed and slapped Jess's shoulder, rocking him back on his heels.

I shook my head. Of course, now they were best buds.

"I'll kiss your mom anytime." Alvaro laughed harder.

I grabbed my beer as I sat on the bed, watching the two men form a bromance.

"All right guys, can we get started?" I took a sip of my dark beer.

39

Callum

"So, you think Chuck is in on it?" Alvaro asked. He had taken a seat by the fire. His large frame made me worry the small wood chair under him might break.

I shrugged. "That's what Harris said. Chuck is part of it."

"How much do you trust Harris?"

My answer had changed since yesterday. "I'm not sure."

Alvaro frowned.

"I think we should take him with us," Jess stated.

"Take him to Jamestown? How would that help?" Alvaro rolled a cigar between his large forefingers. His hands had black cracks on his fingers as if he worked with his hands all day.

"We'd have him with us so we can watch him and also keep him out of Chuck's hands," I said.

Alvaro nodded in thought then shrugged a massive shoulder. "All right, if you think it'll work."

"I think it's the best option than the alternative of him being left here and being caught by Chuck and whoever else. Who knows what they would do to him."

Alvaro took a long drag on his cigar, blowing out puffs of smoke slowly so the tendrils floated to the ceiling like clouds. He checked a heavy-duty military watch on his wrist. "It's 19:00 hours now. Let's meet at portal three in an hour."

Jess and I nodded.

Alvaro stood and headed to the door. "One hour. Bring the usual." The space around him crackled and shimmered as he disappeared. The last traces of his cigar smoke dissipated.

"What kind of power does he have?" I asked Jess.

He grabbed up some clothes and shoved them in a bag. "He can affect the energy and light in a space so he essentially can create mirrors that make him look as if he's disappeared."

That had to be one of the coolest things I had heard in a long time. "Wow."

Jess shrugged. "It's useful in security and sabotage but not always in battle. Though I know of some good stories of him sneaking up on creatures."

We ate the rest of our food and packed our bags full of the essentials, then headed to the tombs to retrieve Harris. There was still a crowd in the dining room, mostly the ones from the Norm Defense. They seemed happy to be in the realm. Mostly eating, drinking, and laughing away, not like we had creatures trying to murder us every day.

We made it outside with no trouble and no sign of Chuck. We followed the path back to Harris' hiding spot and found him sitting on the ground eating a small packet of tuna. He looked so sad I almost felt sorry for him.

"Hey, time to go."

Harris jumped at the sound of my voice. His nerves must have been getting to him.

"Okay, I'm ready." He grabbed his bag and put out the small fire he had built. His usually sparkling eyes were dim with large purple circles around them. His skin was even paler. I guessed from the stress of backstabbing. I tried to feel bad for him but couldn't find the space.

"Come on, we don't have much time." I turned on my heel and

went back down the tunnel. "Do you have a hat or something?" I asked him.

Jess followed. Harris trudged behind. Exhaustion dominated him.

He rubbed his face, then pulled something out of his back pocket. It was a hat. "Yeah." He yanked it on.

Any second I thought he'd fall over from sleep deprivation, but we made it to the portal wall. Luckily, no one was around. We waited beside portal three for Alvaro.

"Man, looks like a waste." Alvaro appeared in front of us. The air shimmered, like scales of a fish, before he fully popped into view. Alvaro's eyes examined Harris from head to toe. "Probably is a good thing he's coming with us."

Harris tugged on his backpack. "I just want my parents back."

Alvaro only nodded and stepped up to the portal. He knocked on the number above the black and blue undulating mass that we had to go through. The portal flashed a white light twice, then stopped.

He gestured to the portal's opening. "It's time. Go on."

Jess went first, then I pushed Harris through. I glanced at Alvaro, who again smoked a cigar. Circles of smoke puffed from his mouth. Definitely an interesting guy.

I stepped through the portal. The portal's essence clung to my skin and sucked me through. My feet hit the solid ground within a few seconds, and I stumbled, having to catch myself before ramming into Jess.

"Whoa, watch your landing." Jess pushed me back up. I sidestepped in case Alvaro came through on my heels.

The lights of Jamestown were blindingly bright. Where Kingston had been built inside of a mountain, Jamestown had been made into a cavern system underground that stretched for some two hundred fifty miles. Forests of stalagmites lined the walls and through the center of the cave systems. Different mineral flowers and structures were sprinkled along the walls and ceiling. The city's homes and structures mostly lined the walls. People ambled along the small walkways that traversed the caverns.

Jamestown was one the largest of the cities in the realm. In size and population. People could arrive through the portals or through an intricate system of tunnels that led to the outside. In all of the hundreds of years, it had yet to be infiltrated by the Nightlins. A smaller Nightlin mountain stood a day's journey from the city.

Alvaro appeared behind us. He took a long drag on his fast-diminishing cigar. "Never can understand why they like having so many lights on." He waved us forward. "This way."

He led us down a small path. His broad shoulders nearly touched the buildings on either side. Passersby had to shrink to pass him. I smiled to myself. The small path branched into a smaller one. Tall skinny buildings lined one side. People bustled in and out of doorways.

In the cavern, the echoes clanged against the walls, though they had sound panels lining the ceiling and walls intermittently to absorb as much sound as possible. Long tapestries hung from doors and windows and billowing fabric draped along the storefronts. Strings of lights lined the tops of the buildings and reflected from the many stalactites.

Alvaro ushered us into a very dingy-looking building that turned out to be a bar. Harris looked sleepier by the second and sighed with relief when we sat down. The interior of the bar reflected more of the realm than the city. Only a dim bulb lit each corner of the space. The rest lay in shadows. Patrons sat along the walls on wood stools and metal chairs. The bar was made of wood and only had three taps. But bottles lined the back wall. We sat at a table in a corner near the front.

"They should be here soon. I'll get us some drinks." Alvaro made his way to the bar and spoke to the bartender who then filled four mugs. The drinks sloshed foam onto our table as he set them down.

Harris picked his up and drank and drank, barely taking a breath.

Alvaro seemed to have a newfound respect for him after that. He slapped Harris' back and laughed. "That's it!"

Two hooded figures stepped through the door. Alvaro waved. "Amigos!"

They weaved through the tables to reach us and pushed their hoods back. A man with black hair cut to his chin and a small goatee bowed slightly. The person next to him was a tall, thin woman with her head shaved. Her large, dark eyes glowered at each of us.

They pulled up two chairs and sat opposite.

"This is Jameson, we call him Jay, and Claire. She's the more dangerous of the two so watch out." Alvaro smiled.

40

Sloane

SOMETHING WAS WRONG. LIKE WRONG. MY MIND FELT FUNNY. Whatever coursed through me burned my insides, as if on fire, but at the same time being suffocated by black mounds of smoke.

They had put me back in the cell with Ashlen. I was sprawled in the middle of the room, and she was curled up in a corner. I flipped to my stomach, trying not to empty my stomach contents at the same time. I inched closer to her and closer. My legs were too heavy so they dragged behind me. I used my elbows to crawl like in the army. The moonlight streamed in through the cracks in the window. I was so thankful for that little bit of light— a speck of hope. A sliver pierced her back.

"Ash?" my throat was so hoarse from screaming and that god-awful stuff they had forced me to drink. I shook her gently.

She moaned and coughed.

Maybe we should be trying to puke everything up? But I hated puking. It was the worst. I grimaced.

"Ash?" my voice sounded more like my own. "Are you okay?" I shook her again, trying to turn her over.

She coughed some more, then spit out something. My eyes tried to focus on what it was. A small clump of black goo sat on the floor.

Then it moved, and I think I peed on myself a little. I shuffled back, and the black thing slithered toward Ashlen again.

"NO!" I shot toward it, not thinking. I couldn't touch it could I? I tried to swat it, but it slithered too fast and latched onto her skin and absorbed.

My mouth fell open. What the hell was that?

Ashlen thrashed on the floor. Sweat ran down her temples and soaked her clothes. She screamed. I tried to calm her, but it was as if she couldn't hear me. She stilled, only her breathing was erratic.

I know I shouldn't be ashamed, but I cried at that moment. Big ugly tears with snot running down my face. I cried and cried. Hopelessness settled over my shoulders. I feared we wouldn't make it out. I wasn't going to see Callum again. I would be losing myself. Probably never seen again.

Ashlen moaned again. "Sloane?" She barely breathed.

"Ashlen?" I cried. I grabbed her and pulled her head into my lap. I brushed her dark hair away from her beautiful face. Her usually unmarred, porcelain skin was covered in black dirt and grime. Sweat and tears stained her cheeks. Her eyes kept switching between black and green. It was an odd thing to see. Was mine doing something just as weird?

"Sloane, something is happening to me," she whispered and coughed. Her limbs shook as she tried to sit up. "What's happening to us?" Her eyes tried to focus on me, but I wasn't sure if she could see me. I held her hands, trying to comfort her.

Should I tell her that I thought we were becoming monsters? Or should I pretend I didn't know?

"It's okay." I whispered then said more assuredly, "It'll be okay." I squeezed her hand.

Something moved under her skin. I tried not to react. But something had freaking *moved* under her skin. I squeezed my eyes shut trying to calm myself and think more clearly.

I shuddered. Surely, someone would come for us. They had to know we needed them. Callum had to come.

I breathed in deep while stroking Ashlen's hair. Her grip tightened around my forearm. Her eyes, black this time, searched mine. Her veins stood out against her white skin. Again, something black moved right beneath her skin. Her lips parted as she screamed. Her nails lengthened. Her teeth looked sharper. She sliced my skin out of fear. I held her as long as I could and cried.

The door opened and two creatures slithered in. They tore her from me. Her screaming became more high-pitched like a frightened bird. How could this be? Her claws scratched the floor and the creatures as she tried to escape.

"Noooo," she wailed as they shut the door and carried her down the hall. The sound of her voice disappeared.

My heart broke at that moment. A throbbing pain hit my chest, and I doubled over. Sobs tore from my throat, and I blacked out, hoping for it all to be a nightmare; hoping it would be over.

A light pulsed in the darkness. A speck of light. I cautiously moved closer. Silence greeted me, wherever I was. I seemed to be in an empty void of space. The speck of light grew larger, then I realized it moved toward me.

A voice I knew said, "This wasn't supposed to happen. You messed it up." His gruff voice held disappointment and incredulity. My grandfather, Charles, stood before me. "I finally had some rest, then I got called back to help you."

I wanted to cry again but nothing came. "I don't know what to do."

He crossed his arms over his chest. "You were supposed to kill them all with Willow."

"I couldn't. James used his powers on me and kept me from using it."

His mouth thinned, and his jaw tightened. "Leave it to James to complicate things." His eyes softened, and he placed his hands on my shoulders. "Sloane, you need him to help get you out. You've been poisoned, and you need to get rid of it."

I shook my head. "He's too far gone. He won't help me. Besides, he doesn't know I'm his daughter."

My grandfather frowned. "Not your father. It may be too late for him. You need fire."

Cal? "How?"

"You have to burn it out." His hands gripped my shoulders tighter.

"I don't know when he will come though. It might be too late."

He shook his head. "He's coming. Don't give up. Burn the poison out. Use your powers to find him and speak to him."

"What? How?" What was he talking about? Panic surged in my gut like bad indigestion.

A sad smile flashed across his face. "Sloane, you're my grand-daughter. I know you're smarter than this." He shimmered slightly. He released me.

"What can I do?" I asked.

But he was already fading. He mouthed something, but I couldn't tell what he said. The light blinked out, and darkness settled around me like a blanket.

I woke up in the cell. The smelly floor let me know I was still in the godforsaken cell. I sat in a ball until my legs grew numb, then stretched my legs out. What had he said? I closed my eyes trying to picture his mouth forming the words. His lips pressed together and moved apart. Two syllables? It ran through my mind over and over, tumbling like clothes in a dryer. Portals? Something about a portal? I hit the back of my head against the wall trying to piece it together.

I had a few days left before they gave me the rest of the black vials. Before I became a monster. Time was running out, and I had to figure it out. Three days. That's all. I breathed in deep and racked my brain for answers.

41

Callum

"We've got to find Sloane and Ashlen as soon as possible. Who knows what kind of hell they're being put through." I said for what felt like the thousandth time. My mind immediately conjured Sloane being sliced into tiny pieces or being fed to monsters.

Alvaro held a hand up. "We know, but we can't show up with guns blazing only to have our asses handed to us and be killed."

"The eclipse is coming soon though. I don't know what they have planned, but it'll be big. We have to get her before then."

Alvaro nodded. "We will. Don't worry."

Waiting was the worst. It felt as if weeks had passed since I last saw Sloane, but it had only been three full days. Seventy-two hours. I knew time wasn't on my side. We needed a plan, but I wanted us to make one on the way there.

We left the bar and went to where Jay and Claire stayed. A tiny home with four rooms total: a kitchen, living room, bedroom, and bathroom. Jay reminded me of a taller and younger Jet Li with a British accent, and Claire was a younger Alfre Woodard with a shaved head. Her smooth, ebony skin had a milky tint that glowed in the darkness. Jay was the other part of the dirty dozen group, and Claire was his partner. They had met in Jamestown and stayed there. The only reason I knew they were in a relationship was that Alvaro had said so. Otherwise, they kept their affection private.

Jay was a Hunter with power over plants and nature. Claire was also a Hunter with a whole lotta strength.

Alvaro spread out a map of the Kingston area on their small kitchen table. He pinned each corner with salt and pepper shakers. He pointed out the Nightlin Mountain and where the different portals were located. We would have to jump to Kingston then jump to the portal by the waterfall, which would be tricky if we ran into Chuck and anyone else on his side.

Claire filled their packs with different necessities while we talked.

"You said the portal to the waterfall is downstairs behind a black door?" Alvaro asked.

I nodded. "Chuck let us in last time. Not everyone is allowed in that way."

Alvaro shrugged. "Yeah, that's because of the pool."

Harris, Jess, and I stared at him.

"What's so special about the pool?" Harris asked.

"It helps keep them young."

My eyes grew larger, and we all looked at each other.

"You've been there?" Jess asked us.

I nodded. "Yeah, we had to go by it on the way to the falls."

"Wow." Jess's eyes grew large, and his lips parted in awe.

"All right, we jump into Kingston, then go down to the waterfall portal, then onto the mountain. I say we start high instead of going underneath as you and Sloane did. They will be ready for that again." Alvaro rolled the map up.

Claire grunted. Alvaro smoked his cigar. Somehow, Harris grew paler; he was already so white.

Harris stuttered, "Will–I–be–be going?"

I looked at him with shock. "Of course, you got them in this mess. You'll get them out."

Red splotches blossomed on Harris' neck and cheeks. His lips turned white. He nodded but didn't say anything else.

Alvaro slapped Harris' back. "Also, we'll need you to be the go around for Chuck."

Harris' mouth fell open and his eyes locked onto mine. "What?"

I may have smiled slightly.

Alvaro said, "Yeah, he thinks you're in hiding and that we don't know so it will be up to you to keep him in the dark and keep him out of our way."

"I don't think I can do it."

"We'll coach you. Don't worry."

"But I caved when Jess and Callum found me." His eyes were as large as the moon. He kept pushing his hair from his face. Pretty sure sweat made his hair stick to his face.

"Ashlen needs your help, Harris. Don't you want to help her?"

"Of course I do." He ran a hand over his face. "She probably hates me."

"Well, you have to help fix it, or you can run off and live in a hole somewhere, like that Morgan guy." I raised a brow.

His posture slumped in defeat. "All right. I'll help." He focused on Alvaro. "But I need help to be convincing."

Alvaro chuckled. "No worries. By the end, you'll be like one of us." He winked and pulled on his cigar, puffing large circles into the air. He looked at Jay and Claire. "You ready?"

Jay nodded. "Yeah, we've got everything we need."

"Let's head out." Alvaro grabbed his bag, snatching a bag of chips on the way to the door.

I gripped his arm before he got too far. "Alvaro, I forgot something."

He took a long drag then blew it out. "Okay, I'm waiting."

He made a point to look at my hand around his arm. I released my grip. "The portal was on a twelve-hour timer. Chuck made us wait until 11 p.m, and when we came back through, it was 11 a.m."

Alvaro looked at his watch. "Fuck. We've got forty minutes. Jay?"

Jay stopped at the door. "Yeah?"

"Need you to gas up the boy now. We don't have long. Forty minutes until the portal is open at the waterfall."

Jay simply nodded and opened the door with Claire on his heels.

"Harris, better catch up with him." Alvaro motioned to where Jay had been.

Harris jumped up and grabbed his things then sprinted from the room after Jay. Alvaro shook his head and pointed his thumb after him. "That's your friend?"

Jess and I glanced at each other, and I answered, "Eh, we thought so, but we aren't so sure."

He nodded in thought, pressing his lips together, then stuck his cigar in the left side of his mouth. "We'll watch out for him." He headed out and closed the door behind us.

The glittering lights above reflected the many colors of the cave: yellows, blues, reds, and greens. People laughed as they walked beside us and in and out of shops and eateries. It was a much happier place than Kingston. We may have been in a cavern below the earth, but it was much lighter than in Kingston. Sloane needed to go one day. She would have loved it.

We walked along the narrow path leading back to the wall of portals. Harris moved closer next to Jay with his head lowered as if he was trying to hear every word. I hoped it would pay off, and he could fool Chuck. The portals glistened before us. Each one was numbered above, just like at Kingston. The blue and black mirrored pools shimmered and moved as if waving us in. Portal three seemed alone. No one stood before it, waiting to jump in. After seeing Jamestown, I could see why no one wanted to go to Kingston. It was comparing real gold to aluminum.

I glanced behind us, marveling at the miles and miles of the cavern that stretched beyond my eyesight. Lights twinkled and laughter filled the air. It wasn't dark and gloomy. Death didn't cling to every surface. Once we brought Sloane back, I was bringing her to the cavern city. There was plenty of space for us here.

"Hey, time to go." Alvaro nudged me.

Jay went first, followed by Claire. I was the last. The eerie coolness pulled me in, making it feel as if I was in one of those sensory deprivation tanks. There was no sound or movement. It lasted mere seconds. It was calming, yet my heart raced in hopes it would be over soon.

42

Callum

As soon as my feet hit the dirt on the other side, I dropped low and ran after the others. We stopped along the wall. Alvaro shoved Harris in front, so he could scout and make sure Chuck wasn't on our tail. We watched him disappear through the doors, then we headed inside. I wasn't afraid of being stopped but knew Alvaro would draw attention merely by his size.

We made it to the dining hall, then headed toward the door that led to the level below. Someone called my name. I glanced over my shoulder to see Irene's red hair moving toward me.

"Callum, what are you doing?" She peered around me to see Jess disappearing down the steps. "Where are you going?"

"I can't tell you that." If there was anyone to trust, it would be Irene, but this wasn't the time to tell her.

A flash of hurt passed through her eyes, then cleared as she schooled her features. Her eyes scanned the room. "I can help. You know I can."

"I know, but there isn't time."

"It's fine. Let me go."

Oh, to hell and back with it. I nodded once, then turned on my heel and trotted down the steps. Irene followed. We caught up with the others, and they all raised their eyebrows when Irene appeared.

Alvaro stepped forward. "Who's this?" His eyes traveled down to her boots then back to her face.

"I'm Irene." She held her hand out to shake his. "I'm coming for the ride. Don't worry. I won't hold you back."

The space between them sparked. And I looked more closely at Alvaro. He seemed riveted with the redhead.

I shook my head. "All right let's go."

"Which power are you?" Alvaro asked Irene.

Air whipped through the hall and around Alvaro. His long hair tangling around his head in answer. He stopped and pushed his hair back into his ponytail. A large smile painted his face.

Irene jogged to catch up. Alvaro looked as if all his dreams had just come true.

He whispered, "Bonita."

Irene rolled her eyes, but a smile tugged her lips.

We reached the black door with no trouble. Jess tried the knob, but it was locked. He rolled his eyes, then held his hand over the locking mechanism, with his eyes closed as he concentrated. Water filled the holes running into the lock. Metal clicked and clanked, and the door swung open.

We filed in. The bright red door to the portal stood in the center of the room still. The red paint glistened in the faint light.

"We have two minutes before it turns on," Alvaro said as he checked his watch.

Jess leaned into me and whispered, "I feel like more should have been guarding this door. Right?"

He was right. I felt the same. Something felt off. This was too easy.

"What can we do?" I asked.

Jess measured everyone up around us, his eyes roaming over each of them. "We've got a good team. Hope it'll be enough for whatever is about to hit us."

My gut roiled with anxiety. I gestured to Alvaro, and he squeezed his way over to me.

"This is too easy. It might be a trap." I said. The others turned to look at us.

He met my gaze and nodded to Jess, then faced the room.

"Be on your guard when we go through. Could be anything."

Everyone unstrapped their weapons, getting ready for battle. The red door sizzled and popped. White light erupted around the door's casing. It was time.

"We have two minutes before it closes," I stated.

Alvaro stepped up and opened the red door. The portal glistened with blues and black.

"Here we go." He stepped through and vanished to the other side.

We went one by one as fast as we could go. Jess decided to go last. I stepped through. The icy depths wrapped around me and yanked me to the other side. An eerie stillness greeted me. The other four fanned out in front of me. Jess popped in behind me. The portal blinked out a few seconds after.

I stilled, listening with every fiber of my being. It radiated from me counting the other five warm bodies around me then went on a search for others. A tiny creature burrowed below us, probably a rabbit. A nest of birds shared a meal in a nearby tree. Then I heard them. Whispers and the thrum of their heartbeats.

"They aren't far." I breathed, barely audible to regular ears.

I pointed east then due north. I signed that there were six. At least it was even-numbered. We moved toward the falls, therefore toward whatever waited for us. We waded through the dense forest. Water rushing over rocks thundered through the trees. Bathed us with its white light, the full moon punctured the darkness. The shadows were in high contrast. Anything that moved my eyes snagged upon. My ears pricked with tension, and my heart raced with anticipation. I gripped my long sword hard. The hard leather handle was already worn from years of fighting.

Footsteps crunched on loose rock, and I halted. We were almost to the falls. The trees swayed in the wind and the clouds rolled by. I tensed, ready to pounce on whatever was about to pop out. Movement caught my eye, and a person stepped through the trees.

Chuck. Shoulders tensed, and hands reflexively grasped their weapons.

"Hey, guys." He stood relaxed. His hand rested on the hilt of his sword. He looked the same as any other time I had seen him. Our Leader and compatriot.

"I don't think we've had the honor of meeting," Alvaro said. He was the only one appearing to be just as casual as Chuck. He hadn't pulled a weapon, he stood with one hand on his hip and his cigar precariously hung from his lips.

Chuck's gaze shifted to Alvaro and nodded. "No, I don't think we have."

An awkward silence fell as neither responded.

"Where are you all headed?" asked Chuck.

I glanced at Alvaro. "We're going to the Nightlin Mountain to get Sloane."

Chuck scanned the area around us. "I told you I'd have a group together to go get them. We just needed some time."

I nodded slowly. "You know me, always ready to take action."

He smirked. "Ah, yes, that's very true."

The air around Irene vibrated as she tensed. I placed a hand on her shoulder hoping to calm her.

"Chuck, why not let us pass so we can get Sloane and Ashlen?" I asked, hoping to dissuade him from whatever he had planned.

"Sorry, Callum, there are bigger plans for them. Especially for Sloane."

Terror seeped in. What had he meant by that?

The trees moved and five men stepped into the moonlight. I had never seen them before. Where had Chuck found these guys? Each male held one to two weapons. Each looked more ominous than the first. One, in particular, seemed excited for a fight as he shifted from foot to foot and kept switching his short sword from hand to hand. Power rolled through the open space and hit me in the chest. Something else was coming. Shadows moved and wavered. Air rustled the leaves and my hair; that would be Chuck's power.

"It doesn't have to be this way. Leave, go back to Kingston and this will be forgotten." A shield sparked to life from Chuck's left hand.

Only, we all knew it wouldn't be forgotten. Either way, we were up shit creek.

Energy popped around Alvaro. Jay lifted a hand. Claire brandished her sword and called her shield forward; it sparked with red light. None of us would be calling our Czars forth if we could help it. No one wanted to pass out afterward, especially a noob like me.

Jess nodded to me, trying to encourage my fire. Water wrapped around his hand and up his arm. I pulled on the fire hiding deep inside. It sprang to life. I was getting more used to it. A ball formed in my palm ready to throw.

The excited one blinked out of existence. A blur ran around our group; guess that answered what power he had. Speed.

"Let's get this over with." Alvaro sparked the air and out of my view.

The air filled with screams. We surged forward. Light meets dark, and assholes meet sphincters. We were the assholes.

43

The Dark

"HER POWER IS GROWING," JAKE MUTTERED, HIS VOICE RASPY AND HARD to understand.

He nodded. "Yes, and you wouldn't let me take it."

Fear glided across Jake's features, then slipped away. "She will help us conquer the other world and realms." He tipped a small rodent into his gaping mouth and crunched. His needle-like teeth speared the mouse instantly.

The other creature stood at the edge of the roofline, spreading its wings wide, to feel the breeze push against them. His claws sank into the softwood and dirt under him. The crescent moon gave a little light that night.

"Once she helps us conquer the other world, you can take her power," Jake said between bites.

"I want it all. You know my patience is thin, but we need the other world and realm, so I will be patient this time." He ground out the words. "But the moment we take the realm, her power is mine." His eyes locked onto a deer grazing way down below in the middle of the tall, grassy plain.

Jake nodded as he popped another small rodent into his mouth. "It will be yours, then I can rule the norm, and you can have this realm."

"What about the other? What will we do about it?"

"She will take care of that one," Jacob said as if an afterthought.

"Make sure she does." The creature spread its wings, readying to take off. "Give her an extra dose tonight so she won't slip back into her weaker self."

Jake nodded and turned to go back inside.

He saw his chance and leapt into the air. His wings buffeted the sky, then tucked against his side as he dove soundlessly for the unknowing deer that would be his supper.

44

Sloane

ASHLEN NEVER CAME BACK. I FELT SICK FROM WORRY AND THAT CRAP they kept forcing down my throat. I had already spewed up whatever contents had been in my stomach for the hundredth time.

My thoughts were all over the place. I'd be thinking of a way out, then they'd jump to killing and death. I wanted no part. If portals were the key, then what could I do? If Callum had to burn it out of me, what then? Something could happen to him. He could die, and I'd never get out. I'd be cursed to be a monster forever. Surely, my grandfather hadn't expected me to be rescued like some sort of damsel locked in a tower. Oh wait, I was locked in a sort of tower... dammit!

I hated being a damsel, especially one of those dumb clueless ones in fairytales! I mean, come on; it had to be more original than that. I hit my forehead on the stone floor again. I was sprawled face-first on the cold stone. My body was racked with heat and sweats every few minutes. The cold floor helped to abate it somewhat.

I rolled onto my back, thinking. I closed my eyes and hollowed that space in my gut. Holding my hands in front of me, I pictured a shield forming. The small round blue-white one that I had made in the cave with Callum. The air hummed and something sputtered. I kept my eyes closed just in case I scared it off. A picture formed in my mind of a round, hard shield and most importantly, light. My hand warmed and pulsed with energy. It felt heavier as I tried forming my shield, though I knew it wouldn't be a real shield. I hoped it would be a portal.

I cracked an eye open. Sweat dotted my upper lip and forehead. My arm shook with the effort. The shield sparked with light and the center undulated like a wave during a storm. My stomach flipped with sickness and excitement rolled into one.

If I could just make it stay open. If I could figure out what it meant. A sound echoed through it. I almost dropped my concentration, and the portal shimmered. I grounded myself and held firm. The stuff in my system bucked. Again, the sound echoed through. It sounded like yells and weapons clanging. What was happening on the other side? A screech echoed down the hall, and my portal shield dissipated in a shower of ash.

A cold sweat washed over me. The door ripped open, and two creatures scuttled in. My uncle, Jacob, was on their heels. I scrambled back, hitting the wall with a smack. The creatures grabbed me, pulling me up and holding my arms on either side. Jacob stopped in front of me. His empty eyes staring.

"Hmm, it's taking longer for you to change. Your friend took no time at all. She must have been weak." His head tilted as if in thought.

My chest squeezed with the thought of Ashlen becoming one of them. Tears leaked down my cheeks. I ground my teeth together, so I wouldn't make a sound. I wouldn't give him the pleasure of it.

His claws shot up and clasped around my throat under my jaw, tilting it up. I thrashed in his grip, but the others grasped harder. Their claws sliced into my skin, and I cried out. Blood trickled down my arms.

"Keep fighting, and you'll die," he croaked.

His claws tightened. The one below my chin pushed upward. He tipped the inky contents into my mouth, then held me up. The tips of my toes brushed the floor. I tried with all my might to kick and punch, but their strength was too much. Another vial poured into my mouth, then another. I cried. The burn and pain drained me, and I stopped fighting as much. My limbs became lead. Two more vials went down my throat.

He dropped me. The other two creatures let me go, and I crumpled to the floor.

"Don't fight it."

The door slammed shut. I was alone. I couldn't move. My mind felt heavy. Thoughts scattered. I faded.

Power. It was all I wanted. More and more power. Power to win and kill. For it to fill my mind and body up with its glorious strength. If I had more power I could defeat them all. I wouldn't need a boy to rescue me. I'd be the hero of my own story. I'd be the one to win.

My skin prickled. Gooseflesh raised my skin and the tiny hairs along my arms. But it wasn't hair. It was ridged. My skin vibrated, and nodules popped up along my arms. Black, oily nodules. My rough, misshapen fingernails lengthened into long pointy daggers. Something along my back bristled. Pain ripped through me.

I fell to the floor as it tore through my shoulders and spine. I cried out. But it was the power finally answering. Thin lacy wings spread from the center of my back. The tips nearly touched the walls.

What was happening to me? What was this? It couldn't be happening.

I cried and cried; because of fear or excitement, I wasn't sure. They felt the same.

My eyesight dimmed. The faint light seeping into the cell burned my eyes. I pressed my hand over the hole at the window to keep the light out. Pain buckled my legs and curled into a ball. My wings encased me in a protective shell.

"Callummmm!" I screamed and screamed his name over and over until my voice grew hoarse, and my mind fell away.

45

Callum

Vines slithered under my feet as Jay used his powers to grab a guy's ankle and send him soaring through the sky. Air whipped around me as Irene and Chuck flew by. Alvaro bent the space around him as he blinked in and out of sight. The excited guy whipped by me and hit me with the flat of his sword. He had become an annoyance.

I threw fireballs left and right.

Claire rushed by, swinging her sword. She cleaved one of the men in half with her brute strength. That was terrifying.

Jess had a guy wrapped in a funnel of water. The shadow man squared off against me. Shadows wrapped around him. He vanished, then appeared out of nowhere. His sword nearly cut my head off. A fireball sailed his way, but he was gone. With each passing second, I grew more frustrated.

It was utter chaos.

Then creatures flew and moved toward us. Limbs cracked. The ground shook. We were about to be dead meat.

"Guys! Something's coming!" I yelled. I pointed in the direction of the movement. My group faced what was coming as the remainder of Chuck's group took a stance.

"I warned you!" Chuck shouted as Nightlins flooded the forest floor.

My heart skipped a few beats as five Nightlins crashed into the melee. Two flew and the other three galloped. I said a silent prayer to the gods there wasn't a Skeletal with them.

Alvaro stood next to me. The white scar along his face pulled tight from his exertion. He heaved in deep breaths. "Two of us need to change. We can't get around it now."

Jess and Claire raised a hand at the same time. Alvaro nodded.

Electricity sparked and popped around them. Claire's energy turned into a red sphere as it took shape. Her Czar's wings unfurled. Its tail whipped around, smacking one of the men. Claire hopped onto its back, and they took off into the air.

Jess's energy was white with pops of purple. The sphere wrapped around him and the energy thundered from the ground, wrapping around his legs and up his arms. His Czar roared to life. Its shiny purple scales reflected the moonlight. Jess jumped onto its back, and they were gone in an instant. His laughter echoed in the breeze.

The Czars and Nightlins crashed in black and sparks of color. We set to work to finish off the men and the Nightlins on the ground. Jay sent vines around Chuck, but Chuck immediately used his air to unwind them or kill off their oxygen. He and Irene were in an endless battle. I kept thinking we were too evenly matched.

Shadows wrapped around me again, but this time I called the fire in, letting it wrap around me. The flames engulfed my body, burning the shadows out. I snatched the guy from the depths. My hand wrapped around his throat, and I squeezed. The tendrils of fire licked his face and hair. Burning my nostrils. I almost gagged. The man screamed. I held on for a second longer until he passed out, then let go.

Alvaro blinked in and out of the air around us as he tried to catch the speedster. Then the unthinkable happened. A flash of red went by as Claire and her Czar were thrown into the trees. The forest echoed with the sound of the trees snapping and of the creature hitting the earth. Sparks erupted in a flash of red, then went out.

I looked to the sky for any sign of Jess. He was still battling, but I could tell he was growing tired. His Czar moved slower with each beat of its wings. We were out of time. I needed to combust. I had to do something.

I scanned the area and ran to the middle of it all. At the same time, I called the heat and fire to burn themselves out. My vision turned white as it burst along my skin, consuming me.

"Take cover!" I yelled, hoping my group would listen.

I pushed and pushed, feeling it build inside. It was almost ready to be let loose.

"Not so fast, Cal." Chuck appeared before me.

The wind wrapped around me in a tight cyclone. Air was being cut off from me. My lungs burned with the need to inhale. It wrapped tighter and tighter around me. The fire sputtered, then died. I coughed and strained to breathe, but he wasn't letting up.

"One day you'll learn Callum." Chuck loomed over me, baring down. The air was being sucked from my body. Then it stopped and the welcoming whoosh of air entered my lungs.

"Restrain this one. He's coming back with us."

I heaved into the grass as Chuck's men locked cuffs around my ankles and wrists, then gagged me. Around me, the rest of my group were either knocked unconscious or being bound with ropes. Claire had been brought back from the woods. She was passed out on the ground with her arms tied behind her. Jay had a black eye and a cut lip. Long gashes cut across Alvaro's chest and one down his leg. With cuts marring his face and one of his arms twisted at an odd angle, Jess was unconscious.

One of the flying Nightlins gestured to us. "Who is coming with us?"

"All of them except this one." Chuck gestured to me. "He's coming back with us to set an example to the others."

The Nightlin spoke incoherently to the other ones, and they got to work gathering up my group. Terror gripped my chest as I watched the creatures picking them up and slinging them on their backs to be taken away. No way it was happening.

The breeze blew and turned colder. A roar erupted, and a larger creature appeared over the treetops. Its massive wings buffeted the trees in large swoops. Sloane's dad. It had to be. I glanced at Chuck, who had spun to see what was coming. The lines in his face were deeper with worry and possibly terror.

The creature banked around us. Its wings beat the air, then he dropped to the ground. The space instantly cooled. My breath came out in puffs of fog. Seeing him reminded me of the last time we had met. Of when he had almost killed me. The fire in my gut blew out. Panic seized my heart, and cold sweat covered my skin, dampening my clothes. I tried to control it. I tried so hard, but my teeth chattering gave me away. Shame flushed my cheeks.

"Uh, my lord." Chuck fell to his knees with his head bowed. "What did we do to honor your presence?"

The creature swung its head to Chuck. Its twin black holes eyed him.

"I heard the battle and came to see who won." Its voice was deep and clipped, making it hard to piece together every word it said.

"As you can see, we did. I was having your creatures take back the losers."

"What of this one?" It pointed to me and drew closer. Its long talons came into view.

"I'm taking him back to show to the rest of my group that he's a traitor."

The creature nodded. "The girl likes this one, though. It may be best to bring him with us."

The girl? Sloane? I looked up then. Its face studied me as if trying to decide if I'd be best alive or dead seasoned with salt. My heart beat a little faster.

A shadow fell across the moon, causing a shadow to fall across our group. The Nightlins shifted uneasily. Another creature flew in a large circle, then dropped to the ground a few feet away. It was smaller than the others. Its wings were thinner and somewhat translucent. As it drew closer, I could make out its knife-like claws that were so long they curled. The legs were still shaped normally, but with large talons for feet. A sheet of black hair fell across its features, making it hard to see what or who it had once been.

Then I saw her. Sloane. My Sloane. The creature. I gasped as the picture came together. She was gaunt. Her usually pale skin had turned grey. Her hair that had been changing to white was now solid black like oil.

Bile rose into my throat, and I swallowed it back down. Her blue eyes were black holes. I looked at Chuck, who also seemed just as shocked as me. The other creatures stood to the side, not moving as if unsure what they were supposed to do.

Sloane's father said something to them. The ones who could fly took off into the air without a second glance. The ones on the ground disappeared into the trees. Only four of us remained.

"What do you think? Should he come back with us?" Her father asked.

My gaze shifted to her. She eyed me with no recognition, and my chest tightened.

"Sloane?" I whispered, barely able to believe my eyes.

She didn't respond, only tilted her head like a predator eyes its meal. I swallowed the lump in my throat.

"Sloane? Are you there?" Would she respond? Did she know me at all? Panic strangled the cry that wanted out. My black eyes tried to absorb every inch of her. She turned to her father, then leapt into the sky. Her wings spread wide, and she disappeared into the clouds.

46

Callum

MY EMPTY SOUL LEFT A VACANT, GAPING CRATER-SIZED HOLE. CHUCK dragged me through the portal by my legs. I didn't care. She had been turned. A monster. What hope was left? Apathy was my new normal. He brought me to Kingston. Dirt and grass covered my body and got in my hair. I couldn't feel the cuts and bruises anymore.

He pulled me along the path to the front gate. I vaguely noticed people working along the gardens and on the building. But their whispers drifted over me. Wind wrapped around my body then lifted me from the ground. I guessed Chuck was tired of hauling my ass.

People gathered around and followed us. We ended up in the dining hall. News had travelled fast as they heard about my predicament. Chuck still had me gagged with a dirty rag, but he needn't worry about me saying anything.

"Everyone, as you can see." Chuck pointed to me. "We have a traitor in our midst."

As the crowd murmured, the tension in the room soured. The air around me pushed my body upward, so I faced everyone.

"He, along with an outside group, tried to give information to the other side. Luckily, we found out before they were able to make contact. We found details of their meetings in Callum's room. As many of you know, the Nightlins have become braver and more active lately, and we believe it is because of Callum and his group of insiders that were helping to provide information to the creatures."

The whispers grew louder, reverberating off the high ceiling. Angry faces focused on me. Raleigh pushed through to the front. Her wide eyes and open mouth held disbelief. She tried to move closer, but someone grabbed her arm.

"We will be having a council meeting later on to decide his fate." He gestured to two big guys to the side. "Take him to the cells."

They picked me up under my arms, carrying me out of the hall. As we left the room, Harris stood at the back door. His large, blue eyes stared in shock. His cheeks turned bright red. We went down the stairs, and down and down. The cells were one level above the tombs. They tossed me into the first one and slammed the door shut without untying me.

I laid my head on the dusty stone floor, staring up at the rotted beams. A small vitamin bulb blinked in the corner. It had been a long time since someone or something had been placed in the cells, much less cleaned. I listened to the air entering and exiting my lungs, to my blood pumping through my heart, to the insects scurrying along the walls. But the only thing I could see was Sloane's face. The black hair. Black eyes. Her wings and claws. She hadn't known me. Any vestige of her was gone.

"Callum?" a voice whispered through the cell bars. Raleigh's big eyes peeked over the rim of the small window. A white scar ran down the side of her face, almost reaching her lips. The only evidence of what she had gone through in the mountain.

I didn't respond.

"Callum, what happened?" Her finger tapped on the wood door. She glanced down the hall. "I know he didn't do anything. Yeah, I know about Chuck. The other one already told me about him." She was talking to her ghosts again. She peered in. "Don't worry, Cal, we'll figure it out. We'll get Sloane and Ashlen back." Then she was gone.

The halls were silent again. Only my breathing disturbed the quiet.

Heat rose to my skin, and I worried I was about to combust and burn the place down, though maybe that wouldn't be a bad thing.

Don't worry, little one. I'm here when you need me. My Czar's voice echoed in my mind. The sound eased some of the stress from my mind.

How? I asked it with my mind.

Now that our connection has been made, you only need to call, and I will answer.

Okay. What should I call you?

In my realm, they call me Hashakar.

Hashakar. I liked it.

The heat abated. My skin cooled, and I knew it was gone until I needed it again.

It felt as if an hour passed when Chuck showed up. He leaned against the door, staring at me.

"I wasn't sure how you'd react seeing her, but I think it worked out for the best. They have big plans for her." He fell silent and watched me. His dark eyes bore into me.

I only stared at the ceiling, wishing he'd be eaten.

"I'll have some food sent down soon and have someone look at your wounds before you heal them over. I haven't decided what to do with you yet. I'll have to see what the council says first." He turned to leave then stopped. "You did well Callum. You almost won. Not many can say that." He turned away. I listened as his feet echoed down the hall and back up the stairs.

I lost it then. Anger, pain, and grief washed over me at once. I couldn't hold it in anymore. My tears mixed with the dust and grime on the cell floor. I curled into myself on the cold stone and let the emotions roll through me. It had been too long since I let go. Once it was over, I packed it back in. All the mistakes I had made ran through my mind. How could I fix it?

Sloane may have been made into a monster, but she certainly could be unmade.

47

HAD I KNOWN THAT GUY? HE FELT FAMILIAR SOMEHOW BUT I COULDN'T quite place him. The soft billowy clouds blew past me, brushing against my wings. It was the best feeling. The crescent moon gave just enough light to illuminate my path back to the mountain. I swooped down and landed on the small tower hidden by the tallest trees. The shutters were already open, waiting for me to come home.

The creature, Jacob, waited for me. He had no wings, so he wasn't able to fly with me.

"How was the flight?"

I tucked my wings carefully behind me. I could smell his jealousy in the air.

"It was great."

"Did you see the Realmers?"

I nodded slowly, unsure why he and the other creature had wanted me to go.

"What did you think?" he asked.

"They weren't very special. I'm not sure how they can be a threat. None of them had wings or claws."

He nodded. "They can be surprising." He turned down the hall. "I have something to show you. A new pet for you."

What could he mean by that?

"I don't like pets."

"You'll like this one."

I followed him down the hall and the rough spiral staircase. Creatures stirred behind closed doors. My talons clicked on the stone floor. The darkness felt welcoming and safe like a warm blanket and cookie. Where had that come from? A cookie?

Jacob stopped at an old weathered door. He glanced at me then pushed the door open. The inside of the room was pitch black until he lit a match and held it to a torch by the door. The orange light cast shadows across the empty room. Well, it was empty except for a small mass huddled in the corner. Jacob stepped inside and called out to it. The shape moved slightly. Its back had the same ridges as Jacob but this creature walked on all fours. It scuttled toward us. Its arms and legs bent at odd angles. Its spine protruded from its back. Long, black scraps of hair hung across its back and touched the floor.

"Its name is Ash."

I nodded and knelt, holding my hand out. Ash was a nice name. For some reason, it sounded familiar.

It moved closer to me, sniffing. The face was gone except for a mouth full of teeth. The rest were holes where the eyes and nose should have been. Its skin was pulled tight across the bones. The paper-thin greyish color showed the bones beneath.

"Hello," I said, trying not to scare it.

It sniffed me some more, then grunted.

Jacob nodded. "I think it likes you. It will stay with you in your room. Come, below is your meeting." He walked out.

I looked back at Ash and waved it toward me. "Come on, time to go." I turned and took a few steps. It followed. Maybe I would like this pet thing.

We kept winding down and down through the maze of corridors. The darkness enveloped us. We reached a thick wooden door with carvings etched across. The scene depicted angels and demons falling.

Jacob pushed through the double doors and we entered a cave. We had to be below the surface. Rocks glittered on the ceiling and floor. Water dripped echoing off the stone walls.

A mass of darkness sat at the end of the cave, unmoving. Jacob moved to the side and waited for I had no clue what. Then air moved in and out of the space as if lungs were breathing. My pet pushed against my leg then moved behind me.

The other creature, James, sauntered in through the doors.

He laid his claws on my shoulder. "You did great. Exactly what we wanted." He turned from her heading toward the black mass.

"My Lord." James knelt and bowed his head.

Horror and awe swept through me as realization spread. The black mass was a living thing. It filled the whole end of the cave, which had to be 100 yards long, making the creature half that size. Jacob stood to attention next to me. His arms folded behind his back the best he could over his large nodules.

The mass stirred and I instinctively took a step back, wanting to give it plenty of space. It was like nothing I had ever seen. Almost like a dragon but made of more shadows and mist. Its massive head swung around to face me. Its eye sockets were empty. Black mist slithered along the cave floor toward me. It wrapped around my body but dispersed just as fast.

Cold sweat ran down my spine. I had to force myself to breathe.

"Here she is. The one to help us get to the other side." James said with a flourish. He swept his arm out pointing to me.

The skeletal face tilted each way as if to get a better picture of me.

"She looksss small," it said through my mind.

I jumped as I registered that it hadn't audibly said anything. Its deep, hollow voice echoed in my brain.

"She is but has lots of power. I'm sure you can tell."

The thing nodded. Black, empty mist billowed, radiating out from it.

"She will make new portals."

James nodded. "Yes, we are certain. She will make them to the normal world, so we can conquer and bring more servants."

This was my purpose? How did they know that? I studied my

hands and claws. The bones showing through my thin skin. My nails had turned black during my change.

"Does she agree?" The thing asked. Its long sharp teeth gleamed through the black mist. Its teeth were longer than I was tall.

James motioned for me to move closer. A second passed before I did. My pet followed close behind. His claws gripped my shoulder and pushed me down, forcing me to kneel.

"Say it," he muttered.

"I- I do." My breath caught in my throat. I stared fixedly at the floor, my heart racing.

James pulled me back to my feet. I couldn't meet the thing's eyes or lack thereof, so I fixed my gaze where its feet should have been.

Mist rolled toward me again. It wrapped around me again but slid around my face as if in a caress. Something inside me told me not to move. I was in the presence of the ultimate predator, who would eat me without a second thought.

The power that emanated from the creature felt stifling. James moved closer to it and motioned for me to move closer. I glanced at Jacob, who patiently stood by the doorway. I made my way over to the large creature stopping beside James.

"Kneel."

I did and waited. He took hold of my wrist. Jacob took the other, spreading my arms out.

"Open your mouth," James commanded.

I glanced at him, then at the creature. I hesitated a second but slowly opened my jaws. My teeth had lengthened and grown sharper during my transition.

The massive creature before me seemed to stand. Its head rose higher and higher as it loomed over me. It breathed in deeply, then exhaled long and loud. Black mist swirled around us. One large tentacle rose above me and stopped at my face. I kept glancing around the room; so unsure of what was to come.

The mist dove for my opened mouth. I couldn't breathe. My lungs felt as if at any second they would burst. Tears I didn't know were in me, leaked from the corners of my eyes, trailing down my bony cheeks. I felt like gagging and throwing up all at once.

"Drink! Drink it in!" James roared.

I did. The pain lessened. My eyes flashed open as power rolled through my veins. Pure power. Somewhere a switch had been flipped, and I couldn't get enough of the mist. I drank as if my life depended on it. In some way it did. My heart beat faster, and my lungs expanded with each inhale. It was over before I wanted it.

I smiled wide as whatever power it had given me blossomed inside. I felt it in my toes; the electric hum sent shivers up my spine. It was as if I had drunk ten Red Bulls. If I went outside for a run, I didn't think I'd stop for hours.

James and Jacob nodded their approval.

48

Callum

The image of Sloane as a monster permeated my mind. It was stuck on repeat. Her massive black gossamer wings beat the air. Her sharp talons curled and uncurled. Her pale skin had been more translucent, and her ocean-colored eyes were gone. Black holes had stared at me as if she hadn't known me. What if she didn't know me? What if it changed her that much?

A coil of dread wrapped around my heart. I breathed in deep then let it out. My tiny cell felt even smaller the longer I occupied it. I was thankful to have on my jacket. The cold dredges of the stone cell seeped into my senses and stole the tatters of warmth I had left. Even my fire had a hard time coming to life.

A small tray had been brought and left, holding soup and bread. I hadn't felt like eating but knew I had to. More time passed before steps and whispers reached my ears.

It was Harris and Raleigh. Chuck didn't think I was much of a risk if Harris and Raleigh were able to come to see me. Granted he did have to make it look to the outsiders as if I was a true traitor, and surrounded by all the Realmers, I didn't have much hope of getting out and escaping, at least not without lots of help.

Harris' dark blond hair appeared in the small cell window.

"Hey," he said.

Raleigh had to stand on her tiptoes to peer in. Her fingers held onto the cell door to help her see. "Cal, we've been brainstorming, but the council is about to meet and decide what to do with you."

I stood. My joints popped as I stretched to touch the low ceiling.

"Any idea what they will do?" I asked.

She shrugged. "Not really. Probably keep you here forever."

I shook my head and moved closer to the small window.

"I tried to find Chuck when we got back here, Callum. I promise I did. I couldn't find him nowheres." Harris' cheeks flushed as he rushed to explain himself.

"I know. He was already on the other side when we got there."

Harris nodded.

Raleigh looked down the hall and began nodding. I tried not to think about ghosts too much but it weirded me out whenever she started talking to things I couldn't see.

"What are they saying Raleigh?" I asked.

She focused her attention back on me. "They say. You might be banished."

I frowned. I hadn't heard of that before.

"How?"

"One of them, a man, talked about banishment in the old days, where they open an old portal, shove you through and not open it again."

"What? They can do that?"

"I really don't know. That's what one of them said." She gripped the bars, "We won't let them so don't worry." Her head whipped to the stairs, and she grabbed Harris. "We better go. We'll be back when we can."

"All right, thanks, guys."

They ran down the opposite way from the stairs. A minute later steps approached from the stairway. A big, burly man stepped into view and unlocked my cell door.

"Time for your meeting. They're in the dining hall."

I nodded and headed in the direction of the stairs. Thoughts crowded my mind as my feet carried me up and up. *Would they banish me? Could they do that?* I hadn't ever done anything bad before. But I was sure Chuck had a hold on whoever occupied the council seats. Politics at its finest. Even in the Night Realm, you couldn't escape it.

As the stairs opened into the dining hall, it looked as if everyone had come to see what would happen to me. The burly guy had to help push me through to the front of the room. People moved out of my way pretty quickly though. Sad or angry faces peered at me. I glimpsed Celest standing in a corner. It had been days since I saw her last. Her arms folded across her chest. She stood, looking impassive. *What would her judgment be?*

Chuck sat in the middle of the long table. Three other men and women were on each of his sides. They seemed familiar but only in a passing glance. Chuck, when he saw me, banged his beer mug on the table to get everyone's attention.

"Attention, everyone. Attention. We will call things to order with the proceedings." He turned to the other members next to him.

The crowd was hushed to a few murmurs.

"Today, the sentence for Callum Livingston will be decided. We will go over the details of the circumstances and vote as a whole; either aye or nay, by show of hands."

Everyone nodded or said aye. Any hope I had fled. I knew Chuck had it rigged. I'd be banished to some hole somewhere. I wanted to laugh. How far I had come. How much we had been through. Now, I was being held for treason. It baffled me. I held my head high though. No one would see me crack. Not now.

"We found Callum Livingston along with three others — Irene, Alvaro, and Jess — in a clearing with the creatures. They attacked us and tried to take us with them to the mountains." Loud murmurs echoed through the halls. Dirty looks turned my way. "We were able to get away but the others took off with the creatures. They killed two of the men with me." Gasps broke from the crowd. "Thom and Sam were good men." Muffled cries rose as I stood there. "What say you, family? What should his punishment be?"

Shouting tore through the space. It was hard to understand everything, but most of them said — kill, stone, or banish.

"Those in favor of kill?" Chuck surveyed the room, ready to count hands.

Several aye's were shouted and hands went up. I swallowed hard. The knives being thrust into my back drove deeper.

"Who's in favor of stoning?"

Only a few hands shot up. Sweat ran down my temples and collar.

"All in favor of banishment?" Chuck seemed to anticipate the answer. His fists clenched, and he rocked on his heels.

The majority of the hands in the room shot up with a raucous aye. Raleigh's petite face peered up at me. Her arms crossed protectively across her chest. Her eyes were watery with unshed tears.

Chuck banged on the table with his mug. "The decision has been made. Callum Livingston, you will be banished from this city." He banged on the table again to adjourn the meeting.

The guards grabbed my elbows to lead me back to the cell. The crowd booed and cheered as I was led away. Harris met me at the end of the row.

He nodded once. "I'm goin' to fix this." His eyes were set and determined.

The cell clanged shut behind me. The sound reverberated off the stone walls. I sank against the wall. Defeated. My hair hung in my face, but I didn't care. The only thing I saw was Sloane; her vacant eyes, her body coursing with black veins. My friends were taken. She was gone, and now I was alone.

49

We traveled back up top to a large room. James led us inside. My pet followed close behind. Jacob closed the door behind us. Time seemed to have no meaning here. We didn't watch the moon or pay attention to the light. We had one focus, and that was to kill the Realmers and to convert more servants.

"We have two more days until the eclipse is here. We have to be ready." James stood against the window, looking out over the forests.

Jacob nodded. "We will don't worry."

James gestured to me with his long claws. "She must be prepared."

Jacob nodded again and looked at me, appraising. "She will be."

I might as well have been invisible. I stroked the top of Ash's head. It nestled against my hand.

A flash of memory took me by surprise. A girl with dark hair and green eyes stood next to me. Her smile was breathtaking as she laughed at something. A man stood to my side. His dark, wavy hair hung in his evergreen eyes. The memory vanished, and I was back in the room with the two creatures.

I frowned and glanced around. Nothing had changed. My pet sat on the floor next to me. The creatures spoke to each other about their plans. I studied my claws again. In an instant, the claws were gone, replaced with pale flesh and short fingernails. I gasped. James and Jacob spun to see why.

I glanced up. "Sorry."

They went back to chatting. My claws were claws again. Black veins thrummed against my pale skin.

"We will use the sword to channel our powers to open the portals to the normal world."

"Where is it?" Jacob asked.

James stooped and pulled out a long object from under a shelf. He uncovered the object, unwrapping the cloth and bits of leather. The end of a sword gleamed in the moonlight that entered through a small crevice. The metal glowed with a soft blue light. It called to me as if it knew me. How could an object know me?

"What is that?" I asked.

James studied me. "An old sword from a Realmer that will help us open the other portals."

"How is that possible?"

"It has special powers that help bond us to the other side." He wrapped the sword back up in the cloth and put it back under the shelf. He turned to me. "Let's go on a hunt. We can show you how we make portals."

I nodded and stood. "Okay."

James pushed the shutters wide open and leapt onto the sill. He didn't check to see if I followed. He fell forward. His wings stayed by his side until the last second, then they whooshed open, catching the wind. He soared around the clearing below, then dropped down.

The newness of my wings hadn't worn off yet. My talons gripped the window, digging into the softwood. I fell, letting the wind rush by me. The trees grew closer and closer until the final moment. My wings buffeted the air. The leaves rustled and the limbs at the treetop creaked in the wind. I soared. James dropped to the ground, and I followed suit. I found him kneeling with grass and dirt in his palms. He acted as if he smelled it. He spun to the east, his nose raised. I waited and didn't make a sound, knowing if I did, he'd have my head.

He sank to the ground and moved slowly toward the treeline. I smelled an animal nearby but couldn't tell what kind. Wet grass and soil covered most of the other scents.

We moved through the woods like two shadows, not making a sound. A beautiful stag stood under a large oak. It had its nose to the ground, searching for food. Its head whipped up as it either heard us or caught our scent. I didn't dare to move. A tense second passed. Ice splintered across the dead leaves toward the stag. It had no clue until it was too late. White ice slid along the dirt and grabbed hold of its legs, keeping it from running away. The deer thrashed once it realized its predicament.

James wasted no time and pounced. He ripped the deer to shreds. Blood and entrails covered the ground and his face. Light pulsed from the deer's body, then rippled along the ground. James inhaled, stretching his wings wide, and the light flowed into him. A ghostly pale fog enveloped him, then pulsed out. He breathed in deep and let the air out slowly.

His eyes flashed open. Two twin grey orbs stared at me, and dissipated, changing back to black holes.

"Now it's your turn," he growled. "Kill and absorb its life source. You'll need it for the exchange."

Exchange? What did he mean? But I didn't ask. I was too afraid. My claws reflected the moonlight. They were longer and sharper. Could I kill? Through the woods, the rustle of small animals rushing through the underbrush reached my ears.

"Listen for the pounding of its heart."

I closed my eyes and listened with every fiber. Leaves rubbed together in the breeze. Small animals ran back and forth on the forest floor. I searched for the bigger animal. A coyote came out of its den. It sniffed the air. Its heartbeat thundered strong and loud.

"Go for it," James murmured.

I took off in one leap. My wings beat the air twice then I floated toward my target. She was crouched watching a rabbit nibble on some grass. I landed with no sound; my heart pounded in my ears. I tread carefully over the leaves and fallen branches. I was maybe twenty feet away. James' presence wasn't too far away, as he watched my progress. If I failed, who knew what he'd do.

The coyote still hadn't caught wind of my presence. I made sure to land on the downside of the wind. The moment she took off after the rabbit I jumped into motion. My talons outstretched as I reached for her. She saw me at the last second as I snatched her up. She yelped and struggled to get free.

Joy and excitement rushed through me. I was so proud. I pinned her to the ground, leering over her. Adrenaline pulsed through my limbs. I had done it. I caught her.

"Finish her. Drink her life away," James snarled behind me.

I glanced at him, then back at the animal in my claws. Blood smeared her coat. My claws had punctured her skin. The smell of her blood in the air made my instincts roar to life, begging me to drink her in. But something stopped me as another distinct smell coated my nostrils. She had pups. I turned to her den and barely made out the small shapes waiting for their mom to return. Their mom. I stared at the animal in my clutches. Her breathing grew ragged. She knew her fate. But I couldn't do it. I faltered. My claws loosened their grip, and she sensed the release and struggled against me.

"What are you waiting for? Finish it."

I tightened my grip on her once more but didn't act. Another memory flashed in my mind. A petite woman with long dark hair and almond-shaped eyes. I could almost picture ethereal wings sprouting from her back. My mom. I gasped. I had a mom. She was there. I sprang back, letting the coyote go. She scrambled to her feet and took off. My breathing hitched in my throat.

"What's wrong with you?" James snarled in my face. His claws gripped my arm, yanking me around to look at him. "Why didn't you kill it?"

I focused my attention on the ground. My shoulders slumped in embarrassment. "I couldn't."

"Couldn't or wouldn't?" he spat. He leapt into the air and took off to the mountain. "Don't come back until you've killed." He roared.

Animals all around me ran for cover. I shrank, feeling defeated. Why was I so weak? Why had I thought about a mother? Around the clearing, the breeze blew the long grass. The moonlight spread across the open plain. Insects crawled along the ground, clueless to monsters above them.

I sighed, and searched again, looking for signs of life.

50

Callum

Whispers echoed down the hall and leaked into my cell. It was nighttime. Surely, everyone had gone to bed.

Raleigh's face peeked above the rim of the cell window. The firelight reflected in her big eyes. "Cal! We're getting you out."

Harris appeared next to her. A wide, goofy grin planted on his face. "Hey, Cal. Told ya I'd fix it."

I stood and stretched. My vertebra popped as my hands reached skyward.

"Guys, you can't be here. You know they'll banish you too if caught."

Harris grasped the window bars. "Man, this is my fault you're here in this mess. I have to help. Doesn't matter what happens to me."

"Right. We're a team. No one gets left behind. Besides, if we get caught we can blame Harris, and they'll throw him out."

"Yeah man — wait a minute! You didn't say that before."

Raleigh only grinned.

"What's the plan?" I asked.

Raleigh glanced at a watch on her wrist. "It's almost 11. We're taking you to the other portal and get you to the other city." Rustling sounded as she dug in her pack for something.

I shook my head. "It won't work."

They both stalled. Raleigh asked, "What do you mean?"

"Chuck is monitoring the portals. He probably knows what you're doing now," I said tiredly, rubbing my face with my hand.

"Not right now. He's up in Patrice's room."

My hand fell to my lap, and my gaze jerked up to meet hers. Why was he up there?

Harris fit a key into the lock and turned it. The cell door swung open.

"What about the guards?"

Raleigh waved me out. "We gave them a sleeping dose, so no need to worry there. Come on. We don't have much time."

She grabbed a pack on the floor and slung it over her shoulders. She pushed a bigger pack into my hands. It was my usual pack I carried. She had stuffed it to the brim. A roll fell out of a pocket and onto the floor. I stooped and grabbed it. Without much thought, I took a bite. It was slightly stale, but I was starving. I inhaled more of it. The roll made it hard to swallow. But I was positive I'd need my fire at some point, and I'd need energy for it.

Raleigh shot toward the stairs. Harris was close on her heels.

My bag weighed so much, but I was so weak it felt heavier. I took off. My legs slammed the stone floor as if I hadn't used them in days, which was true after being kept in that tiny cell for a whole day.

As we came up the stairs, one of the guards was passed out on the floor. His head lolled to the side. Snores disrupted the quiet hallway. He would most likely be beaten once found. I thundered past and up more stairs until we reached the first level.

Raleigh halted, breathing heavy. Her bag rattled with what sounded like metal cans. She peered around the corner both ways.

"Wait. Mary said there's a goon up ahead."

My heart hammered my ribs as my adrenaline rushed through my veins. At any moment I would jump out of my skin.

We held a cumulative breath as we waited. Down the hall, a guard walked by humming a tune. A couple of beats passed.

"Come on," she whispered.

Instead of heading out the front gates, we rounded the corner and headed to the kitchen where the secret door to the tombs led. We pushed some boxes out of the way and lifted the wood door that led down into the dark. Raleigh grabbed my pack and dug around. She lifted my stick light out and waved it under my nose. I snatched it.

"Go!" She pointed into the tunnel. "I'll get the ghosts to cover it back up." She nodded and pointed in the air. I tried not to think about the ghosts she spoke to.

Harris and I jumped in. My stick light bathed the darkness in its white glow. We didn't waste time once Raleigh's feet hit the floor behind us. We took off for the tomb entrance. Harris huffed and puffed behind me. We halted at the massive wood doors. Harris and I grabbed each handle and pulled with all our might. They slowly and painfully opened.

Raleigh threw a hand up. "Wait."

We listened with our ears pricked. Someone walked several yards away, but I was sure they couldn't see the tomb entrance.

"Okay, it's clear," whispered Raleigh. She slipped through the doors and crouched as she ran along the stone wall leading to the garden.

Harris and I followed close behind.

"Yeah, we have to get to portal three," Raleigh said, to no one we could see. "Okay." She faced us. "She's going ahead to scout, then will say when it's safe to go."

We sat crouched at the base of a large boulder. I nodded to her. Harris sat with knees pressed into the ground, his hands braced on the grass, breathing heavily. Sweat ran down his nose and dropped. He wiped feverishly at his face.

Raleigh had her eyes glued to something not too far away. She smiled. "Let's go."

We ran. The portal flickered right before we reached it. The glassy surface undulated in blue and purple hues.

"Thank you, Mary," Raleigh said. She didn't waste any more time and jumped through the portal.

Harris went next, closely followed by me. We burst through the portal in a cloud of dust and sweat. The city of Jamestown blinked and blinded us. People stopped and stared. I was so thankful to be there in the city of sparkling rocks and happy people. Eventually, people carried on and ignored us.

"Now what Raleigh?" I tugged on my heavy pack, trying to situate it easier.

People filed by and wrapped us up in the tempo of the crystal city. "Follow me." She tightened her bag against her back and set off along the path through the crowd.

51

Sloane

THE COLD DARKNESS WRAPPED TIGHTLY AROUND ME. HOURS HAD drifted by. Animals scurried away, running from something. I paused. They ran from me. I was the predator. That didn't feel right. Sounds of water running and the heartbeats of small animals trickled into my ears. It was nice being away from the mountain. The woods felt like home.

I followed my ears to the water, threading through the slender trees and pale moonlight. The canopy broke open, revealing a large creek. Water burbled along the smooth worn rocks. I sat listening, letting the sounds of the forest fill my senses.

An animal cried a few yards away, but I couldn't see it. It was hurt. The smell of blood filled the air around me. My ears strained for any sort of movement or threat. Not hearing anything, I made my way toward the creature. Not far from the creek, a small doe lay on its side trying to breathe. Its legs were bent at odd angles and blood pooled around its body. Teeth marks covered its legs and torso. Something must have tried to kill it but was scared off, maybe? I gazed around the scene, looking for traps. But I didn't see any.

The doe heaved with each breath. Its eyes were wild in the night as it sensed me nearby. It was struggling to call for help. I moved quickly to stand over it. Ready to claim it as mine. But I stopped. What was wrong with me? Why couldn't I claim it like I was supposed to? James would be furious.

I knelt beside the deer and waited. Slowly, she started breathing easier. The light in her eyes dimmed. I placed my claw against her side, trying to ease her anxiety. Her big brown eyes closed slightly. Something wet ran from the corners of my eyes. I wiped them away, realizing they were tears. Tears for a poor animal. I frowned. What was this part of me?

I stroked the doe a few times. Her soft pale, tawny coat gleamed. Her heartbeat slowed even more. And I cried. The loss of her life felt enormous. It felt as if the world was ending.

The weirdest, most, coolest thing I had ever seen happened. The energy from the plants and water around her ran across the ground toward her. As the bioluminescence traveled from far away and into the doe's body, it glowed a soft, bright green and blue. The veins throughout her small form glowed from within. Her eyes glowed green. The cooling blood turned a faint blue.

The last beat of her heart shuddered as it pushed her blood through the valves. Her last breath expelled in one puff of pale white mist, hovering and glowing softly.

I didn't dare move or breathe. I only watched as the pale mist gravitated toward me and hit me square in the chest. The moment it touched my skin, it was as if I had drunk a liter of coffee or ran a mile. Exhilaration coursed through me. I felt alive. Was this what James had been talking about?

I patted the little doe, thanking her for her life. Thanking her that I hadn't had to be the one to take it from her. James didn't have to know how I had gotten it. I was somewhat proud of my little secret.

Gathering my feet underneath me, I pushed off with all my might. I propelled myself into the air. The wind whooshing by me thundered in my ears and made my eyes water. I let a smile slide across my face. Being in the air was where I was meant to be.

I circled the mountain before flying into one of the big open windows. The feel of the wind brushing across my wings was unlike any other feeling in the world. Other creatures flew in and out of the windows now and then. My wings buffeted the air and gently set me on the stone floor.

"Good. You made your kill." James stood against the wall, his arms crossed over his thin chest.

I didn't respond, only waited.

"It happens tonight. We don't have much time. Follow." He turned on his heel and disappeared down the hall.

For a moment, I considered not listening to him but thought better of it. I kept a few paces from him as we traveled down into the depths of the mountain. I had no idea where he was leading me. Along the way, my pet caught up with me. Ash trotted next to me. Its tail swept the floor as we went, making a swish, swish sound. It was a comfort having it close by.

James stopped at a pair of oversized wooden doors. His muscles bulged as he pushed inward. A large cavern opened up. Several portals lined the walls. Some were blinking, others were black as if not on.

"This is where we will conquer the new world. Where we will take what's rightfully ours." James spread his arms out, encompassing the room. "This is where you will show your powers to the world."

His gaze shifted to me, and a terrifying smile slid across his gaunt face. This was going to be incredible. Something to remember forever.

"Come here." James gestured to the center of the space where an urn-shaped vessel sat on a stone table. A knife gleamed in his hand, which I hadn't seen him uncover.

I glanced at the vessel. It was empty. But my anxiety rose from seeing the knife. Ash made a whining noise beside me and pushed against my leg. It agreed with my reservations. I patted its head, more for my reassurance than for its.

"Let me see your hand." James held his palm out and wiggled his fingers.

I hesitated.

"Come on."

I held out my left hand, and he turned it over. Palm up.

"I need your blood for the portals to work." His gaze shifted to mine.

I stilled my breath and nodded.

He held the knife against my palm, making a slash across. Pain sliced up my arm. He made another gash across my palm, marking a red X. I gasped, surprised. Dark blood the color of dark red wine spilled from my palm. Instead of flowing, it squeezed from the cuts in globs like congealed pudding. He kneaded my arm trying to get every drop out. The vessel slowly filled with my blood. Why did my blood look darker?

A devilish grin split James' face. His stare was transfixed on the vessel as it filled. As my blood filled the last of the vessel, he wrapped a cloth around my hand, but the blood had nearly stopped flowing already.

Small traces of blue and green zipped through the contents. That must have been from the poor deer.

James patted my shoulder. "There are a couple of hours before we begin the ceremony, so wait in your room until then."

"Okay." I braced my hand against my chest and turned toward the door. Ash followed close behind.

The maze back up to my room felt never-ending. Had I done the right thing?

52

Callum

I DIDN'T THINK I'D EVER GET OVER THE CONTRAST OF THE TWO CITIES. This one teamed with life, while the other seemed to sleep.

Raleigh encouraged us to follow as she threaded through the throngs of people. The smells of food from houses and merchants wafted through the cobbled streets. People calling to each other and chatting drifted through the cavern in waves. We took a turn on a back alley that ended at a bright green door. Raleigh stopped and rapped on it two times. We waited. The seconds ticked by. A small cutout in the center opened slightly and an eye peered out. It shut almost instantly and the sound of bolts turning echoed off the stone walls. I checked behind us to see if we had been followed but so far nothing.

Brand's weathered face appeared. "Come on." He waved us in as we rushed through the door. He shut and bolted it the moment we were all inside. "Callum, it's good to see you, lad." He clapped my back.

"Brand, thank you." I swept my gaze across the rest of the space. The room we were in was small and mostly bare. A tiny table sat in a corner with a chair. There was no light.

"We never believed anything Chuck said about you."

I nodded my thanks. Miranda walked through the opposite doorway. Her dark skin glowed softly from the light emitting from the other room.

"Callum, good to see you in one piece." She wore her usual Hunter attire: Black leather boots, a long-sleeve black shirt, and black leather pants. Her muscles pulled the fabric tight.

"Let's go into the other room. It's homier." Brand ushered us through the opposite door.

The room was lit with string lights, hanging from the ceiling. The walls were painted a deep blue. A sofa and chair were nestled in a corner, and a large round table sat in the opposite corner near a small kitchenette. Rory stood at the sink, washing veggies. He nodded to me. His shirt this time read, 'Here for a good time, not a long time.'

"What up Cal." He shut the water off and moved to sit in a chair.

"Hey Rory, surprised to see you here."

He shrugged his shoulders in answer. I was glad to see at least three others felt I was free from judgment.

I settled into the sofa. My body was sore from laying on the hard floor and honestly, from all the crap it had been through. The soft cushions felt amazing, and I wanted nothing more than to sleep.

Raleigh set her bag on the floor. "We don't have much time until the eclipse in the Norm. We need a game plan to rescue Sloane and Ash." She sank onto the cushion next to me.

"And the others," I said. My eyes closed and my head tilted back.

"And the others," she repeated. "We have a few hours until they go through the portals. I'm not sure what we can do."

Brand sat in one of the chairs, his hands folded on his knees. "We can't do anything from this side. We need to get to the Norm Defense and start our defenses there. We have no way of getting into Nightlin territory and actually accomplishing something."

Brand was right.

"How many others are there?" I massaged my hands and cracked my knuckles. Being in such a confined space as that cell was not part of my plan.

Raleigh looked around the room. "This is it so far."

I frowned. Five people out of thousands weren't going to have much of an impact.

"We have a few more people on the way. The people of Jamestown will most likely help once they know what's happening," Brand stated.

"How can we tell them?" I brushed my dark sweaty hair from my forehead. I needed a bath, so bad.

"I have a meeting with their leader in a few minutes. She should be here soon," Miranda said. "You'll need to help fill in everything that's been happening. They have a direct portal to the Defense, so it won't take us long."

I nodded. The anxiety that had built up behind my eyes slowly ebbed away. A small plan was forming.

Knock, knock.

We all fixed our attention on the door.

Miranda pushed from the wall. "That's probably her."

We waited as she opened the door and muffled voices carried through. A woman's voice asked, "Hi, Miranda."

Miranda answered, "This way." She appeared in the doorway, followed by a short, older woman. Her clothes were bright reds and blues, opposite from all of our black clothes.

Her dark, big eyes surveyed us. She had deep laugh lines around her mouth and eyes. Her white hair was cut short into a bob. She smiled easily at us. "So, this is your team?"

Miranda said, "Yes, this is Callum, Raleigh, Harris, Rory, and Brand." She pointed to each of us. "This is Ellen."

Brand stood and bobbed his head, his hand held out to her. "Ello, madam."

She smiled and took his hand, shaking it.

"Please, sit." Brand gestured to an empty chair.

"Miranda said this meeting was very important that lives depended on it?"

We all nodded in agreement.

"We don't have much time, so I'll jump to the reason why I asked you to come here." Miranda stood against the wall, her hands in her pockets. "The Nightlins are opening more portals and there is a solar eclipse coming in the Norm, which you know isn't good for us."

"A solar eclipse?" Ellen asked. "What makes you think this?"

I spoke up this time, "We have heard from several sources, and I have been in the Nightlin Mountain on the Kingston side. They are preparing for something big. I'm sure you heard about them opening new portals over our city?"

Ellen spread her hands across her lap, smoothing the material, "Yes, I'm afraid we did hear. Truly disheartening." Tiny studs lined her earlobes and along the ridge. A small stud pierced her nostril.

I sat forward. "We need your help. Any you can give."

She glanced at Miranda. "What else can you tell me?"

Miranda looked at me, then Brand. "We believe — we know Chuck is on the wrong side."

Silence fell as her words sunk in. Ellen's grey eyes grew slightly larger. Her lips pressed together in a tight line.

"You know I never liked him. Something was always off about him." Ellen sat a little straighter.

Miranda nodded. "That's why I felt like we could trust you."

Ellen sat back and her shoulders slumped. Her eyes narrowed. "What do you need?"

Our small group looked at each other.

"We need people, and we need to get to the Defense. And start setting up a defensive strategy."

Ellen nodded and stood. "Okay, follow me. No time to lose." She headed to the door and turned back. "Coming?" Her eyes twinkled with amusement.

We stood at once and gathered what little we had. As we made our way out the front door, two large men stood on either side waiting.

"Jack, lead us back to the house." Ellen motioned to one of the men. The one, covered head to toe in tattoos with black hair and eyes, bowed and headed down the small avenue.

It seemed surreal for things to be happening so quickly, but time was of the essence.

53

Callum

We threaded our way through the streets, taking so many turns. I wasn't sure I'd be able to find my way back. In the center of the city was a massive building made from rocks and stalagmites. Purple and blue crystals were placed around the double doors. Two women stood on either side wearing dark blue shirts and pants with their weapons at their sides, and hands folded behind them.

The doors opened to tall ceilings and a circular room with halls branching out. Ellen made her way to the most central one. We followed her into a large amphitheater with rows and rows of seats. A small semi-circular stage sat at the front. A small group of people stood around it.

Ellen stopped right before them. "This is part of my team. You might recognize some faces."

The group of about twenty people turned to face us. They ranged from old to young. From stout to wispy.

I recognized one face in particular. His solid black eyes were a giveaway. Morgan focused on me, and he nodded once. His face had been cleaned, and beard trimmed. He looked more presentable, less of the rugged mountain man from before.

A woman stepped forward. "Hi, I'm Sarah, I'm part of the Dirty

Dozen. And I'm ready to get my friends back." She pounded her fist into her palm.

A man stepped through the group. His salt and pepper hair was cut short to his scalp and his blue eyes were almost ice-colored. "I'm Chris, another Dozen member, hoping to get the rest of 'em back." He placed a hand on Sarah's shoulder and squeezed it.

"I've read about some of your adventures," I said.

Chris and Sarah glanced at each other with a slight cringe disrupting their calm faces.

"Uh, sorry about that," Sarah said.

"It was nothing. Mostly about James and Jacob."

A beautiful dark-haired woman squeezed through the people. Celest. Instinctually, I stepped back.

"What are you doing here?"

She spread her hands wide. "I'm on your side."

Ellen parted the group. "She's been working for us and feeding us some of Chuck's entail."

My mouth was slightly ajar. Unbelievable.

She smiled somewhat ashamedly. "Do you forgive me?"

Raleigh spoke, "If you're really on our side then I'm glad." She stepped closer to Celest. "But if you backstab us, I will cut your throat."

Celest's face grew slightly ashen. "I respect that, Raleigh. I wouldn't dare double-cross this group or you."

Their gazes locked for what felt like a full minute before Raleigh relaxed.

Ellen's voice rose above the whispers and chatter. "We don't have much time until the eclipse is here. We need everyone here on board with our mission. Realmers are being held at the Nightlin Mountain near Kingston. They believe that Realmers are being changed to Nightlins so instead of killing on sight we need to catch them." The group fell quiet as if hanging on her every word.

Celest said, "It is my understanding that the Nightlin Mountain has fallen quiet. I'm afraid we may be too late."

Murmurs of dismay echoed in the hall.

"We will send a team to the mountain and one to the Defense." Ellen gestured to some guards on the far wall. "This is our time to finally take a stand against whatever these creatures are. The eclipse will give them more power, so we have to act fast. Callum knows more so we will be following his lead." She nodded to me.

All eyes swiveled to me. I hoped I wouldn't lead them astray. Sure as shit hoped I didn't fuck it all up. We'd have one chance, one opportunity. In the great words of Marshall Mathers, would we capture it or let it slip?

54

Sloane

It was happening. Finally.

I stood with my mouth slightly ajar as the portals along the wall sparked and blinked open. They were breathtaking. The creatures beside me screeched and cawed with their excitement. It was a big day. A day everyone would remember for all of history to come. Even the people I didn't know about.

The new power inside me thrummed with possibility and promise. It breathed and expanded with each pulse. James stood beside me and squeezed my shoulder; his claws barely scraped my skin. I smiled as well as I could with my new teeth. My legs were still something to get used to. My wings ruffled and shifted, trying out the new expanse and freedom that they lent.

James had given me the long sword with beautiful details etched into the blade. It now hung from my hip in its scabbard. I tugged on the extra weight trying to find the right angle for it to hang. Something like static electricity shocked me, and I flinched from the cold metal. A tiny breath of light seeped from the crack between the hilt and scabbard. That wasn't right.

My nerves were on edge from all the excitement.

The portals sparked a blueish-green. It was almost time for us to conquer the new world. For us to recruit some new specimens while feeding on the helpless humans. An emotion roiled through me. What was it? Sadness? Anger? Surely, not. I should be happy this was what we had been working for the whole time.

The eclipse was almost upon us then, we could soar free. Soar through the portals to the other world, to the humans, and conquer them. Night would be all around. No threat to us. Even the Realmers were taken care of. The Realmers. I was forgetting someone. Who was it? A flash of green eyes disrupted my thoughts. But it was gone. I shook my shoulders to help shake the feeling.

A creature nipped at my long claws. I smiled and patted its scaly, blackhead. The creatures screamed and charged the portals. Red light streamed through the open portals in an eerie haze.

Freedom was almost here.

55

Callum

I DECIDED TO BE PART OF THE GROUP HEADING TO THE NIGHTLIN Mountain. I wanted to see for myself. Had to see. Raleigh, Harris, Celest, and Miranda joined me. The rest, including Rory, headed for the Norm Defense.

Ellen showed us the portal to lead us close to the mountain. We jumped in without a second thought and burst through the other side at a run. I didn't heed the limbs or the sounds of us crashing through the undergrowth. Sloane was only a short distance away. The lake glimmered ahead of us, and we stopped.

"Listen, I can carry at least two people on my czar," said Miranda. "Callum, can you call your czar?"

I closed my eyes and reached for the thread inside that called my czar and felt the reassuring answer. "Yes. He's there."

"Okay, let's go. We head for the top." She didn't wait a second more. White electrical currents erupted from the ground at her feet and massive wings unfurled. She hopped on its back in one fluid motion. She didn't wait for the others to give their acceptance. Her czar scooped them up in its razor-sharp claws and took off like a shooting star toward the mountain's dark point.

Celest turned to me, "You sure you've got it?"

"Yeah, he'll answer. He's waiting."

A corner of her mouth pulled back. "Sloane is a strong girl. We'll get her back." She stretched her arms out with her palms facing the ground. Deep purple currents snapped up and latched onto her arms and legs. A tall elegant czar stepped from the shadows and bowed its head. Its long tail had small purple feathers sprouting along the ridges and scales. Celest stepped on its leg and the beast helped push her onto its back. The wind knocked me back a step as the creature beat the air with its wings and shot upward.

"All right. Our turn. Don't fail me now."

Little one, I said I would answer when you called. Don't lose faith now.

Its answer rumbled through my mind and down my spine.

I grasped the gold-orange thread inside and tugged hard. Electricity shot from the ground like a tangled mess. The orange and gold threads latched onto my legs and hands. The weight felt heavy and somewhat unsure. *Hashakar.* He answered with a roar that reverberated through my skull. Heat and fire poured from my palms and he took shape. Translucent wings spread wide. Strong legs flexed with unbridled power. Relief washed over me as he stood before me.

I didn't waste time. I jumped onto his back and his muscles bunched under me as he leapt from the ground. A cool wind rushed past us. The Nightlin Mountain sat in front of us. A purple and white light not too far ahead.

I spotted the small tower poking through the trees. Its windows were wide open. That was my first clue that something was wrong. Miranda and her czar tossed Harris and Raleigh inside. She jumped from its shoulders and the massive creature disintegrated into sparks. Celest jumped through the window rolling and popping up on her knees. Her purple czar spun away and dissolved. I didn't want to say goodbye to Hashakar.

I am always with you. Go on.

I patted his neck then vaulted for the window. I barely caught the sill. I yanked myself over the side and tumbled onto the floor.

"Might need to work on your dismount," said Harris.

I narrowed my eyes at him.

Orange light pulsed from outside, and I caught the last glimpse of my czar erupting into ash. A pang of sadness tore through me.

No time. Go.

"Wait." I held my hand up telling everyone to stop. I listened with every ounce of my hearing. Water dripped far below, air blew through the cracks in the rocks, but no heartbeats. I frowned. "There's nothing."

Miranda unsheathed a long sword and small blade. "You lead."

I drew in a deep breath and headed toward the far door. Stopping before opening it, I listened once more. Nothing. Only the sounds of absence.

I pulled the door open and stepped through. Stale air met me. I retraced my steps down the stairwell that Sloane and I had raced up in our haste to get away. Our slow steps echoed off the rock walls no matter how quiet we padded down. At each door I stopped and quieted my mind, letting my ears reach out to listen for a pin drop or tiny flutter of a heartbeat. Only little insects answered back. We continued down. Hope slowly dissolved like foam from a wave.

But then I heard a tiny crackle of something I didn't quite recognize. I ran toward it. Ripping the door open, I sprinted down the hall. It hit me. Portals. Several of them. I rounded the corner and almost ran into another door. I wrenched it open and skidded to a stop. An eerie red haze lit the empty room. The stone walls were awash with the kaleidoscope of reds, oranges, and shadows.

The group behind me gasped. They stopped on my heels and caught their breaths.

"We are too late," Miranda said.

"I don't believe it." Celest slumped. Her sword dangled from her grip.

Harris stood with his mouth agape.

"Where are Sloane and Ashlen?" Raleigh took a step forward and stopped thinking better of it. "What can we do?"

I shook my head. "We go through and meet them on the other side."

Miranda tightened her grip on her blades. "Yes, we will meet them. The others are at the Defense by now."

We looked at each other assessing the other.

I nodded. "Let's go." I stepped forward, and the others followed. Something tickled the back of my mind. I stopped.

"What's wrong?" Raleigh asked.

"I heard something." I faced the door, straining to hear the soft noise. I braced myself. "Something is coming this way."

Miranda faced the door. "What is it?"

Celest moved to the opposite side.

"I'm not sure… but it isn't good."

Cold dread slid down my back and settled between my shoulder blades. A long-forgotten whisper echoed through the halls. Insects scuttled into cracks.

Miranda started to close the door.

"That won't help."

She peered back at me. Horror and panic slid across her smooth features. Celest eyed me.

"What can we do?" Raleigh whispered.

"I — don't know." The hairs along my arms and neck rose. "It's almost here." I glanced at the red portals behind us. "It's coming fast."

"Do we stay or take our chances in the Norm?" Miranda took a step back to line up with me.

"It's probably the same stakes, so what's everyone's vote?"

We met each other's gaze. Fear and dismay permeated the stale air. I eyed the door again.

"It's here."

ACKNOWLEDGMENTS

Thank you so much to all the readers who gave these books a chance! Thank you to Allison Dublin, Rachel Ramey, Lacey Krauch, R. Jones, and Brittany Smith for editing, critiquing, and spending so much time talking me through this! You've all been the best!

Book 3 in the series coming soon.

ABOUT THE AUTHOR

K.R. Bowman has been writing stories since she was a child, always with her head in the clouds, dreaming up different worlds. She has a Bachelor's in Interior Design that she uses for her day job. Her loves are traveling and discovering new pieces of the world. She currently lives in the south, where she drinks way too much sweet tea.

She loves all types of fiction but mostly writes fantasy, sci-fi, and mystery with a female lead. She loves action and adventure, and characters that feature a quirky underdog.

Printed in Great Britain
by Amazon